Recent Titles by J. A. Jance from Severn House

IMPROBABLE CAUSE
INJUSTICE FOR ALL
A MORE PERFECT UNION
TRIAL BY FURY

TRIAL BY FURY

TRIAL BY FURY

J. A. Jance

This title first published in Great Britain 2000 by
SEVERN HOUSE PUBLISHERS LTD of
9–15 High Street, Sutton, Surrey SM1 1DF.
This first hardcover edition published in the USA 2000 by
SEVERN HOUSE PUBLISHERS INC of
595 Madison Avenue, New York, N.Y. 10022.
Originally published in paperback format only
in the U.S.A. by Avon Books Inc.

British Library Cataloguing in Publication Data

Jance, J. A. (Judith A.)
    Trial by fury. - (A   J. P. Beaumont mystery)
    1.   Beaumont, J. P. (Fictitious character) - Fiction
    2.   Detective and mystery stories
    I.   Title
    813.5'4 [F]

    ISBN 0-7278-5609-X

Printed and bound in Great Britain by
MPG Books Ltd, Bodmin, Cornwall.

To Will, who used to be the strong, silent type.

CHAPTER
1

I was hung over as hell when Detective Ron Peters and I hit the crime scene at ten after eight on a gray and rainy Seattle Monday morning. Peters, my partner on Seattle P.D.'s homicide squad, was quick to point out that it could have been worse. At least I had some hope of getting better. The black man lying behind the dumpster at the Lower Queen Anne Bailey's Foods didn't.

He was dead. Had been for some time. The sickish odor of decaying flesh was thick in the air.

Partially wrapped in a tarp, he lay propped against the loading dock, the whole weight of his body resting on his shoulders, his broad head twisted unnaturally to one side.

The human neck is engineered to turn back and forth and up and down in a multitude of combinations. This wasn't one of them. I didn't need the medical examiner's officer to tell me his neck was broken, but it would require an autopsy to determine if a broken neck was actually the cause of death.

Fortunately, the medical examiner wasn't far behind us. Old Doc Baker, his full head of white hair wet and plastered flat on his head, turned up with a squad of youthful technicians. Baker supervises departmental picture-taking and oversees the initial handling of the corpse.

Crime-scene etiquette comes with its own peculiar pecking order. In phase one, the medical examiner reigns supreme. Baker barked orders that sent people scurrying in all directions while Peters and I stood in the doorway of the loading dock trying to keep out of both the way and the rain.

The store manager, with a name tag identifying him as Curt, came to stand beside us. He chewed vigorously on a hangnail. "This is real bad for business," he said to no one in particular, although Peters and I were the only people within earshot. "Corporate isn't going to like it at all!"

I turned to him, snapping open my departmental ID. "Detective J. P. Beaumont," I told him. "Homicide, Seattle P.D. Is this man anyone you recognize?" I motioned in the direction of the dead man.

It was a long shot, checking to see if Curt recognized the victim, but it didn't hurt to ask. Every once in a while we get lucky. Someone says sure, he knows the victim, and provides us with a complete name and address. Having that kind of information gives us a big leg up at the beginning of an investigation, but it doesn't happen often. And it didn't happen then.

Curt shook his head mournfully. "No. Never saw him before. But it's still bad for business. Just wait till this hits the papers."

"Optimist," Peters muttered to me under his breath. To Curt, he said, "Who found him?"

"Produce boy. He's upstairs in my office."

"Can we talk to him?"

"He's still pretty shook up. Just a kid, you know."

We followed Curt through the store, deserted except for a few anxious employees who watched our progress down an aisle stacked high with canned goods. At the front of the store, he led us through a door and up a steep flight of steps to a messy cubbyhole that served as Curt's office. From the debris and litter scattered on the table, it was clear the room doubled as an employee lunchroom.

The produce boy was just exactly that, a boy, a kid barely out of high school to look at him. He sat by a scarred wooden desk with his tie loosened and his head resting on his arms. When he raised his head to look at us, a distinctly greenish pallor colored his face. The name tag on his blue apron pocket said *Frank.*

"How's it going, Frank?" I asked, flashing my ID.

He shook his head. "Not so good. I've never seen anybody dead before."

"How'd you find him?"

"The lettuce," he said.

"Lettuce?"

"Not lettuce exactly. The produce trimmings. I was taking them out to the dumpster in a lettuce crate. That's when I saw him."

"What time?"

"After seven sometime. Don't know exactly. I don't wear a watch."

"And you didn't move him or touch him in any way?"

"Are you kidding? I dropped the crate and lost my cookies. Right there on the loading dock. Then I ran like hell."

"What time?" Peters asked, turning to the manager.

"Twenty after seven. I checked when I dialed 911."

We asked the full quota of questions, but there was nothing either Frank or his boss could add to what they'd already told us. Finally, thanking them for their help, we left the office and returned to where Doc Baker was still throwing his considerable weight around.

"What's it look like?" I asked when he heaved himself to his feet, motioned the techs to pack up the body, and came over to where Peters and I were standing.

"Death by hanging from the looks of it," he said. "Rope burns around his neck. That's probably how it got broken. I'll be able to tell you for sure after the autopsy."

"When will you do it?" Peters asked.

Baker scowled. "Don't rush me. This afternoon, probably. We have another one scheduled for this morning. What was it, a full moon over the weekend?"

Peters shook his head. "You've got it wrong, Doc. According to what I read, rapes and robberies go up during a full moon, not murders."

Baker gave Peters another sour look. They never really hit it off. Baker didn't have much patience with Peters' photographic memory for everything he'd read, and Peters regarded Baker as a pretentious old fart. Young detectives who hang around long enough, however, eventually figure out that Howard Baker is a very *wise* old fart.

Keeping out of the cross fire, I asked, "What's the approximate time of death?"

"Off the top of my head, I'd say he's been dead for two days or so. I'll have more exact information later."

Over the years, I've learned to rely on Doc
Baker's educated guesses. He may be a pom-
pous son of a bitch at times, but autopsy find-
ings tend to verify his "top of the head"
theories. I'm willing to give credit where credit
is due.

We watched as technicians carefully placed
paper bags over the victim's hands to protect
any trace of evidence that might have remained on his skin or under his fingernails.
As they wrestled with the body, I realized this
was a big man, well over six feet tall. He must
have been in his late thirties or early forties.
His close-cropped, wiry hair was lightly sprin-
kled with gray.

"Any identification?" Peters asked.

Doc Baker, observing his technicians, appeared to be lost in thought. There was a long
pause before he answered. "No. No identification. Nothing. Plucked clean as a chicken.
Watch and rings are gone, although he evidently wore both. No wallet. They even took
his clothes, every stitch."

Baker paused and looked at me, one bushy
eyebrow raised questioningly. "Robbery,
maybe?"

"Maybe," I said.

Once the body was loaded, the next wave
of technicians moved into the picture. The
crime scene investigators from the Washington State Patrol's crime lab took over the territory. The rain had solidified into a steady

downpour, but the team tackled the dumpster in hopes of finding some clue that would help identify the victim.

Peters turned to me. "We'd better get busy, too," he said.

My hangover hadn't improved, but I knew better than to expect Peters to give me a break in that regard. He's a man who doesn't drink very much, and he doesn't have a whole hell of a lot of patience with people who do.

We walked across the lot to where uniformed officers had cordoned off the area. Just beyond the group of banked patrol cars, Arlo Hamilton, Seattle P.D.'s public information officer, held forth for a group of reporter types. He raised a hand to momentarily silence further questions. Extricating himself from the group, he walked over to Peters and me.

"Any idea who it is?" Arlo asked.

"None whatsoever," Peters answered.

Hamilton turned back to the reporters. "That's it. No further information at this time. The autopsy is scheduled for this afternoon." There was general groaning and grumbling as the reporters dispersed. Hamilton came back to us, shaking his head. "I got called in twice over the weekend. Here we go again, first thing Monday morning."

"Doc Baker says it must have been a full moon," Peters told Hamilton with a sarcastic grin.

"Right," Hamilton replied, then strode away.

We stopped in the drizzly parking lot and looked around. Two sides of Bailey's Foods face Seattle Center. A third side is bounded by the backs of businesses that front on First Avenue North, while the fourth side is lined with backs of apartments and businesses that front on Mercer. There was nothing to do but hit the bricks with our standard question: Had anyone seen or heard anything unusual over the weekend?

The answer was no. Time and again. Everywhere we went, from little old retired ladies to a burly night watchman who was pissed as hell at being awakened out of a sound sleep. They all told the same story. No one had heard any unusual noises. Well, maybe it had been a little extra noisy Friday and Saturday nights, but that was to be expected. After all, the state high school basketball championships were being played in the Coliseum. Aside from that, there was nothing out of the ordinary. No strange vehicles. No strange noises. Business as usual.

Except for one dead man with a broken neck. He had evidently crept into the parking lot like fog. On little cat feet.

Who he was or where he'd come from, nobody seemed to know. Or care.

C H A P T E R
2

An army travels on its belly. J. P. Beaumont can go only so far on an empty stomach. On a good day. My endurance is reduced in direct proportion to the amount of MacNaughton's consumed the night before—in this case, far too much.

By noon we had worked our way through most of the businesses and several almost deserted apartment buildings on Lower Queen Anne. Famished, I called a halt.

"We'll come back later, after people get home from work. How about breakfast?"

Peters shrugged. "It's up to you."

Leading the way to the Mecca Cafe, I ordered a full breakfast and conned a sympathetic waitress out of a pair of aspirin. Peters ordered herb tea. Tea, but no sympathy.

"You drink too much, Beau," he said.

"Lay off," I told him.

"I won't lay off. You were fine when you left the house. What happened?"

I had spent Sunday afternoon helping Peters reassemble a secondhand swing set for his daughters, Heather and Tracie. The girls had supervised from the sidelines. They're cute little kids, both of them. They were underfoot and in the way, but being around them made me realize once more exactly what I'd lost. I had finished the evening at the Dog House, my home-away-from-home hangout in downtown Seattle, crying over spilt milk and singing solos with the organist. Cold sober I don't sing. I know better.

"Guess I got to feeling sorry for myself," I mumbled.

"Sorry!" Peters exclaimed. "What the hell for? You're set. You wouldn't have to work another day in your life if you weren't so goddamned stubborn."

"Sure, I'm set. Now that it's too late."

"Too late?" Peters echoed.

"Too late for me and my kids. Did I build the swing set for my own kids? No way. I was working nights as a security guard, trying to make ends meet. Karen had to ask a neighbor to help her put it up. No Little League games, no school programs. Now I've got both money and time, and where the hell are my kids? In California with Karen and their stepfather."

I dunked a piece of toast in my egg yolk and waited to see if Peters would jump me for eating eggs, too. He was quiet for a moment, stirring his tea thoughtfully. "Maybe you should join a health club, play racketball, get involved in something besides work."

"And maybe you should give up Homicide and go in for family counseling," I retorted. On that relatively unfriendly note, we left the Mecca and went back to work.

After lunch we spent some time in the Seattle Center Administration Office and got the names of all the security people who had worked Friday's games. It was nice to have a list of phone numbers to work from for a change. They let us use a couple of empty desks and phones. We sat right there and worked our way through the list. For all the good it did us. None of the security guards could remember anything unusual, either.

When we left there, we finished our canvass of the neighborhood as much as possible considering the time of day, eventually returning to the car in the Bailey's Foods parking lot. A man wearing a faded red flannel shirt over khaki pants and topped by a dingy Mariners baseball cap was leaving a nasty note under the windshield wiper.

"This your car?" he asked.

"Belongs to the mayor," Peters said, unlocking the driver's door.

"City cars park free on city streets," the man continued plaintively. "Not on private property. Was gonna have you towed."

"Look," Peters explained, "we're with Homicide. We're working a case. Didn't the store manager tell you?"

"Got nothin' to do with the store. Parking's separate. Good for half an hour, while you shop. That's it. You gonna pay me or not?"

Peters glowered. "We're here on official business."

"Me, too," the man whined. "My boss says collect. I collect. From every car. You included."

I reached into my pocket. "How much?"

"Two bucks." The man glanced triumphantly at Peters, who climbed into the driver's seat, slamming the door behind him. I waited while the man counted out my change.

"You work over the weekend?" I asked.

"Me? I work every day. I've got four lots here on Queen Anne Hill that I check seven days a week, part-time. Keeps me in cigarettes and beer. Know what I mean?"

I nodded. "Did you tow any cars from here over the weekend?"

He lifted his grimy baseball cap and scratched his head. Peters had started the car. Impatiently, he rolled down the window. "Coming or not?" he demanded.

"In a minute," I told him. I returned to the parking attendant. "Well?"

"What's it worth to you?" he asked.

I had no intention of putting a parking attendant on the city payroll as an informant. "How about if I don't let my partner here run over your toes on the way out?"

Glancing at Peters, who sat there gunning the motor, the attendant mulled the idea, then reached into a pocket and retrieved a tattered notebook. He flipped through several pencil-smudged pages before stopping and holding the notebook at arm's length.

"Yup, three of them Friday night, four on Saturday, and one on Sunday. Sunday's real slow."

"Where to?" I asked.

He stuffed the notebook back in his pocket. "Like I said. That'll cost you."

It's a wonder some people are smart enough to get out of bed in the morning. He was standing directly in front of a green-and-white sign that said "Violators will be towed. At owner's risk and expense. Lincoln Towing."

"That's okay," I said. "We'll figure it out."

"It's about time," Peters grumbled when I finally got into the car. "Where to?"

"Lincoln Towing," I told him. "Over on Fairview. They towed eight cars out of the lot over the weekend. Maybe one of them belongs to the victim."

Peters put the car in gear, shaking his head in disbelief. "Come off it, Beau. Doc Baker said he was dumped here. After he died. Why would his car be left in the lot?"

"Humor me. Unless you've got a better idea."

He didn't. We drove through what Seattlites jokingly refer to as the Mercer Mess, a city planner's worst nightmare of how to stall traffic getting off and on a freeway. It's a tangle of one-way streets that circle this way and that without any clear direction.

Lincoln Towing actually sits directly in front of traffic exiting Interstate 5 and coming into the city. At the Fairview stoplight, Lincoln Towing's Toe Truck, a tow truck fitted out as a gigantic foot complete with bright pink toes four feet tall, may very well be the first sight some visitors see as they drop off the freeway to enter Seattle.

Lincoln's Toe Truck lends a whimsical bit of humor. As long as you're not one of Lincoln Towing's unwilling customers. Then it's no laughing matter.

The man who got out of a taxi and stomped his way into the Lincoln Towing office directly ahead of us wasn't laughing. He was ready to knock heads.

"What the hell do you mean towing me from a church parking lot! It isn't Sunday. I was just having breakfast down the street."

A girl with a wholesome, scrubbed appearance greeted his tirade with a sympathetic smile. "The lot is clearly marked, sir. It's private property. We've been directed to tow all unauthorized vehicles."

He blustered and fumed, but he paid. By the time he got his keys back, it was probably one of the most expensive breakfasts of his life. He stormed out of the office. The clerk, who had continued to be perfectly polite and noncommittally sympathetic the whole time she was taking his money, turned to us. "May I help you?"

I opened my ID and placed it on the counter in front of her along with the list of license plate numbers from our surly parking lot attendant. "We understand you towed these cars over the weekend. They're all from the Bailey's Foods lot on Queen Anne Hill."

She picked up the list and looked it over. "What about them?"

"Could you check them against your records. See if there was anything unusual about any of them?"

She went to a computer terminal and typed the license numbers into it. A few minutes later she returned to the counter, shaking her head. "Nothing out of the ordinary about any of them, except one."

"Which one?"

"A Buick. It came in early Saturday morning."

"What about it?"

"It's still here."

"That's unusual?"

She smiled. "Sure. Most of them are like that guy who just left. They get here by taxi half an hour to an hour after the car. They can't wait to bail it out."

"But the Buick's still here, and that's unusual?"

"Not that unusual," she replied. "Sometimes you run into a drunk who takes a couple of days to sober up and figure out where he left the car. That's probably what happened here."

"Which Buick?" I asked.

She pointed. "The blue one. The Century. Over in the corner."

"Mind if we take a look?"

"I don't know why not." She shrugged and called over the intercom for someone to escort us. A young fellow in green Lincoln Towing coveralls led us to the car. We peered in through the windows. An athletic bag sat on the floor of the backseat. An airline identification tag was still attached to the handle. It was turned in the wrong direction for us to read it.

"Would it be possible for you to open it up so we could see the name on that tag?"

"Well . . ." The young man hesitated.

"It could be important," I urged. "Something may have happened to the driver."

He glanced from me to the window of the office over my shoulder. "Okay by me," he said.

He opened the front car door, reached in, and unlocked the back. Using a pen rather than a finger, and careful to touch only the smallest corner of the name tag, I flipped it over. The name Darwin Ridley was written in heavy felt-tipped pen along with an address and telephone number in Seattle's south end.

I read them to Peters, who jotted them down. Nothing in the car appeared to have been disturbed.

"Thanks," I said to the Lincoln Towing guy and backed out of the car.

"No problem," he said, then hurried away.

Peters scowled at the name and address. "So what now? Motor Vehicles?"

I nodded. "And check Missing Persons."

Peters shook his head. "I still think you're way out in left field. Dead men don't drive. Remember? Why would the car turn up in the same parking place as the corpse? It doesn't make sense."

"The car's been here since Saturday morning. Nobody's come to claim it. Something may have happened to the owner, even if it isn't our victim."

"All right, all right. No use arguing."

"Besides," I said, "you've got nothing better to do this afternoon."

We returned to Lincoln Towing's office and dropped off a card, asking the clerk to please notify us if anyone came to pick up the Buick. Then we headed for the Public Safety Building, where Peters went to check with Missing Persons while I dialed the S.P.D. communications center for a registration check from the Department of Motor Vehicles. I also put through an inquiry to the Department of Licensing on a driver's license issued to Darwin Ridley.

I've reluctantly come to appreciate the value of computers in police work. By the time Peters finished with Missing Persons, I knew via computer link that the Buick was registered to Darwin T. Ridley and his wife Joanna. The address on the name tag and the address on the vehicle registration were the same.

Peters, shaking his head, came to sit on the edge of my desk, his arms folded obstinately across his chest. "Missing Persons's got nothing. What a surprise!"

Margie, our clerk, appeared from nowhere. "Did you guys pick up your messages?"

She had us dead to rights. We shook our heads in silent, sheepish unison. "So what else is new? The medical examiner's office called and said they've finished the autopsy. You can go by and pick up preliminary results if you want."

"Or even if we don't want, right?" Peters asked.

"Right," she answered.

We headed out for the medical examiner's office. It's located at the base of Harborview Medical Center, one of several medical facilities in the neighborhood that have caused Seattle locals to unofficially revise First Hill's name to Pill Hill.

Doc Baker's receptionist led us into his office. As usual, we found him tossing paper clips into his battered vase. He paused long enough to push a file across his desk.

Peters picked it up and thumbed through it. "Death by hanging?"

Baker nodded. "Rope burns around his wrists and ankles. I'd say somebody hog-tied that poor son of a bitch and lynched him. Hanged by the neck until dead."

"You make it sound like an execution."

Baker tossed another paper clip into the vase. "It was, with someone other than the state of Washington doing the job—judge, jury, and executioner."

"Time of death?"

"Two o'clock Saturday morning, give or take."

"Any identifying marks?"

He sent another paper clip flying. This one

bounced off the side of the vase and fell to the floor. "Shit!" Baker bent over to retrieve it. "Not so as you'd notice," he continued. He tried again. This time it landed in the vase with a satisfying clink. "Surgical scar on his left knee that would be consistent with a sports injury of some kind."

"Nothing else?"

"Nothing. Not even dental work. Didn't have a single filling in his head."

"Got good checkups, right up until he died."

Baker glowered at Peters. "That's pretty unusual for a man his age."

"And what's that?" I asked.

"How old? Oh, thirty-nine, forty. Right around there."

"Anything else?"

"Last meal must have been about noon. We're working on stomach contents."

"Drugs?"

"Morphine, as a matter of fact. Not a lethal dose, but enough to knock him colder than a wedge."

"A junkie, then?"

Baker shook his head. "No way. We found only the one puncture, in his buttocks. Very difficult to self-administer, if you ask me. No other needle marks."

"How much did he weigh?" I asked, thinking of the driver's license information in the notebook I carried in my pocket. I didn't pull it out and look at it though, for fear of tipping my hand prematurely.

"Two twenty. Six foot four. Big guy."

"Anything else?" I asked.

Baker lobbed another paper clip into the vase. "The killer took his time. Hanging victims don't come out squeaky clean. This guy was hosed down before somebody wrapped him up in the tarp."

"Any identification on the tarp?"

"Sure, Beau, the tarp had a goddamned serial number on it! What do you think?"

I shrugged. "It could happen."

"One more thing," Baker added. "We found some flakes in his hair."

"Dandruff?" Peters asked.

Baker glowered. "Blue flakes. We're sending them down to the crime lab. It could be from whatever the noose was tied off to."

We'd pretty much worn out our welcome with Baker. "Great," I said, getting up. "Let us know if you find out anything more. We'll do the same."

I led the way. Once outside the building I paused long enough to take the notebook out of my jacket pocket and check my notes. Darwin Ridley's weight was listed as two ten and his height was listed as six four.

"Well?" Peters asked.

"It's possible. Weight is off by ten pounds,

but lots of folks fudge on weight by a pound or two."

"So what do we do?" Peters glanced at his watch. "We can either go by that address down in Rainier Valley, or we can go back up to Queen Anne and see if any of the residents are home now. Can't do both. Tracie and Heather have a dental appointment right after work."

"Cavities?" I asked.

"Two each. No perfect checkups in our family. I'll need to be on the Evergreen Point Bridge by four-thirty to beat the worst of the rush."

By working in Seattle and living on the east side of Lake Washington in Kirkland, Peters seemed to spend the better part of half his life parked on the floating bridges, going in one direction or the other. It was almost three o'clock.

"Let's go back to Queen Anne and see if we can find out anything more. I can check Ridley out by myself after you leave."

Peters scratched his head. "You know, every time you say that name, it seems like it's one I should recognize, but I just can't place it."

"Ridley?"

He nodded. "It'll come to me eventually."

We walked back to the car. Little patches of midafternoon sun had broken through the clouds and rain. It felt almost like spring as we once more tackled the questioning process on Queen Anne Hill. A few more people were home, but it didn't do us much good. They hadn't heard or seen anything unusual, either.

It was frustrating but certainly not unexpected. I decided a long time ago that only people with a very high tolerance for frustration survive as homicide detectives.

I've worked Homicide the better part of twenty years. I must qualify.

CHAPTER
3

Peters bailed out of the office at about four-fifteen. Taking kids to dentists was one part of parenthood I had brains enough not to envy. I completed our share of paperwork and handed it over to Margie for typing.

I decided to walk back to my apartment and take my own car down to Rainier Valley to check on Darwin Ridley. People who know Seattle only from television weather reports assume we live under unfailingly gray and dreary skies. The network weather reports never mention that our clouds often burn off during the day, giving us balmy, springlike afternoons, while the rest of the country remains frozen in the grip of winter.

This was one of those afternoons. If it hadn't been for the departmental issue .38 in my shoulder holster, I would have stripped off my jacket and slung it over my arm as I sauntered down a noisy Third Avenue. From either side of the street and from below it as well came the rumbling sounds of construction, the jackhammer racket of a city changing and growing. Harried pedestrians bustled past, blind and deaf to the process.

I entered the lobby of the Royal Crest and experienced a twinge of regret. Within weeks I'd be moving into a new place at Second and Broad, leaving behind the apartment that had been my haven ever since the divorce. Maybe being over forty makes the prospect of change, even change for the better, extremely uncomfortable.

It was rush hour. Honking horns told me that traffic was heavy everywhere, including the usually free-moving Fourth Avenue. It didn't make sense for me to leave my apartment and jump into the fray. I wasn't in that much of a hurry.

Instead, I made a pot of coffee and flopped into my ancient leather recliner, a relic from my first marriage, and the only stick of furniture I had managed to salvage from the house in Sumner when Karen threw me out. The recliner was brown and stained and scarred with years of use—ugly but honest. I had served notice to the interior designer working with me on the new place that where I went, so did the recliner.

With a steaming mug of coffee for company, I settled back to mull the Bailey's Foods case and try to get a handle on it. Being a detective with Homicide is very much like playing chess with a dozen opponents. The game requires anticipating all the moves, yours and the other players' as well, without ever getting a clear look at the board or knowing exactly who all the players are.

Was Darwin Ridley the dead man? A routine check of police records had turned up nothing but a couple of unpaid parking tickets. Ridley appeared to be a fairly law-abiding man. The name and address in Rainier Valley provided a very slender lead. Only the slimmest circumstantial evidence suggested we were on the right track. My first move was simple: Ascertain whether or not Darwin Ridley was alive. If he was, that was that, and we could go barking up another tree.

If lightning did strike, however, and it turned out Ridley was our victim, then the game would become infinitely more complicated.

Grieving families must be handled with utmost care, for two reasons. First, the sudden violent death of a loved one is possibly the worst shock a family ever withstands. Survivors are faced with a totally unanticipated death that leaves them with a lifetime of unresolved feelings and unsaid good-byes.

The second reason isn't nearly as poignant. The killer may very well be lurking among those grieving relatives and friends. Most homicide victims are murdered by someone they know rather than by a total stranger. Separating real grief from phony grief is an art form in its own right.

So I sat there waiting for the traffic to die down and puzzling about an unidentified man by a grocery store dumpster who would never get the chance to flaunt his set of perfect teeth in some old folks' home. And about a towed Buick Century, sitting forgotten in a corner of the Lincoln Towing lot. And about a man named Darwin Ridley, who was either dead or alive. By six o'clock, I was ready to find out which.

My Porsche was happy to be let out of the garage, but it protested being held to city speed limits. Or maybe it only seemed that way because I was hearing the call of the open road myself and wanted to be on a freeway going somewhere. Anywhere.

I found Ridley's house with no trouble, a neat, old-fashioned brick Tudor, situated near Lake Washington but minus the high-priced view. There was a two-car carport attached to the house. In it, shining in the glow of an outdoor light, sat a sporty bronze-and-cream Mustang GT. The other half of the carport was empty. Early evening dusk revealed a well-tended front yard, trimmed by a manicured hedge. Several lighted windows in the house indicated someone was home. Pulling into the carport, I parked behind the Mustang.

The house looked peaceful enough, so much so that I almost dreaded ringing the bell. Whatever the outcome, having a homicide detective pay a call tends to disrupt a family's ordinary evening routine. I more than half wished Darwin Ridley himself would open the door.

He didn't.

Instead, an attractive black woman, still puffing with exertion, came to the door. Her hair was held back by a purple sweatband. A fine film of perspiration beaded her upper lip.

She flung open the door angrily, as if expecting someone she knew but wasn't too happy with. Then, seeing a stranger, she slammed it almost shut.

"Yes?" she asked guardedly through the crack.

"I'm Detective Beaumont, Seattle P.D." I held my ID up to the open slit of the door. "Are you Joanna Ridley?"

There were long, brilliantly colored fingernails on the hand that took my ID into the house and then passed it back to me without opening the door further. "What do you want?"

"I was hoping to speak to your husband."

"He's not here."

"Do you know when he'll be back?"

"No."

She wasn't exactly brimming over with spontaneous information. "Could I speak with you then, Mrs. Ridley?"

Reluctantly, she inched the door open a little wider. In the glow from the porch light, she looked up at me defiantly, her full lips pursed, eyes smouldering. Her hair was pulled back from a high, delicately curved forehead. I was struck by her resemblance to that classic bust of Nefertiti I had seen when it came through Seattle with the King Tut exhibit years ago.

Joanna Ridley was an exotic beauty, with wide-set eyes glowing under magenta-shaded lids. Her look of absolute disdain brought me back to earth in a hurry.

"Why do you want to talk to me?" Her arch tone was almost a physical slap in the face.

"We're conducting an investigation, Mrs. Ridley. It's important that I talk to you."

"I suppose you want to come in?"

"Yes."

She stepped aside to allow me inside. My gaze had been riveted to her face. It was only when I looked down to gauge the step from the porch up into the house that I realized one of her hands rested on a wildly protruding tummy. Joanna Ridley was more than slightly pregnant. She was very pregnant.

She wore a huge pink sweatshirt that hung almost to her knees. An arrow pointed downward from the neck, and the word *Baby* was emblazoned across the appropriate spot. Her legs, what I could see of them, were well-shaped and encased in a pair of shiny, royal blue leotards. Joanna Ridley was the complete technicolor lady.

Padding barefoot ahead of me, she led the way into the living room. A rubber exercise mat lay in the middle of the floor. On the VCR a group of blurred aerobic exercisers were frozen in midair. She switched off the VCR and the screen went blank. I wondered if unborn babies liked aerobics, if they were willing or unwilling participants in America's latest health-nut fad.

Joanna Ridley spun around to face me. Her question was terse. "What do you want?"

"Do you have any idea how we could reach your husband?"

"No."

"Has he been gone long?"

Some of the defiance left her face. Awkwardly, she squatted down beside the exercise mat, folded it, picked it up, and wrestled it behind the couch. Once more her hand returned unconsciously, protectively to the swell of baby in her abdomen. I got the distinct impression she was avoiding the question.

"A couple of days," she said evasively.

"How long?" I insisted.

"I saw him last Friday morning, at break-fast, before he left for school. He's a teacher. A coach for Mercer Island High School."

"He's been gone since Friday and you haven't reported him missing?"

She shrugged. "He lost."

"I beg your pardon?"

"The game. The Islanders lost Friday night. The first round of the championship. He'll come home when he's good and ready."

"He does that? Just disappears?"

She nodded. "When they win, he celebrates. When they lose, it's gloom and doom. He hides out afterward. He usually doesn't miss school, though," she added.

"He did today?"

Joanna Ridley turned her back on me and walked to the couch. She sat down, curling her legs under her in a way that should have been impossible for someone in such an advanced stage of pregnancy. Maybe doing aerobics does make a difference. Uninvited, I helped myself to a chair.

She took a deep breath. "They called look-ing for him. Left a message on the machine. I didn't return the call."

There was a brief silence between us while I wondered exactly how pregnant she was and whether the female reproductive system would withstand the shock my intuition told me was coming. If Darwin Ridley was missing, had been since Friday, I had a feeling I knew where he was, and I didn't know how she'd take it.

Looking for a way to delay or soften the blow, I cleared my throat. "As I said, Mrs. Ridley, we're conducting an investigation. Would you happen to have a recent photograph of your husband?"

Despite her bulging center of gravity, Joanna Ridley gracefully eased her way off the couch. She left the room and returned a few moments later carrying an eight-by-ten gilt-framed photograph, which she handed to me. Staring back at me was a good-looking middle-aged man with a sprinkle of gray in his curly hair. His mouth was set in a wide grin. With perfect teeth.

"It's a good picture," I said.

She took it back from me and examined it closely herself, as though she hadn't looked at it for a long time. "It is, isn't it."

"Did your husband ever have any kind of surgery?"

She looked at me thoughtfully, considering before she answered. "On his knee," she said at last. "An old football injury."

"Right or left?"

"Left." Suddenly, she seemed to lose all patience with me and my apparently inane questions. "Are you going to tell me what's going on?"

"Mrs. Ridley, I'm sorry to have to say this, and at this point let me stress that we're not sure, but we have reason to believe your husband may be the homicide victim who was found on Queen Anne Hill early this morning."

Her slender fingers tightened around the picture frame, gripping it until the knuckles showed light against the darker skin. She stepped backward, sinking heavily onto the couch.

I hurried on. "We need someone to make a positive identification. This afternoon we discovered that over the weekend your husband's car was towed away from the same parking lot in which the victim was found."

"You think he's dead?" She choked over the last word.

"As I said, Mrs. Ridley. We're not sure. From looking at the picture, I'd say it was the same man, but that doesn't constitute a positive identification. There's certainly a strong resemblance."

She leaned back against the couch, resting her head on the wall behind her, closing her eyes. Her breathing quickened. I was afraid she was going to faint. Alarmed, I got up and went to her.

"Are you all right, Mrs. Ridley? Can I get

you something? A glass of water? Something stronger?"

She looked up at me through eyes bright with tears. "Where is he?"

"The medical examiner's office. Harborview Medical Center."

"And you came to take me there?"

I nodded. "If you're up to going. You could send someone else—a relative, a close friend. A person in your condition . . ."

She stood up abruptly. "I'll go."

"You're sure it won't be too hard on you?"

"I said I'll go," she repeated.

She paused by the door long enough to pull on a pair of leg warmers and some short boots. She draped a long yellow wool shawl over her shoulders. "I'm ready," she said.

Outside, I helped her into my car. Sports cars are not built with pregnant ladies in mind, whether or not they do aerobics. There was absolute silence between us during the drive to Harborview. She asked no questions; I offered no information. What could I say?

A brand new, peach-fuzzed night tech in Doc Baker's office came out of the back as we entered. "What can I do for you?"

"I'm Detective Beaumont. Seattle P.D. I believe we have a tentative identification on the Queen Anne victim."

"Great!" He glanced at Joanna Ridley's somber face. She stood there silently, biting her lower lip. He curbed some of his youthful enthusiasm. "Sure thing," he said. "If you'll wait here for a couple of minutes..."

He disappeared down a short hallway. I offered Joanna a chair, which she refused. Instead, she walked over to the doorway and stood peering out. Harborview Medical Center sits on the flank of First Hill. Even from the ground floor she could look down at the city spread out below and beyond the early evening hazy glow of parking lot lights. Eventually, the tech came back for us.

"Right this way, miss," he said. I winced. He wasn't going to win any prizes for diplomacy, or for observation either, for that matter.

He led us down the same hallway and stopped in front of a swinging laboratory door. He pushed it open and held it for her to enter. Joanna seemed to falter. I didn't blame her. Eventually, she got a grip on herself and went inside. I followed her, with the tech bringing up the rear.

A sheet-draped figure lay on a gurney in the far corner of the room. "This way, please," the tech said.

Joanna Ridley didn't move. She seemed frozen to the spot. I stepped to her side and took hold of an arm, just above the elbow. Gently, I led her forward.

The tech moved to the head of the gurney and held up a corner of the sheet far enough to expose the still face beneath it. In the quiet room, Joanna gave a sudden, sharp intake of breath and turned away.

"I need to lie down," she said.

C H A P T E R
4

I led Joanna Ridley into a small, private waiting room and helped her lie down on a dilapidated couch. The tech brought a glass of water. "Is she going to be all right?" he asked nervously. "I can call somebody down from Emergency."

Glancing back at her, I saw tears streaming down her face. She didn't need a doctor or a whole roomful of people. "No," I told him. "She'll be okay. I'll let you know if she needs help."

The tech backed out of the room. I set the water down on a table without offering any to her. She didn't need plain water, either.

For several long minutes, I waited for her sobs to become quiet. Eventually, they did, a little. "Mrs. Ridley," I asked gently, "is there anything I can do to help? Someone I can call?"

Her sobs intensified into an anguished wail. "How could this happen when the baby . . ."

She broke off suddenly, and my adrenaline started pumping. "The baby! Is it coming now? Should I call a doctor?"

Joanna shook her head. "My baby's not even born yet, and his father's . . ." She stopped again, unable to continue.

My own relief was so great, I walked to the table and helped myself to her glass of water, all of it, before I spoke, offering what comfort I could. "It'll be all right. You'll see. Really, isn't there someone I can call?"

Her sobbing ceased abruptly. Raising herself up on one elbow, she glared at me angrily. In her eyes I was something less than an unfeeling clod. "You don't understand. My baby's father is dead."

Unfortunately, I did understand, all too well. I knew far better than she did what was ahead for both her and her baby. From personal experience. Except my mother hadn't had so much as a marriage certificate to back her up when I was born. Society was a hell of a lot less permissive back in the forties.

"My mother did it," I said quietly. "You can, too."

She looked at me silently for a long moment, assimilating what I had said. Then, before she could respond, the technician burst into the room. "Dr. Baker's on the phone. He wants to talk to you, Detective Beaumont." The tech bounded back out of the room with me right behind him. "He wants to know who it was," he said over his shoulder.

"How the hell did he find out?"

"He told me to call if we came up with something."

"What do you mean *we*?" I fumed.

He led me into another office, picked up a telephone receiver, and held it toward me. I snatched it from his hand.

"Beaumont," I growled into the phone.

"Understand you've got a positive ID. Good work, Beau. That was quick. What have you got?"

"Who the fuck do you think you are, calling me to the phone like this? I just barely found out myself. All I know so far is a name and address."

"Well, get on with it for chrissakes."

"Look, Baker. That poor woman just learned her husband's dead. I'll start asking questions when I'm damn good and ready."

"Don't be a prima donna, Beau. Give me what you have."

"Like hell!"

I flung the receiver at the startled tech, who stared at me dumbfounded. I hurried back down the hall to the room where Joanna Ridley waited. The phone rang again, but I didn't pause long enough to hear what the tech said to his irate boss. Besides, I was sure Baker's next phone call would be to either Captain Powell or Sergeant Watkins.

Hustling back into the waiting room, I startled Joanna Ridley, who was dabbing at her eyes with a tissue. There was no time to waste in idle explanations. "Come on," I said, helping her up. "Let's get out of here."

"Where are we going?"

"I'll take you home. We've got to go now, before we're overrun with cops and reporters."

The tech had followed me. We ran into him head-on in the doorway. He was carrying a metal clipboard and had a pen poised to take down information. "Detective Beaumont, you can't leave."

"Oh, yeah? Watch me!"

"But I need some information . . ."

"You'll have it when I'm damn good and ready."

"What's going on?" Joanna managed as I hurried her, half-resisting, out the door and down the hallway.

"This place is going to be crawling with officers and reporters in about two minutes flat."

The technician trailed behind us, whimpering like a scolded puppy. "But Dr. Baker says . . ."

"Piss on Doc Baker. You had no business calling him! Now get out of here."

I helped Joanna into the car and slammed the door behind her for emphasis. The technician was still standing with his mouth open and clipboard in hand when I fishtailed the Porsche out of the parking lot and onto the street.

Dodging through a series of side streets, I paused at a stop sign on Boren, signaling for a right-hand turn, planning to drive Joanna Ridley back down to her home in Rainier Valley to talk to her there.

"I don't want to go home," she said.

Surprised, I glanced in her direction. She seemed under control. "Are you sure? I'm going to have to ask you some questions. It might be easier."

A marked patrol car, red lights flashing, raced past us on Boren. Obviously, Baker had sounded the alarm and troops were out in force to pull J. P. Beaumont back into line. I waited until the car turned off toward Harborview before I eased the Porsche out into the intersection and turned left.

"I understand what you did back there," Joanna said quietly. "Thanks."

"No problem."

I wondered where to take her. Obviously, we couldn't go to the department, and my own apartment was a bad idea as well. I settled on the only logical answer, the Dog House.

The Dog House is actually a Seattle institution. It's a twenty-four-hour restaurant three blocks from my apartment that's been in business for more than fifty years. I've needed almost daily help from both McDonald's and the Dog House kitchen to survive my reluctant return to bachelorhood.

You'll notice I said the kitchen. The bar at the Dog House is a different story.

Steering clear of the scene of my previous night's solo performance, I took Joanna Ridley through the main part of the restaurant and into the back dining room. It was closed, but I knew Wanda would let us sit there undisturbed.

She brought two cups of coffee at the same time she brought menus. Joanna accepted coffee without comment, but she refused my offer of food. Groping for a way to start the conversation, I asked what I hoped was an innocuous question. "When's the baby due?"

It wasn't nearly innocuous enough. Just that quickly tears appeared in the corners of her eyes. "Two weeks," she managed. She wiped the tears away and then sat looking at me, her luminous dark eyes searching my face. "Is it true what you said, that your mother raised you alone?"

I nodded. "My father died before I was born. My parents weren't married."

She lowered her gaze and bit her lip. Her voice was almost a whisper. "Are you saying that'll make it easier, that we were married?"

"It'll be better for the baby," I returned. "Believe me, I know what I'm talking about."

Wanda poked her head in the doorway to see if we were going to order anything besides coffee. I waved her away. I decided I'd offer Joanna Ridley food again later, if either of us had the stomach for it, but now was the time to ask questions, to begin assembling the pieces of the puzzle.

"Mrs. Ridley," I began.

"Joanna," she corrected.

"Joanna, this will probably be painful, but I have to start somewhere. Do you know if your husband was in any kind of difficulty?"

"Difficulty? What do you mean?"

"Gambling, maybe?" Even high school teams and coaches get dragged into gambling scams on occasion.

Joanna shook her head, and I continued. "Drugs? One way or another, most crimes in this country are connected to the drug trade."

"No," she replied tersely, her face stony.

"Was he under any kind of medical treatment?"

"No. He was perfectly healthy."

"You're sure he wasn't taking any medication?"

Again she shook her head. "Darwin never

used drugs of any kind. He was opposed to them."

"The medical examiner found morphine in his bloodstream. You've no idea where it could have come from?"

"I told you. He didn't use drugs, not even aspirin. Is that what killed him, the morphine?"

It was my turn to shake my head while I considered how to tell her. "He died of a broken neck," I said softly. "Somebody tied a rope around his neck and hung him."

Joanna's eyes widened. "Dear God!" She pushed her chair back so hard it clattered against the wall. Dodging her way through empty chairs and tables, she stopped only when she reached the far corner of the room. She leaned against the two walls, sobbing incoherently.

I followed, standing helplessly behind her, not knowing if I should leave her alone or reach out to comfort her. Finally, I placed one hand on her shoulder. She shuddered as if my hand had burned her and shrugged it away.

She turned on me then like a wounded animal, eyes blazing. "It'll always be like that, won't it! We're accepted as long as we're smart enough to know our place, but cross that line, and niggers are only good for hanging!"

"Joanna, I . . ."

She pushed her way past me, returned to our table, and grabbed up her shawl. Just as suddenly as the outburst had come, it subsided. Her face went slack. "Take me home," she said wearily. "There are people I need to call."

I dropped money on the table for the coffee and trailed her outside. When I caught up, Joanna was standing by the Porsche, fingering the door handle. "Since when do cops drive Porsches," she asked when I walked up to open her car door.

"When they inherit them," I replied. I helped her into the car and closed the door behind her.

Sliding into the driver's seat, I glanced in her direction before I started the engine. She sat with her head resting against the carseat, her long, slender neck stretched taut, eyes closed, her face impassive. That unconscious pose elicited once more the striking similarity between Joanna Ridley and that ancient Egyptian queen, but this was no time to tell her how beautiful she was. Joanna Ridley was in no condition to hear it.

"I didn't finish asking all my questions," I said, starting the car and putting it in gear.

"Ask them tomorrow. I'm worn out."

"Somebody will come stay with you? You shouldn't be alone."

She nodded. "I'll call someone."

We drove through the city. It was early, not more than eight o'clock or so, but it seemed much later. I felt incredibly tired. Joanna Ridley wasn't the only one who was worn out. She just had a hell of a lot better reason.

I drove back to her place and pulled up in front of her house. "Would you like me to come in with you?" I asked. "I could stay until someone comes over."

"Don't bother," she said. "I can take care of myself."

I started to get out to open the door for her, but she opened it herself, struggled out of the low-slung seat, and was inside the house before I knew what had hit me. I sat there like a jerk and watched her go.

It wasn't until I turned the car around that I noticed the light in the carport was out. I couldn't remember her switching it off when we left the house, but she must have. As a precaution, I waited in the car with my hand on the door handle long enough to see her pick up a phone, dial, and begin talking.

She'll be all right, I said to myself as I put the car in gear and drove up the street. What Joanna Ridley needed right then was family and friends, people who cared about her and would give her the strength and courage to pick up the pieces and go on with her life. What she didn't need was an aging police watchdog with a penchant for finding bogey-men under every light switch.

Right that minute Joanna Ridley needed J. P. Beaumont like she needed a hole in her head.

CHAPTER
5

One of the drawbacks of living in the royal Crest is the lack of soundproofing. I can hear my phone ringing the moment the elevator door opens. It's always a horse race to see if I can unlock the door and grab the phone before whoever's calling gives up. My attorney keeps suggesting I get an answering machine, but I'm too old-fashioned. And too stubborn.

Detective Peters was still on the phone when I picked it up. He was hot.

"God damn it, Beau. What the hell are you up to now? I've had calls from Watty and Captain Powell, both. They're ready to tear you apart. Me, too. They demanded I tell them what *we* had. Remember me? I'm your partner."

"Hold up, Peters. It's not my fault."

"Not your fault! I heard you told Doc Baker to piss up a rope."

"Not in those exact words."

"Jesus H. Christ, Beau. What's going on?"

"It's Ridley, all right."

That stopped Peters cold. "No shit! The basketball coach? I remembered where I'd heard the name while I was stuck on the bridge, but there was no way to get hold of you. Who identified him?"

"His wife. He'd been missing since Friday, but she didn't report it. Thought he was sulking over losing the game. She figured he'd come home eventually."

Peters gave his customary, long, low whistle. "Have you sealed the car?"

"Not yet. I just dropped Joanna Ridley back at her house."

"Should I come on in? That Buick shouldn't sit outside any longer than it already has."

I glanced at my watch. It was nine o'clock and I was tired, but there was a lot of merit in what Peters said. Every effort has to be made to preserve evidence. "What about your girls?"

"Mrs. Edwards is here. The kids are asleep, and Mrs. Edwards is watching television." Mrs. Edwards was Peters' live-in housekeeper/babysitter. "I'll meet you at Lincoln Towing in twenty minutes."

As an old Fuller Brush salesman, I recognize

an assumed close trap when I see one. Not do you want to meet me, but when will you meet me.

I needed to hit my second wind pretty damn soon. I was going to need it. Peters is a hell of a lot younger than I am, and he's disgustingly immune to vices of any kind. Including booze. I avoided my recliner. I didn't dare sit down and get comfortable for fear I wouldn't get back up. Instead, I made a cursory pass at the refrigerator in a vain search for food before driving to Lincoln Towing's Fairview lot.

I waited outside the lot itself, watching the eager beaver fleet of tow trucks come and go. Peters must have flown low across the bridge. He was there in far less than twenty minutes. His first question nailed me good. "Did you have her sign a voluntary search form?"

"You can't expect me to remember everything," I told him. He glared at me in reply, and we went inside together.

The night clerk wasn't thrilled at the added paperwork involved in our securing Ridley's Buick. She did it, though. Once the car had been towed to the secured processing room at Fifth and Cherry, I was ready to call it a day.

"No way," Peters said, opening the passenger door on my Porsche and climbing inside. "I'm not letting you out of my sight until we've mended some fences along the way, starting with the medical examiner's office."

We found the same night tech sound asleep in the employee's lounge. The bell over the front door didn't faze him. He awoke with a start when I gave his shoulder a rough shake. "I thought you wanted information," I told him.

He stumbled sleepily to his feet and went in search of his clipboard. I couldn't help wondering if Doc Baker knew his baby tech took a little evening nap on company time. Eventually, the tech returned relatively awake and prepared to take down my information.

I filled in as many blanks on his form as I could, based on what information I had gleaned from Joanna Ridley. It consisted of the usual—name, address, phone number, next of kin—enough to clear the medical examiner's office of one of its prime responsibilities: Identification of the victim.

As Peters and I left the office, I paused in the doorway. "By the way, you might want to call Doc Baker with that now. He's probably waiting to hear from you." The tech didn't look eager to pick up the phone to call Doc Baker's home number.

"You ever hear of winning friends and influencing people, Beau?" Peters asked as we walked outside.

"I don't like people who sleep on the job. Where to next?"

If I had any delusions of going home right

then, Peters put a stop to them with what he said next. "We'd better check in with the department and let them know what's up. Officially."

We were ready to climb into the car. I looked at him across the roof of the Porsche. "What the hell happened to you, Peters? You used to be a lot more flexible, remember? You didn't always do things by the book."

He grinned at me. "Two and a half years of hanging around with J. P. Beaumont. That's what happened. Somebody in this outfit has to go by the book, or we'll both get our asses fired."

Back on the fifth floor of the Public Safety Building we sorted through our individual fanfolds of messages.

"Call," Peters said. "Five bucks says I take it."

"You're on."

"Full house." Triumphantly, Peters turned his messages faceup on the desk. Three from Sergeant Watkins, two from Captain Powell. "See there?"

"Read 'em and weep," I told him, turning over my own—four of a kind, all from Captain Lawrence Powell. With a grimace of disgust, Peters slapped a five-dollar bill on the desk in front of me.

One of the other detectives sauntered over to our cubicle. "I don't know what you two have been up to, but people are gunning for you. I'd lay low if I were you."

We never had a fighting chance of lying low. We were right in the middle of writing our reports when Sergeant Watkins showed up in a stained sweat suit and worn running shoes. He hadn't bothered to dress for the occasion. He ignored Peters and came straight after me.

"You interested in the Officer Friendly program in Seattle Public Schools?" he demanded. "By the time Doc Baker finishes with you, that may be the only job in the department you're qualified for."

"Doc Baker was out of line," I returned. "So was his tech. They had no business demanding information before I had a chance to question the individual."

"*Doctor* Baker," Watty corrected, enunciating every syllable clearly to be sure I understood his meaning. "Doctor Baker happens to be the King County medical examiner, and don't you forget it."

He glanced down at the forms we were working on. He sighed and headed for his desk, still growling at us over his shoulder. "When you finish those reports, you could just as well bring them by so I can see what you've got."

It was eleven by the time we were perched

on the front of Watty's desk, waiting while he scanned our reports.

"A high school basketball coach. Holy shit! I'd better get Arlo Hamilton on this right away. Can you two be here for a press briefing at eight tomorrow morning?"

We both nodded. Unlike crooks, cops don't get time off for good behavior. By the time I drove Peters back to his Datsun at Lincoln Towing, I could barely hold my head up.

"You satisfied?" I asked. "Is everything by the book now?"

"As much as it's going to be," Peters replied mildly. "What do you want to do tomorrow? Go to Ridley's house or stop by the school?"

"The house first," I answered. "We'd better get that voluntary search form before this gets any deeper."

Peters rolled his eyes and grinned. "Wonders will never cease."

I drove back to Third and Lenora and put the Porsche to bed in its assigned place in the parking garage. I walked onto the elevator only because it would have been too much trouble to get down on my knees and crawl. A phone was ringing when the elevator door opened. It's always my phone.

"Hello," I snarled into it.

"Don't sound so happy to hear from me." It was Ralph Ames, my attorney, calling from Phoenix. Ralph Ames' law firm, and more importantly, Ralph's personal attention, had been a gift to me from the same lady who left me the Porsche. I'm not one of his more dependable clients.

"I understand you didn't make your closing interview this afternoon."

"Damn it, Ralph. I got busy here and completely forgot about it. Can we reset it?"

"No sweat," Ralph told me cheerfully. "Only you'll have to swear on a stack of Bibles that you'll show up this time."

"I swear. Just let me know when it is."

When I got off the phone I was careful to steer clear of any hair of the dog. I figured I'd need to be on my toes early and long the next day. A clear head was essential. I fell into bed, but by then I was too wound up to sleep.

My mind slipped into overdrive and busily tried to sift through all the information it had received that day. So far the only person firmly fixed in my memory bank was Joanna Ridley. What was it she had said when she blew up at me there in the waiting room? Something about crossing a line. What line had Darwin Ridley crossed? And why had it been fatal? That was one of the tough questions I'd have to ask his widow the next day.

It was late when I finally drifted off. I was still awake when the last of the serious drinkers left Palmer's Tavern across the street. It seemed like only minutes later when I surfaced in a dream with Anne Corley.

She never changes in my dreams. She's always young and beautiful and vibrant, and she's always wearing that same, tantalizing red dress.

In the dream, I'm always so glad to see her it's pathetic. She smiles and reaches out to take my hand. Over the months I've learned to force myself awake then, to propel myself out of the dream before it has a chance to turn ugly.

I awoke shaking and dripping with sweat. I know better than to try to sleep again after one of those dreams. I always return to that same instant like some crazy broken record.

Instead, I stumbled out of bed, took a long hot shower, shaved, and dressed. I was at the Dog House ordering breakfast by five-thirty, along with a generous slice of Seattle's colorful cast of late-night/early-morning characters.

I appropriated the discarded remains of a newspaper from the table next to me. I ignored the news as I always do. Daily doses of news are bad for me. Instead, I worked *The New York Times* crossword puzzle over coffee, bacon, and eggs.

It's one way to take your mind off your troubles.

CHAPTER
6

The murder of a prominent man is always news. The murder of a winning high school coach is news with a capital *N*. The department's conference room was jammed to the gills for the promised briefing, with the attendees nothing short of a *Who's Who* in Seattle media, from television reporters to print pukes. Including Maxwell Cole, my all-time least favorite newspaper columnist.

Max is part of a long-running rivalry that dates back to college days. His position as crime columnist for the *Seattle Post-Intelligencer* has kept us at odds for as long as I've been with Seattle P.D. He has a way of getting under my skin. And staying there.

Arlo Hamilton, Seattle P.D.'s public information officer, is a reasonable sort, but I could see he was losing patience as Max asked questions that were nothing less than an ill-disguised tirade—the media busily manufacturing news to suit themselves.

"One of my sources stated that Mr. Ridley was ..." He paused for dramatic effect and consulted a small notebook. "I believe the word he used was *lynched*. Doesn't that sort of take you back to the Old South? Is it possible this homicide was racially motivated?"

"As I said before, Mr. Cole, at this time we have no motive in this crime. The exact cause of death is being withheld pending investigation."

"But wouldn't you say lynching is a step backward to the Ku Klux Klan mentality of the sixties?"

"I wouldn't say anything of the kind."

"You're ruling out race as a possible motive, then?"

I was glad Arlo was running the press conference instead of me. About then I would have told Max to fuck off. Hamilton managed to remain unruffled. "We are investigating all possibilities at this time. No potential lead will be ignored, racial or otherwise."

Arlo glanced around the room, hoping to shut Max down by calling someone else. Max blithely launched into another question.

"Two years ago, during the height of the Neo-Nazi scare, there was talk of creating an all-white preserve here in Washington. Could this action be connected with one of those groups?"

"As you know, Mr. Cole, members of those groups were apprehended, tried, and found guilty of numerous crimes. Those who didn't die during the initial siege of their headquarters are in prison for long terms. I don't think we need worry that Mr. Ridley's death is part of a Neo-Nazi plot. Any other questions?"

Fortunately, someone else raised his hand, and Hamilton gratefully acknowledged him. "Were police officers in attendance at the basketball championships in Seattle Center Friday night?"

Hamilton nodded.

"The Mayor's office has been concerned about special event security at the Center. Has security been beefed up?"

"Yes, it has. The horse patrol was there as well as several officers patrolling the grounds on foot. None of them saw anything out of line."

"You're saying that it wasn't a lack of security?"

"Look, you guys, give me a break. Don't read between the lines. We had numerous officers at the Center, but until we know exactly what happened, I can't say whether it was a security problem or not."

It was clear the newshounds had Arlo's scent. There was no need for Peters and me to hang around for the bloodletting. I reached over and tapped Peters on the shoulder. "Let's get out of here."

He followed me to the door. I didn't notice that Maxwell Cole had trailed after us until he showed up at the elevator lobby. Everything about Max is big, from the layer of flab that spills over the top of his belt buckle up to and including his ego. He wears a waxed, handlebar mustache that tends to be littered with bits and pieces of his most recent meal—egg yolk in this particular case.

"How's it going, J. P.? You two working this one? I saw you hanging around the briefing room."

"Look, Max, we've got a long day ahead of us. Get lost."

"Come on, J. P. Give an old fraternity brother a break. All I need is an angle. Race would be dynamite. It would bust this town wide open."

I try not to deal with Maxwell Cole in anything but absolute contempt. Lesser insults go straight over his head. "We're booked up already, Max. We don't need you to start a race war just to keep us busy."

The elevator door slipped open. We got on and left him standing there in the hallway. "Think he got it?" Peters asked once the door closed.

"Beats the hell out of me."

We went on down to the garage and checked out a car. The first order of business had to be the voluntary search form from Joanna Ridley. That would enable the crime lab to go to work on Darwin Ridley's Buick.

Several cars were parked on the street outside Joanna Ridley's house, including an immense old Lincoln. I led the way to the door and rang the bell. A tall but stoop-shouldered black man opened the door and peered down at us through gold-rimmed glasses. "What can I do for you gentlemen?" he asked.

"We're with Seattle P.D.," I said, offering him my ID. "We're here to speak to Mrs. Ridley."

"Joanna's not feelin' too well."

Joanna Ridley appeared in a doorway behind him, wearing a flowing blue caftan. Her eyes were swollen, and she wore no trace of makeup. She looked haggard, as though she hadn't slept well, either. "It's all right, Daddy," she said. "I'll see them."

The old man stepped to one side, allowing us to enter the house. The living room was filled with nine or ten people, all of them involved in various conversations that ceased as Joanna led us through the gathering to a small study that opened off the living room. She closed the door behind us, effectively shutting out the group of mourners gathered to comfort her.

"Mrs. Ridley, this is my partner, Detective Ron Peters. We brought along a form we need you to sign so we can search your husband's car." I extracted the folded form from my jacket pocket and handed it to her. I watched as her eyes skimmed the lines.

"It'll save us the time and effort of getting a search warrant," I explained.

A scatter of pens and pencils lay on the desk. Without hesitation, she put the paper on the desk, located a pen that worked, and scrawled her name across the bottom of the form.

"Will that do?" she asked, handing it back to me.

"For a start. We also need to ask some questions, if you don't mind." She took the chair behind the desk. Peters and I sat on a couch facing her. With determined effort, Joanna Ridley managed to retain her composure.

"To begin with, you told me yesterday that, as far as you knew, your husband had no drug or gambling connections. Had you noticed anything unusual in your husband's patterns? Any threats? What about money difficulties?"

She shook her head in answer to each question.

"Any unusual telephone calls, things he might not have shared with you?"

There was the slightest flicker of something in Joanna's expression, a momentary waver, before she once more shook her head. A detective lives and dies by his wits and by his powers of observation. There was enough of a change in her expression that I noted it, but there was no clue, no hint, as to what lay behind it. I tried following up in the same vein, hoping for some sort of clarification.

"Anyone with a grudge against him?"

This time, when she answered, her face remained totally impassive. "Not that I know of."

"How long had you two been married?" Peters asked.

"Fifteen years." Peters' question came from left field. It moved away from the murder and into the personal, into the mire of Joanna Ridley's private loss and grief. She blinked back tears.

"And this is your first child?"

She swallowed. "We tried, for a long time. The doctors said we'd never have children."

"How long did your husband teach at Mercer Island?"

She took a deep breath. "Twelve years. He taught social studies at Franklin before that. He was assistant basketball coach at Mercer Island for eight years, head coach for the last two."

"Didn't they win state last year?" Peters asked. "Seems like I remember reading that."

Peters' memory never fails to impress me. He impressed Joanna Ridley, too.

She gave him a bittersweet smile. "That's true, but people said it was only a holdover from the previous year, the previous coach. Darwin wanted to do it again this year so he could prove . . ." She stopped abruptly, unable to continue.

"I know this is painful for you," Peters sympathized. "But it's important that we put all the pieces together. You told Detective Beaumont here that you last saw your husband Friday morning at breakfast?"

She nodded. "That's right."

"You didn't go to the game?"

"I don't like basketball."

"You didn't attend his games?"

"Our work lives were separate. I stayed away from his career, and he stayed away from mine."

"What do you do?"

"I'm a flight attendant for United. On maternity leave."

"Joanna," I cut in, "something you said last night has been bothering me, something about crossing a line. What did you mean?"

Joanna Ridley was not a practiced liar. She hesitated for only the briefest moment, but caution and wariness were evident in her answer. "Blacks go only so far before they hit the wall. It was okay to come from Rainier Valley and go to Mercer Island as assistant coach, but not head coach."

"There were problems, racial problems?"

"Some."

"And you think your husband's death may be racially motivated."

"Don't you?" she asked in return.

I could tell she was concealing something, hiding what she really meant behind her curt answers, her troubled gaze. Finally, biting her lip, she dropped her eyes and sat looking down at the bulge of baby in her lap.

At last she looked back up at us. "Is that all?" she asked. "My guests are waiting."

It wasn't all. It was a hell of a long way from being all, but we had reached an impasse, a place beyond which progress was impossible until Peters and I had more to go on.

"For the time being," I said, rising. Peters followed. I handed her my card. "Here's my name and numbers. Call if you remember something else you think we need to know."

She took it from my hand and dropped it onto the desk without looking at it. Her expression said that I shouldn't hold my breath.

When she made no offer to get up, I said, "We can find our way out."

She nodded, and we left.

"We said something that pissed her off," Peters mused as we climbed into the car. "I don't know exactly what it was."

"She lied," I told him.

"I know, but why?"

"There must have been phone calls, or at least, one call. And then later, when I asked her about what she said last night. That was all a smoke screen."

Peters nodded. "I thought as much."

There was a brief silence in the car. In my mind's eye I played back the entire conversation, trying to recall each nuance, every inflection. Peters was doing the same thing.

"Something else bothered me," Peters said.

"What's that?"

"The part about her not going to the games, not liking basketball."

"Karen wasn't wild about homicide," I said. "Wives aren't required to adore whatever it is their husbands do."

"Point taken. So what now? Run a routine check on her?"

"Sounds reasonable."

"By the way," Peters added, "how come you didn't mention she was pregnant last night?"

"Didn't I?"

"No."

"I must be getting old. The mind's going."

Peters chuckled, and there was another short silence. "I hope she's not the one," he said at last. "She seems like such a nice lady."

"Appearances can be deceiving," I said.

I felt Peters' sharp, appraising look. "Ain't that the truth!" he said.

I didn't answer. Didn't need to. Anne Corley had taught me that much.

In spades.

CHAPTER
7

We took the signed search form back to the Public Safety Building and hand-carried it through the process. Once it had crossed all required desks and swum upstream through all necessary channels, we followed the State Patrol's criminalists into the processing room.

Over the years, you get used to the unexpected. When you're dealing with homicide, there's no telling what'll turn up in the victim's vehicle—the murder weapon, incriminating evidence, perhaps even another victim. That's happened to me more than once.

Peters and I had already seen what was in the car itself, but we were most curious about what might be hidden out of sight in the trunk. We were prepared for anything, except for what we found—a trunkful of Girl Scout cookies. Fifteen boxes in all.

We weren't the only ones who were surprised. It set the guy from the crime lab on his ass as well. "I'll be damned!" he said.

He conducted a quick inventory: Five Mints, three Carmel Delights, three Peanut Butter Patties, two Lemon Creams, and two Short Bread. The entire selection. If there was a hidden message concealed in the variety of cookies, the pattern eluded us.

On the other hand, the contents of the athletic bag turned out to be quite revealing—sweats, a clean shirt, a change of underwear and socks, toothbrush, toothpaste, and a bottle of Chaps. Darwin Ridley had intended to smell good, if not during the game, then certainly after it. And it appeared that he had planned to spend the night away from home regardless of whether or not the Islanders won.

We left the lab tech to his detail work. Peters and I drove across the floating bridge to Mercer Island. During the early years of Seattle, there was a group of visionaries who had wanted to turn Mercer Island into a vast park to benefit the whole city. That idea was squelched on the premise that no one in his right mind would travel that far for a picnic. Now, depending on rush hour traffic, Mercer Island is one of Seattle's closest suburbs. It's also one of the poshest.

Mercer Island High School is tucked back

into the island's interior. On that particular day, it was a hotbed of activity. A whole contingent of reporters had beaten us to the punch. They hovered in eddying groups, hoping to capture a newsworthy comment from a grief-stricken team member or student. News vehicles occupied every visitor parking place as well as a good portion of the fire lane.

Peters and I parked a block or so away on the street and walked. We located the principal's office from the crowd milling around the door, both inside and out. A harried clerk stood behind a counter, attempting to maintain some semblance of order. Peters and I shoved our way through the mob, many of whom we recognized from the early morning press conference.

"We need to see the principal," Peters said brusquely to the clerk when we finally reached the counter.

"You and everybody else," she replied sarcastically.

He handed her the leather wallet containing his ID. She took off her glasses to examine it and then gave it back. She replaced her glasses, settling them firmly on her face. "All right. Let me check with Mr. Browning."

She disappeared into an inner office and returned moments later. "He'll see you now," she announced.

The only thing big about Ned Browning was

his voice, which rumbled from an incongruously diminutive chest. His elfin features smacked of Santa Claus. His handshake, however, was that of a born wrestler.

"You're here about Mr. Ridley's death?" We nodded. Obviously, Ned Browning wasn't one to beat around the bush. "I'm sure you understand what an effect this terrible loss has had on our student body today." He spoke with the measured cadence of an old-time educator, one used to having his listeners' undivided attention. Or else.

"I considered dismissing school entirely when we first were notified of the situation. It's difficult to know what's the best thing to do in a case like this."

He paused and rubbed his chin, staring fixedly at us.

"Not canceling school was probably a good idea," I said. "It's best to keep things as close to normal as possible."

My comment was greeted with all the enthusiasm Ned Browning might have given an unfortunate truant's overused alibi. He ignored it totally. He continued speaking as though I'd never opened my mouth.

"The trouble is, this team has faced a similar problem once before. Some of these boys were already playing varsity ball when their previous coach, Mr. Altman, died of a heart attack.

"Of course, that was last year. It happened

during the summer. It wasn't a situation like this where he was here one day and gone the next. We had the benefit of some adjustment time before school started in the fall. Not only that, Mr. Ridley had worked with the team for several years as the assistant coach. There was enough continuity so they were able to put together a winning team. They won the state championship last year. Were you aware of that?"

Peters and I nodded in unison. Browning went on. "I've sequestered the entire team as well as the squad of cheerleaders in Mr. Ridley's classroom. Of all the students, they're probably the ones who are most upset. They're the ones who worked most closely with him.

"Our guidance counselor, Mrs. Wynn, is with them. I thought it best to keep them together and isolated for fear some of your friends out in the other room would get hold of them." Ned Browning nodded slightly in the direction of the outer office. All of his actions were understated, self-contained.

"Believe me, Mr. Browning, those jerks out there are anything but friends. If we could talk with each member of the team . . ."

Browning cut me off in mid-sentence. "They're not there for your convenience, Mr. . . ."

"Beaumont," I supplied. "Detective Beaumont."

"Thank you, Detective Beaumont. These are adolescents who have suffered a severe loss. I've assembled them for the purpose of enabling them to begin working through their grief. It's the idea of peer group self-help. I won't tolerate any manipulation by you or anyone else. Is that clear, Mr. Beaumont?"

There was no Santa Claus twinkle in Ned Browning's eyes. They were sharp and hard. He meant what he said. I couldn't help feeling some real respect for this little guy, doing the best he knew for the benefit of those kids. I wondered if they appreciated him.

"Mr. Browning," Peters broke in, "neither Detective Beaumont nor I have any intention of manipulating your students, but we do need to interview them, all of them. It's the only way we'll get some idea of what happened Friday night."

For a time Browning considered what Peters had said. Finally, making up his mind, he nodded. "Very well. I'll take you there, but you must understand that the well-being of these young people is my first priority."

He rose. His full height wasn't more than five foot seven. "This way," he said. He led us out through a back door, avoiding the crowd surrounding the front counter. What had been Darwin Ridley's classroom was at the end of a long, polished corridor. Browning stopped before the closed door.

"What did you say your names are again?"

"Beaumont," I said. "Detectives Beaumont and Peters."

He ushered us inside. The room was hushed. There must have been twenty or so people in the room, standing or sitting in groups of two or three, some of them talking quietly, some weeping openly. The group was made up mostly of boys with five or six girls thrown into the mix. All of the faces reflected a combination of shock, grief, horror, and disbelief.

In the far corner of the room, a woman in her mid-thirties stood with one comforting hand on the heaving shoulders of a silently weeping girl. Browning gestured to the woman. She gave the girl a reassuring pat and walked toward us.

"This is Mrs. Wynn, one of our guidance counselors. She's also the advisor to the cheerleading squad. Candace, these are Detectives Beaumont and Peters from Seattle P.D. They need to interview those students who were at the game Friday."

Candace Wynn had a boyish figure and a headful of softly curling auburn hair. An impudent cluster of freckles spattered across her nose. Those freckles were at odds with the hostile, blue-eyed gaze that she turned on us.

"That's absolutely out of the question!"

"Candace, of course we will cooperate fully

with the authorities in this matter."

"But Ned . . ." she began.

"That, however, does not mean we will allow any exploitation. My position on the media remains unchanged, but we have an obligation to teach these young people their civic responsibility."

The previous exchange had been conducted in such undertones that I doubt any of the kids had overheard a single sentence. Browning raised his hand for attention. His was a small but totally commanding presence. The students listened to his oddly stilted remarks with rapt concentration.

"My intention was that you should gather here and not be disturbed. However, I have brought with me two detectives from the Seattle Police Department. They are investigating Coach Ridley's death. It's important that we work with them. All of us. They have asked to spend time with you today, to discuss anything you may have seen or heard in the course of the game at the Coliseum Friday night."

He paused to clear his throat. A whisper rustled through the room. "We at this school have all suffered a severe loss. Those of you in this room, the ones who were most closely connected with Coach Ridley, are bound to suffer the most. Grief is natural. We all feel it, but it's important that we put that grief to a constructive use.

"Mrs. Wynn will be here throughout the interview process. I urge you to cooperate as much as possible. Helping these men discover who perpetrated this terrible crime is perhaps the only practical outlet for what we're feeling today. Detective Beaumont?"

I stepped forward, expecting to be introduced, but Browning continued. "Before you begin asking your questions, Detective Beaumont, I think it only fair that the students be allowed to ask some of you. All day long we've been subjected to a barrage of rumors. It would do us a tremendous service if we had some idea of what's really going on."

I'd been snookered before, but let me tell you, Ned Browning did it up brown.

Where, oh where, was Arlo Hamilton when I needed him?

CHAPTER
8

I've never faced a tougher audience. Browning was right. Those kids were hurting and needed answers. As a group they had taken a closer look at death than most kids their age. Adolescents aren't accustomed to encountering human mortality on a regular basis. Two times in as many years is pretty damn regular.

They needed to know when Darwin Ridley had died, and how. Evidently, some helpful soul had spread the word that Ridley was despondent over the loss of the game and had committed suicide on account of it. The asshole who laid that ugly trip on those poor kids should have been strangled.

I answered their questions as best I could, fudging a little when necessary. I knew what would happen as soon as they stepped out of Ned Browning's artificial cocoon and the media started chewing them to bits. The principal stayed long enough to hear my introductory remarks, then left when Peters and I started our routine questioning process.

It took all afternoon to work our way through the group, one at a time. It was a case of patient prodding. The kids were understandably hesitant to talk to us. Candace Wynn, the guidance counselor, hovered anxiously on the sidelines.

Peters was a lot more understanding about that than I was. I had no patience with what I viewed as a direct impediment to our conducting a thorough investigation. As a consequence, we split the room by sex. I talked to the boys, the team members, and Peters dealt with the girls, the cheerleaders—helpless chicks to Mrs. Wynn's clucking mother hen. At least it kept her out of my hair.

Surprisingly, in spite of all that, we did get a few answers fairly early on. One of the first team members I interviewed was a gangly kid named Bob Payson, captain of the basketball team. I asked him if **he** had noticed anything unusual about Darwin Ridley's behavior the night of the game.

Payson didn't hesitate for a moment. "It was like he was real worried or upset or something."

"He was preoccupied?" I asked.

Payson nodded.

"Before the game? After it? During?"

"The whole time," Payson answered. "He was waiting at the gate when the team bus got there."

"The gate?"

"To Seattle Center. The team buses all stop at that gate there on Republican."

"Across from Bailey's Foods?"

Payson nodded. "That's right."

"He didn't ride on the bus with the team?"

"That was weird, too. Always before he rode the bus, but not this time."

My ears pricked up at that. Something out of the ordinary. Something different in the victim's way of doing things the night of the murder. Most human beings are creatures of habit. They don't like change, they actively resist it wherever possible. A change in Darwin Ridley's behavior the night he died might well be connected to his murder.

"So he didn't ride the bus, and he seemed worried when you saw him?"

"Yeah. He was looking up and down the street like he was waiting for someone. He told us to go on in and suit up, that he'd be inside in a minute."

"Was he?"

"No. He didn't come in for a long time. In fact, he got to the dressing room just before we had to go out and warm up. He didn't even have time to give us our pep talk."

"That was unusual?"

"You'd better believe it."

"He was a good coach?"

"The best."

"So what happened during the game?"

"We were leading by two points at halftime. He talked to us then, told us we were doing great." Payson paused.

"And then?" I prompted.

He frowned. "Just before time to go back on court, someone came to the door and talked to him."

"Did you see who it was?"

"No. They knocked. He opened the door and talked through the crack to whoever it was. After they left, he went over and sat down on one of the benches. He told us to go on, that he'd be out in a minute. He looked real upset."

"There wasn't anyone in the hallway when you went out?"

"No. At least I didn't see anybody."

"And did he come right out?"

"I don't know exactly when, but it was after the half started."

"That was unusual?"

"I told you. Coach Ridley was a good coach. He never missed part of a game before that, as far as I know."

"What about after the game?"

"We were pissed."

"Why?"

"The ref made a bad call in the last two seconds. They won by two points. On free throws."

Payson was suddenly quiet. He sat there fingering the intertwined *M* and *I* emblazoned in white felt on his maroon letterman's jacket. He seemed close to tears.

"What is it?" I asked.

"He just walked off. I couldn't believe it. He never said anything to us. Not good game. Not nice try. Nothing. Not even a word about the bad call. It was like he couldn't wait for the game to be over so he could be rid of us."

Payson was quiet again. There was more to his silence than just grief over the death of someone close to him. It wasn't an end of innocence, because I'm not so sure innocence exists anymore. But it was the end of something else—of youthful hero-worship, maybe—and the beginning of a realization of betrayal. It's hell growing up.

"He didn't even leave us the damn cookies," Payson managed.

"Cookies?" I almost choked on the word. "Did you say cookies?"

Payson grinned sheepishly and swiped at his eyes. "Girl Scout cookies. Pretty stupid, huh? But it was a tradition. Every member of the team got his own personal box of cookies after the first game in the tournament—win or lose, it didn't matter."

I hadn't expected an answer to the Girl Scout cookie question this early in the investigation. "Why Girl Scout cookies?" I asked.

"Coach Altman, our first coach. His wife was a Girl Scout leader, and he always brought cookies. Coach Ridley said he was going to do the same thing. And he did, last year. I guess this time he just forgot."

"He didn't forget," I said.

Bob Payson's eyes lit up. "He didn't?"

"The trunk of his car was full of Girl Scout cookies. Something kept him from giving them to you, but he didn't forget." It was small enough comfort, but Payson seemed to appreciate it.

Embarrassed, he mopped a tear from his face. "Knowing that makes me feel better and worse, both. How come?"

I shook my head. "Beats me," I said. "Can you think of anything else, Bob?"

"No. Can I go now?"

"Sure," I said, "you've been a big help. Thanks."

As Payson got up, I glanced across the room to where Peters was talking to one of the cheerleaders. She had broken down completely. She had buried her face in her arms and was sobbing uncontrollably. Candace

Wynn patted her shoulder and gently straightened the girl's hair.

All other eyes in the room turned warily toward the weeping girl. Raw emotion can be pretty tough to take, especially when everyone is feeling much the same thing, but only one or two have nerve enough to express those feelings.

The counselor leaned down and spoke into the girl's ear. She quieted some, and I went on to the next boy on the team. Peters finished with the cheerleading squad long before I had worked my way through the team. In the course of the interviews it became apparent to me why Bob Payson was captain. None of the other boys was either as observant or as articulate as Bob had been. They told me more or less the same things he had, but without some of the telling details.

By three o'clock, parents began arriving to take their kids home. I could see Ned Browning's handiwork in that as well. One way or another, he was going to make sure the likes of Maxwell Cole didn't lay hands on any of his "young people" as long as they were in the school's care and keeping.

Unfortunately, I knew the news media a little more intimately than Ned Browning did. I guessed, and rightly so, that reporters would make arrangements to snag the students at home if they couldn't reach them at school.

Had Ned and I discussed the matter, I could have told him so.

By the time the last of the students had left, Peters and I were wiped slick. As usual, we had worked straight through lunch and then some. Candace Wynn looked like she'd been pulled through a wringer, too. We invited her to join us for coffee at Denny's, a suggestion she accepted readily. It wasn't totally gentlemanly behavior on our part, though. We still hadn't interviewed her.

I waited politely until she had swallowed a sip or two of coffee before I tackled her. "Mrs. Wynn," I began.

"Call me Andi," she said. "I hate my name."

"Andi, then. Were you at the game?"

She nodded and smiled. "Where the cheerleaders go, there go I."

"Can you tell us anything about that night, anything odd or unusual that you might have noticed about Mr. Ridley."

Her eyes clouded. "You'll have to bear with me," she said. "We were good friends. It's hard to . . ."

"We understand that," Peters interjected. "Your point of view might be just that much different from the kids', though, you could give us some additional insight."

She sighed. "I knew him a long time. I never saw him as upset as he was that night."

"Any idea why?"

"No. I tried to talk to him about it during halftime, but he just cut me off."

"Are you the one who came to the dressing-room door?"

Andi gave me an appraising look, as though surprised that I knew about that. She nodded. "He said he couldn't talk, that he was busy with the team. He shut me out completely."

"What about after the team left the dressing room? Did you see him talking with anyone in the hallway? Something or someone made him late for the second half."

"I knew he was late, but I didn't see anyone with him."

"Could he have been sick? Did he say anything to you?"

"No."

"Did you talk to him after the game at all?"

"I left during the third quarter. My mother's sick. I had to go see her. I was late getting back."

"So you never talked to him again, after those few words at the dressing room door."

"No." She choked on the word. "Something was wrong. He looked terrible. If only I . . ." She stopped.

"If only you what?"

"If only I could have helped him." She pushed her coffee cup away and got up quickly. "I'm going," she said. "Before I embarrass myself."

"We appreciate your help, Andi," Peters said.

"It's the least I can do."

We watched her drive out of the parking lot in a little red Chevy Luv with a bumper sticker that said she'd rather be sailing. As she pulled onto the access road, Peters said, apropos of nothing, "How many women do you know who drive pickups?"

I shrugged. "Not many, but it figures. She's a guidance counselor. My high school counselor at Ballard wore GI boots and drove a Sherman tank."

Peters laughed. "Come on now, Beau. Mrs. Wynn isn't that bad. I think she's cute. And she really seems to care about those kids."

On our way back to the Public Safety Building, Peters and I compared notes from our respective interviews. The cheerleading squad had been able to tell Peters very little that the team hadn't already told me, except they said Darwin Ridley had been five minutes late coming into the game after halftime.

The cheerleaders had taken a short break at the beginning of the third quarter, and they had followed Darwin Ridley onto the court. None of them were able to tell who or what had delayed him between the dressing room and the basketball court.

It wasn't much of a lead, but it was something. It gave us another little sliver of the picture. It didn't tell us what exactly had gone awry in Darwin Ridley's life that last day of his existence, but it was further testimony that something had been sadly amiss.

All we had to do was find out what it was. Piece of cake, right?

Sure. We do it all the time.

C H A P T E R
9

I could probably get away with saying that I went to Bailey's after work that day because I'm a dedicated cop who doesn't leave a single stone unturned. I could claim that once I'm on a case, I work it one hundred percent of the time. I could say it, but it wouldn't be true.

The visit to the store was necessary because I was out of coffee. And MacNaughton's. And the state liquor store is right across the street from Bailey's parking lot.

So much for dedication.

To my credit, I did have my mind on the case. In fact, I was mentally going back over Bob Payson's interview, word for word, trying to see if there were any additional bits and pieces that could be pulled from what he had told me. I was so lost in thought, that I almost ran over the poor kid.

"Would you like to buy some Girl Scout cookies?"

The girl standing in front of two cartons of cookies was around eleven or twelve years old. She had a mop of bright red curls that could have come straight from Little Orphan Annie. She also had an award-winning smile. I'm a sucker for a smile. I stopped and reached for my wallet.

"How much are they?"

"Two fifty a box."

"And what kinds do you have?"

She gave me the complete rundown. I took two boxes of Mints and handed her a twenty. She rummaged in a ragged manila envelope for change.

"Do you sell here often?" I asked.

"I'm here every day after school. My mom brings me over. I earn my way to camp by selling cookies."

I felt my heartbeat quicken. Adrenaline does that. It's got nothing to do with heart disease. "Were you here last week?"

Handing me my change, she nodded. "All last week and all this week. It's a good place."

"You're serious about this, aren't you?"

"I've signed up to sell one thousand boxes. That way my mom doesn't have to pay to send me to camp."

She finished speaking and turned away from me to ask someone else. I had already bought. She couldn't afford to waste time with me at the expense of other potential paying customers. She homed in on a little old lady coming out of the store, carrying a cloth shopping bag filled with groceries.

"Did you save me some?" the woman asked, handing over the correct change.

"Right here," the girl replied, picking up an orange box and tucking it inside the woman's shopping bag. With the transaction complete, she turned back to me.

I took a wild stab in the dark. "What's the most you've ever sold at one time?"

She never batted an eyelash. "Fifteen boxes."

My heart did another little flip. I don't believe in coincidences. It's an occupational hazard. "No kidding. When?"

"Last week. A man and a woman bought fifteen boxes. They wrote a check."

Out of the corner of my eye I saw a woman emerge from a parked car and walk in our direction. Her total focus was on me, but she spoke to the girl. "Do you need anything, Jenny?" she asked.

"More Mints and some Carmel Delights," the girl answered. "And would you take this twenty?" Jenny handed over the twenty I had just given her and the woman returned to her car.

"Is that your mother?" I asked.

Jenny nodded. "She stays with me every day while I sell cookies."

The mother returned with four boxes of cookies cradled in her arms. She eyed me warily as she put them in the cartons at Jenny's feet.

"What are you, the hidden supply line?"

The woman gave me a half smile and nodded. "It works better if people don't realize we have a full carload of cookies right here. That way they think they're buying the last Mint."

"This is quite a little entrepreneur you have here," I said.

"Jenny's a good kid, and she has a lot of spunk. I don't mind helping her. She's willing to help herself."

Jenny was no lightweight salesperson. She had just finished nailing a woman with a baby in her grocery cart for four packages of cookies. She gave her mother the ten.

There was a quiet space, with no customers coming or going. The sun had dipped behind the roof of the Coliseum, and it was suddenly chill. Jenny gave a shiver.

"How many boxes in a carton?" I asked.

"Twelve," Jenny answered.

"How would you like to sell two cartons all at once?"

"Really? You mean it? Plus the ones you already bought?"

"Sure. But it'll cost you. I'll need you to tell

me everything you can remember about the man and woman who bought those fifteen boxes."

Jenny's mother stiffened. "Wait just a minute . . ."

I reached into my pocket and extracted my ID. "It's okay," I said. "I'm a cop, working a case. I really will buy the cookies, though, if you're willing to help me."

Jenny looked from me to her mother and back again. "Is it okay, Mom?"

Her mother shrugged. "I guess so. It's about time we left here anyway. It's starting to get cold."

Jenny packed up her supplies. I wrote the Girl Scouts a check for sixty bucks, and we transferred twenty-four assorted boxes of cookies from their trunk to the backseat of the Porsche. I made arrangements to meet them at Dick's for a milkshake and hamburger. My treat.

While Jenny mowed through her hamburger and fries, I chatted with her mother, Sue Griffith. Sue and Jenny's father were divorced. Sue had custody, and she and Jenny were living in a small apartment on Lower Queen Anne while Sue finished up her last year of law school. There was no question in my mind where Jenny got her gumption.

Showing great restraint, I waited until Jenny had slurped up the very last of a strawberry shake from the bottom of her cup before I turned on the questions. "Tell me about the man who bought the cookies," I said.

"It wasn't just a man. It was a man and a woman."

"Tell me about them."

She paused. "He was tall and black. He had a sort of purple shirt on. And high-topped shoes."

"And the woman?"

"She was black, too. Very pretty. She's the one who wrote the check."

"What was she wearing, did you notice?"

"One of those big funny sweatshirts. You know, the long kind."

"Funny? What do you mean, funny?"

"It had an arrow on it that pointed. It said *Baby*."

I had seen a sweatshirt just like that recently. At Darwin Ridley's house, on the back of his widow, who never went to his games, not even statewide tournaments.

"What color was her shirt?" I asked.

"Pink," Jenny told me decisively. "Bright pink."

It was all I could do to sit still. "What time was it, do you remember?"

"Sure. It was just before we left. Mom brings me over as soon as I get home from school and have a snack. We're at the store by about four-thirty or five, and we stay for a couple of hours. That way I catch people on their way home from work."

"So what time would you say, six-thirty, seven?"

She nodded. "About that."

"Jenny," I said. "If I showed you a picture of those people, would you recognize them?"

Jenny nodded. "They were nice. The nice ones are easy to remember."

Across the table from me, Sue was looking more and more apprehensive. "What's all this about?" she asked. "This isn't that case that was on the news today, I hope."

"I'm afraid so."

"I don't think I want Jenny mixed up in this."

"Jenny's already mixed up in it," I said quietly. "Aside from his basketball team, your daughter may have been one of the last people to see Darwin Ridley alive."

Jenny had watched the exchange between her mother and me like someone watching a Ping-Pong game. "Who's Darwin Ridley?" she asked.

"I believe he's the man you sold all those cookies to," I told her.

"And now he's dead?" Her question was totally matter-of-fact.

"Somebody killed him. Late Friday night or Saturday morning."

Kids have an uncanny way of going for the

jugular. "Was it the woman in the pink shirt? Did she kill him?"

I've suspected for years that kids watch too much television. That question corked it for me, convinced me I was right. The problem was, it was closer to the truth than I was willing to let on. I already knew Joanna Ridley was a liar. I wondered if she was something worse.

"It's not likely it was his wife," I said, waffling for Jenny's benefit. "At this point it could be almost anybody. We don't know."

"I hope she didn't do it," Jenny said thoughtfully. "I felt sorry for her."

"What do you mean?"

"The man was in a hurry. He seemed angry. He kept looking at his watch and saying he had to go. She said he should go, that she'd pay for the cookies and leave them in his trunk."

"Did she?"

Jenny nodded, big-eyed. "I helped her carry them to the car. She started crying."

"Crying? Are you sure?"

"Yes, I'm sure." Jenny sounded offended that her veracity had been called into question.

"What happened then?"

"After she put the cookies in one car, she got in another one."

"What kind?"

"Brown-and-white car, I think."

"And did she leave right away?"

"No. She sat there for a long time, leaning on the steering wheel, crying. She finally drove away."

I turned to Jenny's mother. "Did you see any of this?" I asked.

She shook her head. "I must have been in the car, studying. When Jenny needs something, she whistles."

"What about the check?" I asked.

Sue answered that question. "I turned it in to the cookie mother yesterday. She said she had to make a deposit this morning."

I made a note of the cookie mother's name and number. For good measure, I had Jenny go over the story one more time while I took detailed notes. "Is this going to help?" Jenny asked when we finished and I had closed my notebook.

"I certainly hope so," I said.

"And can I tell the kids at school that I'm helping solve a murder?" she asked.

"Don't tell them yet," I told her. "I'll let you know when it's okay to say something."

Jenny looked at me seriously. "Can girls be detectives when they grow up?"

"You bet they can," I told her. "You'll grow up to be anything you want to be. I'd put money on it."

Sue Griffith got up. Jenny did, too. "We'd better be going," Sue said.

"Thanks for buying all those cookies," Jenny said. "But if you run out, I'll still be selling next week. The sale lasts for three weeks."

Jenny Griffith was evidently born with selling in her blood. I had a Porsche full of Girl Scout cookies to prove it.

I never did remember to buy the coffee. The coffee or the MacNaughton's, either.

I called Peters as soon as I got home. "Guess what?" I said.

"I give up."

"Joanna Ridley was at the Coliseum on Friday."

"I thought she didn't like basketball."

"We've got a Girl Scout who says someone who looked like Joanna Ridley paid for the cookies we found in his trunk. By check."

"She wrote a check?"

"That's right."

"So what do we do now, Coach?" Peters asked.

"I'd say we take a real serious look at the Widow Ridley and find out what makes her tick."

"Starting with United Airlines?"

"That's as good a place to start as any."

"How about the neighbors?"

"Them, too."

Peters hesitated. "What would she have to gain, insurance maybe?"

"It wouldn't be the first time," I replied.

"I've never dealt with a pregnant murder suspect before. The very idea runs against the grain."

"Murder's against the grain," I reminded him. "Pregnancy's no more a legal defense for murder than Twinkies are."

Peters hung up then, but I could tell it still bothered him. To tell the truth, it bothered me. Joanna Ridley bothered me. I recalled her house, the way she had looked when she answered the door, her reactions when she finally learned what I was there for. I would have sworn she wasn't playacting, but as I get older, the things I'm sure of become fewer.

I kept coming back to the bottom line. Joanna Ridley had lied to us, more than once. In the world of murder and mayhem, liars are losers. And they're usually guilty.

Just thinking about the next day made me weary. I stripped off my clothes and crawled into bed. I wasn't quite asleep when the phone rang.

"How's it going, J. P.?"

"Maxwell Cole, you son of a bitch! It's late. Leave me alone. I've got a job to do. I don't need you on my ass."

"Look, J. P., here I am calling you up to lend a little assistance, and you give me the brush-off."

"What kind of assistance?"

"You ever heard of *FURY?*"

"What is this, a joke?"

"No joke. Have you ever heard of it?"

"Well, I've heard of Plymouth Furies and 'hell hath no fury.' Which is it?"

"It's an acronym, *F-U-R-Y*. The initials stand for Faithful United to Rescue You."

"To rescue me? From what?"

"J. P., I'm telling you, this is no joke. These people are serious. They're having their first convention in town this week. They're up at the Tower Inn on Aurora."

"So what are they rescuing? Get to the point, Max."

"They're white supremacists. I interviewed their president today. No kidding. They want blacks to go back where they came from."

"Jesus Christ, Max. What does all this have to do with me? I need my beauty sleep."

"They said it's possible one of their members knocked off Darwin Ridley."

"Send me his name and number. I'll track him down in the morning."

"J. P. . . ."

"Get off it, Max. You know how this works. Some kooky splinter group claims responsibility for a crime and manufactures a whole armload of free publicity. Don't fall for it. And don't complicate my life. I've got plenty to do without chasing after phony suspects who are playing the media for a bunch of fools."

"Are you saying . . ." he began.

"If the shoe fits!"

With that, I hung up. The phone began ringing again within seconds, but I ignored it. It
rang twenty times or so before it finally
stopped.

Within minutes, I was sound asleep and
dreaming about Girl Scout cookies.

CHAPTER
10

There's only one thing to do with that many Girl Scout cookies—take them to the office and share the wealth. So I drove to the Public Safety Building and parked the Porsche in the bargain basement garage at the foot of Columbia. I've noticed that my 928 commands a fair amount of respect from parking garage attendants.

This one held the door open for me as I got out. Then I crawled back inside and dredged out the two cartons of cookies. When the kid handed me my parking ticket, I gave him a box of cookies.

"Hey, thanks," he said, grinning.

"Just handle my baby with care," I told him.

"We always do," he replied.

I was halfway up the block when I heard squealing tires as he jockeyed the Porsche into a parking place. There was no accompanying sound of crumpling metal, so I didn't worry about it.

Peters glanced up from his newspaper as I put the cookies on my desk. "Want one?" I asked.

"Are you kidding? That much sugar will kill you, Beau. What are you doing, peddling them for one of your neighbors?"

"Peddling, hell! I'm giving this stuff away, all in the line of duty."

"Don't tell me you bought that many cookies last night when you were talking to that little girl about the Ridleys."

"She's a terrific salesman."

"And you're an easy mark."

For the remainder of the morning, while Peters and I valiantly worked at running a check on Joanna Ridley and tried to dredge a copy of the check out of a combination of Girl Scout and bank bureaucracy, our two desks became the social hub of the department. Word of free cookies spread like wildfire, and everyone from Vice to Property managed to stop by with a cup of coffee. Including Captain Lawrence Powell.

He wasn't above taking a cookie or two before he lit into us. "Whenever you two finish socializing, how about stopping by my office for a little chat."

Larry Powell's glass-enclosed, supposedly

private office offers all the privacy of a fishbowl, which is what we call it. It isn't sound-
proofed, either. You don't have to be a
lip-reader to know everything that's going on
behind Powell's closed door.

"You're out of line, Beau," he said. "Dr.
Baker has sent a formal complaint to the
chief."

"That jerk," I said.

"Detective Beaumont, this is serious. Just
because you can literally buy and sell city
blocks in this town doesn't give you the right
to run roughshod over elected public offi-
cials."

"Look, Larry, we're not talking net worth
here. Baker demanded information before I
had it. Then he pitched a fit because I wouldn't
give it to him."

"This is a sensitive case, Beau. If you're going to go off half-cocked, I'll pull you two off
it and give it to someone who isn't as hot-
headed."

"It wouldn't be such a sensitive case, as you
put it, if Peters and I hadn't figured out who
he was. Darwin Ridley was just an unidentified corpse by a garbage dumpster until we
got hold of him, remember?"

"We're making progress," Peters put in
helpfully, hoping to defuse the situation a little.

Powell turned from me to Peters. "You are?"

"We've been working one possibility all morning."

"Well, get on with it, then, but don't step on any more toes. You got that?" Powell had worked himself into a real temper tantrum.

"You bet! I've got it all right." I steamed out of the fishbowl with Peters right behind me. Making a detour past our cubicle, I grabbed up our jackets, tossed Peters his, and shrugged my way into mine.

"Where are we going?" Peters asked.

"Out!" I snapped.

It took a while for the attendant to free my Porsche. It had been buried among a group of all-day cars as opposed to short-term ones. Once out of the garage, I hauled ass through Pioneer Square, driving south.

"I asked you before, where are we going?"

"Any objections to letting Joanna Ridley know we know she's a lying sack of shit?"

"None from me."

"Good. That's where we're going."

"Do you think it'll work?" he asked.

"She's no pro. She's not even a particularly good liar. It won't take much to push her over the edge, just a little nudge, especially in her condition."

Peters nodded in agreement.

By the time we got off the freeway, fast driving had pretty well boiled the venom out of my gut. It wasn't the first time I'd heard sly references to the fact that having money had somehow spoiled J. P. Beaumont. Money doesn't automatically make you an asshole. Or a prima donna, either. Damn Doc Baker anyway.

We drove across Beacon Hill, one of the glacial ridges that separates Puget Sound from Lake Washington. When we stopped in front of Joanna Ridley's house, there were no cars there at all. I was disappointed. I had geared myself up for a confrontation. Now it looked as though it wasn't going to happen.

We had turned around and were heading back to the department when we met Joanna Ridley's Mustang GT halfway down the block. She was alone in the car.

"We're in luck," I said.

I made a U-turn and parked in the driveway behind the Mustang. When we stepped onto Joanna's front porch, she greeted us with what could hardly be called a cordial welcome. "What do you want?"

"We need to talk."

She stood looking up at us questioningly, one hand resting on the small of her back as though it was bothering her. "What about?"

"About last Friday."

"I've told you everything I know."

"No, you didn't, Joanna. You didn't tell us you had gone to the Coliseum and talked to your husband. In fact, you told us you never went near his games."

Defiance crept across her face. "So I went there to talk to him. What difference does that make?"

"Why did you lie to us? You said the last time you saw him was at breakfast."

She dropped her gaze. With eyes averted, Joanna turned to the front door. She unlocked it, opened it, and went inside, leaving us standing on the porch. Peters and I exchanged glances, unsure whether or not we were expected to follow.

"After you," Peters said.

We found Joanna Ridley sitting on the couch. Her face was set, full lips compressed into a thin line, but there was no sign of tears. Peters sidled into a chair facing her, while I sat next to her on the couch.

"How did you find out?" she said, her voice barely above a whisper.

"It doesn't matter. The point is, we know you were there. We have a witness who saw you there. You signed a piece of paper."

She looked at me for a long minute. "The cookies," she said. "I forgot about the cookies. I wrote a check."

Putting her hand to her mouth, she started to laugh, the semihysterical giggle of one

whose life has been strung so tight that the
ends are beginning to unravel. The giggle
evolved into hysterical weeping before she finally quieted and took a deep, shuddering
breath.

"I don't know why I'm laughing. I went to
tell him I wanted a divorce, and I didn't even
do that right," she said finally. "I ended up
paying for all those damn cookies."

"You didn't mention a divorce to us before."

"I didn't tell anyone. Why tell? If Darwin
was dead, what did it matter?"

"But it could have some bearing on how he
died, Mrs. Ridley. Do you mind if I ask why
you wanted a divorce?"

"Mind? Yes, I mind."

"But we need to know," Peters insisted. "It
could be important."

She sat silently for what seemed like a long
time, looking first at Peters then at me. At last
she shook her head. "Darwin was screwing
around," she whispered. Once more Joanna
Ridley began to cry.

Suddenly, I felt old and jaded. It didn't seem
like that big a deal. Husbands screw around
all the time. And wives put up with it or not,
divorce them or not. And life goes on. In most
cases.

Darwin Ridley had not survived his indis-
cretion, however. I wondered if we might not

be treading on very thin Miranda ice. We had
not read Joanna Ridley her rights. I was beginning to think maybe we should have.

Peters and I waited patiently, neither of us
saying a word. Eventually, she quieted, got
control of herself.

"Does it have to come out? About the divorce, I mean."

I did my best to reassure her. "We'll try. If
it has nothing to do with the murder itself,
then there's no reason for it to go any further
than this room."

She got up and walked away from us. She
stood by a window, pulling the curtain to one
side to look out. I knew what she was doing—
distancing herself from us while she waged
some ferocious internal war. Finally, she
turned to face us.

"I guess I could just as well tell you," she
said softly. "You'll probably find out anyway.
I had a phone call that afternoon, about three-
thirty or a quarter to four. From a man. He
said I'd better keep that motherfucking son of
a bitch away from his daughter."

"Talking about Darwin?"

She nodded.

"That's all he said?"

"No, he said I could tell that black bastard
that his daughter wouldn't be at the Coliseum
to meet him, that she wouldn't be at the game,

and that if Darwin even so much as spoke to her again, he was a dead man."

Stopping, Joanna looked at me, her eyes hollow. "That's the other reason I went to the Coliseum. To warn him."

"I don't suppose the caller left his name and number," I said.

Joanna shook her head. "This came yesterday." Like a sleepwalker, she rose, crossed the room into the little study, opened a desk drawer, and extracted a large manila envelope, which she brought back to me. Her name and address were typed neatly on the outside. There was no return address in the upper left-hand corner. The postmark was illegible.

When I opened it, a single photograph fell out.

At first glance, it seemed to be a picture of a man embracing a woman in what appeared to be a motel room. Closer examination revealed the man to be Darwin Ridley, but the woman wasn't a woman at all. She was a girl. A blonde girl. She was still wearing a bra, but the camera had caught her in the act of slipping out of her skirt. A short, gored, two-toned skirt.

A cheerleader's skirt.

I shook my head and handed the picture over to Peters. He looked at it and dropped the picture on the coffee table like it was too hot to handle.

Captain Powell's sensitive case had just turned into Maxwell Cole's dynamite. I wondered briefly if it was too late to get the captain to put two other detectives on the case instead of us. I didn't think I wanted to be anywhere within range when this particular shit started hitting the fan.

I looked at Joanna Ridley then, standing there with her pregnant silhouette framed against the curtained window, with the muted sunlight filtering through her backlit hair. She was a picture of totally vulnerable, abject despair.

And in that instant, I knew what she was feeling.

She had lost the man she loved, and now even her memories of him were being shredded and torn from her. I knew all too well that sense of absolute loss.

I got up and went to her. Somebody needed to do it, and Peters wasn't going to. He didn't understand what was happening. I reached out for her and held her. She fell against my chest, letting my arms support her, keep her from slipping to the floor. Everything that stood between us, every conceivable barrier, disintegrated as I cradled her against me.

"Did you kill him, Joanna?" I asked, murmuring the question through her hair.

"No, I didn't."

From that moment on, I never doubted for a minute that she was telling the truth.

CHAPTER
11

By the time Joanna drew away from me and I led her from the window back to the couch, Peters was ready to go straight up and turn left. He was there to investigate a homicide, not to offer emotional support and comfort to a bereaved widow, one he considered to be a prime suspect. I couldn't have explained to him what had just happened. I couldn't explain it to myself.

With an impatient frown that was far more exasperation than concentration, he picked up the picture once more and examined it closely. His brows knit.

"Can you tell which cheerleader it is?" I asked him. After all, Peters had been the one who had spent the afternoon interviewing the Mercer Island cheerleaders the day before.

He shook his head. "Not for sure." He

glanced at Joanna, who was gradually pulling herself together. "Do you know?" he asked Joanna.

"No." Her voice was flat, her face devoid of expression.

Peters, reluctant to give up that line of questioning, took another tack. "Your husband never mentioned any of the cheerleaders to you by name?"

"Never."

Peters passed me the picture again. I examined it more carefully this time, looking at it less for its shock value than as an integral part of the puzzle that marked the end of Darwin Ridley's life.

I studied the background of the picture. Definitely a motel, and not a particularly classy one at that. The picture had evidently been taken through a window from outside the room. I don't know a lot about cameras, but I recognized this was no Kodak Instamatic. The clarity of detail, the finite focusing even through glass said the picture had been taken with topflight equipment. Scrutinizing the background of the picture, I wondered if someone in the crime lab could blow the photo up large enough to read the checkout information in a framed holder on the room door behind the fondly embracing twosome.

"Could we take the picture, Joanna? It

would help if we knew where and when this was taken. And by whom."

All the fight had been taken out of her, all her strength. She nodded in agreement.

"Did you have separate checking accounts?" Peters asked suddenly. "Checking accounts or charge cards, either one?"

"No." Joanna looked genuinely puzzled. "Why?"

"He had to pay for motel rooms some way or other. Do you mind if I look through his desk?"

"Go ahead."

Peters went to the little study, leaving Joanna and me alone. "Had you been planning to divorce your husband before the phone call?" I asked.

Joanna shot a darting look in my direction. "We were having a baby," she replied, leaving me to draw my own conclusions.

"But you believed the man who called you. Instantly. Even before he sent you the photograph."

"It wasn't the first time," she said quietly.

"Another cheerleader?" I asked.

"I don't know. I don't care. Maybe the same one. It doesn't matter. The marriage counselor said Darwin was going through a mid-life crisis, that he'd get over it eventually if I was patient."

A part of me objected to the term mid-life

crisis. It's a handy rationalization that covers a multitude of sins. I've used it myself on occasions, some of them not very defensible. "Counselor?" I asked.

"We went to the counselor together, last year, a lady family therapist. I could tell something was wrong, but I didn't know what it was. All I knew was that I wanted to stay married. Being married was important to me."

"And in the course of counseling you found out your husband was having an affair." It's an old story.

She nodded. "He promised he'd break it off. He said it was over, and I believed him."

"And you decided to have a baby to celebrate," I added.

"We both wanted one," she said. "We had been trying for years. It was an accident that I turned up pregnant right then. Besides," she added, "I thought a baby would bring us closer together."

The look on her face, far more than what she said, told me exactly how badly Joanna Ridley had been taken in by the old saw that babies fix bad marriages. It certainly hadn't worked in this case. My heart went out to the lady who would be raising her child alone.

Sometimes, life isn't fair. Make that usually.

The doorbell rang, and Joanna hurried to answer it. Meanwhile, Peters returned from his examination of the desk. "Nothing there," he said.

Joanna ushered a heavy-set woman into the room. She was evidently a neighbor. In one hand she held a huge pot that contained an aromatic stew of some kind. In her other hand she carried a napkin-covered plate heaped high with some kind of baked goods. She glared at us, making it clear that we were unwelcome interlopers.

"You have anything to eat today, Joanna, honey?" she asked, still glowering at us, but speaking to Joanna.

"No, I . . ." Joanna trailed off.

"Now you listen to Fannie Mae, girl. You got to keep up your strength, for you and that baby. I'll just put this food in the kitchen." She bustled out of the room. Joanna returned to the couch.

"What did you do after you left the Coliseum?" Peters asked as soon as she sat back down.

Joanna regarded him coolly. "I drove to Portland," she replied.

"Portland, Oregon? Why?"

"To see my father."

"And did you?"

Joanna's eyes never strayed from Peters' face. "No. I drove past the house, but I didn't go in."

"Wait a minute. Let me get this straight.

You left the Coliseum after talking to your husband, drove all the way to Portland to talk to your father, and then didn't go in to see him once you got there?"

"That's right."

"Why not?"

"Because I changed my mind. I realized I'd **never** go through with it, the divorce, I mean."

If I had been trying to sell Peters Fuller Brushes right then, I would have known I'd blown the sale. He lay his finger next to his nose, the palm of his hand covering his mouth. He wasn't buying Joanna's story. Not any of it.

"What time did you get back?" I asked, stepping into the conversation.

"Midnight. Maybe later."

"Did you see anyone along the way? Someone who would be able to say that they saw you there during that time?"

She shrugged. "I stopped for gas in Vancouver, but I don't know if anyone there would remember me."

"What kind of station, Joanna?" I prompted. "Can you remember?"

"A Texaco. On Mill Plain Road."

"How did you pay? Credit card? Cash?"

"Credit card. I think I used my VISA."

"Could you give us that number?"

Joanna retrieved her purse from a table near the front door where she had left it when she first entered the house. As we had talked, there had been sounds of activity in the kitchen. Now Fannie Mae reappeared, carrying a tray of coffee cups, a pot of coffee, and a plate of homemade biscuits. Joanna dictated the number to Peters while I helped myself to coffee, biscuits, and honey. Naturally, Peters abstained. Health-food nuts piss me off sometimes.

Within minutes several other visitors showed up, and it seemed best for us to leave. I wasn't looking forward to being alone with Peters. I figured he'd land on me with all fours. I wasn't wrong.

"You've really done it this time!"

"Done what?" I made a stab at playing innocent.

"Jesus, Beau. We never even read her her rights."

"We didn't need to. She didn't do it."

"What? How can you be so sure?"

"Instinct, Peters. Pure gut instinct."

"I can quote you chapter and verse when your instincts haven't been absolutely, one hundred percent accurate."

I could, too, but I didn't tell Peters that. Instead, I said, "Ridley was too big. With the morphine, he would have been all dead weight. She couldn't have strung him up, certainly not in her condition."

"She could have had help."

"She didn't."

Peters wasn't about to give up his pet suspect. "What about her father? The two of them could have done it together. She said she got back around midnight. The coroner said he died about two A.M. Portland doesn't give her an alibi, if you ask me."

I thought about Joanna's father, the kindly, stoop-shouldered old man who had let us in the house the day before. "No way," I said. "It's got to be somebody else."

We let it go at that. Neither of us was going to change the other's mind.

Before leaving Joanna's house, we had decided to stop by Mercer Island High School in hopes of determining the identity of Darwin Ridley's cheerleader. With that in mind, I turned off Rainier Avenue onto an on-ramp for I-90. Unfortunately, I had been too busy talking to notice that traffic on the ramp was stopped cold, three car lengths from the entrance.

Unable to go forward or back, we spent the next hour stuck in traffic while workers building the new floating bridge across Lake Washington escorted traffic through the construction, one snail-paced lane at a time.

We should have phoned first. We got to the school about twelve-fifteen, only to discover that Candace Wynn wasn't there. Her mother was gravely ill, and Mrs. Wynn had taken the day off.

Ned Browning's clerk wasn't exactly cordial, but she was somewhat more helpful than she had been the previous day. She gave us Mrs. Wynn's telephone number in Seattle. We tried calling before we left the school, but there was no answer.

Back in the car, we started toward Seattle. Thinking the other bridge might be faster, we avoided I-90 and circled around through Bellevue. Unfortunately, a lot of other people had the same idea, including two drivers who managed to smack into one another head-on in the middle of the Evergreen Point span. It wasn't a serious accident, but it was enough to tie us up in traffic for another hour, along with several thousand other hapless souls.

It was a flawless spring day, without a cloud in the sky, with Lake Washington glassy and smooth beneath us, and with Mount Rainier a snow-covered vision to our left. Unfortunately, Peters was still ripped about Joanna Ridley, and I was pissed about the traffic, so we weren't particularly good company, and we didn't spend that hour admiring the scenery.

We finally got back to the department around two. I took Joanna's photograph and envelope down to the crime lab to see if they could lift prints or magnify the photo enough to read the print in the notice on the motel room door. Meanwhile, Peters settled down in our cubicle to try to track down Candace Wynn. By the time I got back to the fifth floor, he had reached her and made arrangements for us to meet her at a Greek restaurant in Fremont in half an hour.

Fremont is a Seattle neighborhood where aging hippies who've grown up and gone relatively straight try to sell goods and services to whatever brand of flower children is currently in vogue. Costas Opa, a Greek restaurant right across from the Fremont Bridge, is quite a bit more upscale than some of its funky neighbors. It was late afternoon by then. The place was long on tables and short on customers when we got there.

We sat at a corner window table where we could see traffic coming in all directions. Across the street, Seattle's favorite piece of public art was still wearing the green two days after St. Patrick's day. *Waiting For The Interurban* is a homey piece of statuary made up of seven life-size figures, including a dog, whose face is rumored to bear a remarkable resemblance to one of the sculptor's sworn enemies. They stand under what seems to be a train station platform, waiting for an old Seattle/Tacoma commuter that has long since quit running.

Throughout the year, concerned citizens and

frustrated artists make additions and corrections by adding seasonal touches to the statues' costumes. That day, they all wore emerald green full-length scarves.

I expected Candace Wynn to drive up in her red pickup. Instead, she arrived on foot, walking the wrong way up a one-way street. The Fremont Bridge, a drawbridge, was open. Candace darted through stopped vehicles to cross the street to the restaurant.

Her outfit wasn't well suited for visiting invalid relatives. She wore frayed jeans, a ragged sweatshirt, and holey tennis shoes. Sitting down, she ordered coffee.

"I'm in the process of moving," she explained, glancing down at her clothes. "The house is a mess, or I'd have invited you there."

"You live around here?" Peters asked.

She pointed north toward the Ship Canal. "Up there a few blocks, in an old watchman's quarters. View's not much, but I couldn't beat the rent. I'm moving back home, though, at the end of the month."

"Back home with your mother?"

She nodded.

"How is your mother?" I asked. "I understand she's very ill." Sometimes it surprises me when the niceties my own mother drilled into my head surface unconsciously in polite company.

Candace Wynn's freckled face grew serious.

"So, so," she said. "It comes and goes. She's got cancer. She's back in the hospital right now. I'll be home to help her when she gets out. I was up with her all last night and couldn't face going to school this morning. Once I woke up, though, I decided to tackle packing. It was too nice a day to waste."

I had to agree with her there. If you've ever spent time with a cancer patient, you should know better than to squander a perfect day being miserable over little things like stalled traffic.

Somehow I had forgotten. I had spent the day blind to blossoming cherry trees and newly leafing trees. It took Andi Wynn's casual remark to bring me up short, to make me remember.

We had yet to ask her a single question, but already I was prepared to mark the interview down as an unqualified success. Whether or not she identified Mercer Island's precociously amorous cheerleader.

CHAPTER
12

After the waiter set down her coffee, Candace Wynn took one demure sip and then looked expectantly from Peters to me and back again. "You said you needed to talk to me."

I gave Peters the old take-it-away high sign. After all, Candace Wynn knew Peters somewhat better than she knew me. Besides, Peters' earnest, engaging manner encouraged people to spill their guts. I had seen it happen.

"That's right; we do," Peters said. "How long have you been at Mercer Island?"

"Ten years."

"All that time as counselor?"

"No. I've only been in the counseling department for the last year and a half. Before that, I taught math."

"And what about the cheerleaders?"

"I've had them the whole time. I was a

cheerleader at Washington State in Pullman."
She stopped and gave Peters an inquiring
look. "I thought this was going to be about
Darwin."

"It is, really, in a roundabout way," Peters
said. "You told us yesterday that you were a
friend of his. How good a friend, Mrs. Wynn?"

"Andi," she reminded him. She shrugged.
"Fairly good friends. When I started teaching
there, a bunch of us used to play crazy eights
in the teachers' lounge in the morning—Coach
Altman, Darwin, and a couple of others. You
get to be friends that way."

"Playing cards?"

"That's right. And in the afternoons, some
of us would stop by the Roanoke and play a
few games of pool."

"Including Darwin Ridley and yourself?"
Peters asked.

Andi nodded. "Yes."

"Did you know anything about his personal
life?" Peters continued.

"Some, but not very much."

"Have you ever met his wife, Joanna?"

"No. I never even saw her. She didn't come
to school, and she never showed up at any of
the faculty functions, at least not any of the
ones I went to."

"And she never came to the Roanoke?"

"No."

"Did you know she's pregnant?"

Andi looked at Peters. She seemed a little surprised. "Is she? I didn't know. That's too bad," she said.

Peters nodded in agreement. "Yes, it is. Did Darwin ever indicate to you that his marriage was in trouble?"

Andi Wynn sipped her coffee and considered the question before she answered. "I remember him mentioning that they were going for marriage counseling. That was some time back. A year ago, maybe a year and a half. He never said anything more about it. Whatever the problem was, they must have straightened it out."

I was growing restless, sitting on the sidelines. "Tell us about your cheerleading squad," I said.

"The cheerleaders? What about them?"

"Give us an idea of who they are, what they're like."

"They're mostly juniors and seniors . . ." she began. Then she stopped and looked at Peters. "You talked to most of them yesterday. What more do you need to know?"

"Most?" Peters focused in on the important issue. "I only met most of them? Where were the others?"

"Two were missing. One was home sick. She has mono. The other quit, transferred to a different school."

Peters had gotten out his notebook and flipped through several pages. "What are their names?" he asked, his pen poised above the paper.

"Those who weren't there yesterday?" Peters nodded in reply. "Amy Kendrick and Bambi Barker."

"Bambi? As in Walt Disney?"

"That's right."

"Which one has mono?" Peters asked.

"Amy."

"So Bambi transferred to another school," I said. "Recently?"

"Monday of this week."

"What is she, a junior?"

Andi Wynn shook her head. "A senior."

"And she's transferring this late in her last year? What's her problem? Flunking out? Having trouble with grades?"

"No, nothing like that. Her father just up and shipped her off to a private school in Portland, a boarding school."

"Which one?" Peters asked, still holding his pen.

Andi frowned. "St. Agnes of the Hills. I think that's the name of it."

Peters wrote it down. "Do you have any idea why she was sent away?" he asked.

"Not really. Her father's Tex Barker, though."

Peters dropped his pen on the table. The name meant nothing to me, but I saw the spark of recognition flash in Peters' eyes. "Wheeler-Dealer Barker?"

"That's the one."

I was tired of sitting on my hands. "Who the hell is Wheeler-Dealer Barker?"

"Beau here doesn't watch TV, Andi," Peters explained with a smile. Andi Wynn smiled back.

"Okay, you two. Stop making fun of me. Who's this Barker character?"

"He runs Tex Barker Ford in Bellevue," Peters told me. "His commercials are reputed to be some of the worst in the country."

"That bad?"

Peters and Andi nodded in unison. "Somebody gives out awards for the worst television commercials. It's like Mr. Blackwell's worst-dressed list. Barker won one last year, hands down."

"What else do you know about him?" I asked. Because of Peters' voracious reading, he always seemed to know something about practically everything. Wheeler-Dealer Barker was no exception.

"He came up here from Texas four, maybe five, years ago and bought up a failing Ford dealership on auto row in Bellevue. Within months, he had moved it from the bottom of the heap to one of the top dealerships."

"So the commercials haven't hurt him."

"Are you kidding? He's like that character

with his dog Spot, one of those guys people love to hate, but they do business with him right and left. I understand he's made offers on two more dealerships, one in Lynnwood and the other down in Burien."

"And he lives on Mercer Island?" I asked, turning once more to Candace Wynn. "How did the daughter of someone like that fit in on Mercer Island?"

"Bambi landed in the in-crowd and stayed there. She never had any problem."

The picture Joanna Ridley had handed me passed through my mind. Bambi Barker had problems, all right, I thought to myself. Lots of them. They just didn't show. "When did you find out Bambi was being transferred?" I asked.

"She was at school Friday morning. I saw her. Then, right about noon, her father came to pick her up. I didn't see it, but I understand there was quite a scene in the office. Yesterday, her mother officially checked her out of school. You know, got the withdrawal forms signed, turned in her books, cleaned out her lockers, that kind of thing."

"Did you talk to her, the mother?"

Andi nodded. "Briefly. Tried to anyway. I tried to explain how tough it would be for Bambi to change schools this close to graduation, but she said it was too late, that they had taken Bambi down to Portland over the weekend."

"And this school..." Peters paused and consulted his notes. "St. Agnes of the Hills, you said. Where is it?"

"Somewhere in Beaverton, I guess." Andi paused, thoughtfully. "I still don't understand. What exactly does all this have to do with Darwin? I thought he was the main reason you wanted to talk to me."

I took the plunge. Peters would have walked around it all day. "Did you ever hear any rumors about Bambi Barker and Darwin Ridley?" It was the most delicate way I could think of to phrase a most indelicate question.

For a moment or two Andi Wynn looked at me as though she didn't quite grasp what I was saying. "Rumors?" she asked. "What kind of rumors?"

Peters cleared his throat. "We've been informed by a reliable source that there's a possibility that Bambi and Darwin Ridley were having an affair."

Shock waves registered on Andi's face. "That's a lie!"

"It's not a lie, unfortunately," I said. "We've seen proof. We just didn't know who the girl was. Now we do."

Candace Wynn drew herself up sharply and looked me right in the eye. "You don't expect me to believe that, do you? Darwin Ridley was a fine man. His memory deserves to be treated with respect."

"Andi, it's not a matter of disrespect . . ." I began, but she didn't wait long enough to hear me out. Instead, Candace Wynn angrily shoved her chair back from the table, rattling the silverware and glasses on the table next to us. She bounded to her feet.

"I won't listen to this! Not a word of it!" With that, she turned on her heel and stamped out of the restaurant.

"Nice going, Beau," Peters said. "What do you do for an encore?"

I watched Candace Wynn storm across the street and out of sight behind a wall of buildings. I shrugged. "After all, she's the cheerleading advisor. If she'd been doing her job right, maybe she would have noticed something funny was going on."

Peters leaped to Candace Wynn's defense. "You expect her to be psychic? Ridley wasn't exactly advertising the fact that he was screwing around. His wife didn't know about it. The girl's parents apparently didn't know. Why should a teacher? From the sound of it, she's got her hands full with a dying mother."

I have to confess, I didn't have a pat answer for that question. Why should Candace Wynn have known? I said nothing, and my mind went wandering down another track.

"What else do you know about this what's-his-name, Wheeler-Dealer? Would he really mail a copy of that picture to Joanna? A picture of his own daughter? I'm a father. It doesn't sound to me like something a father would do, not even a shitty father."

Peters agreed and offered an alternate suggestion. "Maybe somebody else sent pictures to both of them."

I gave that idea some thought. It seemed somewhat more plausible. "But who?" I asked.

Peters shrugged. "Your guess is as good as mine. What now?"

"We'd better drag our butts down to Portland and talk to Bambi Barker."

"Today?" Peters asked in surprise, glancing at his watch. It was already well after three.

"Why not today? If we left right now, we could just beat the traffic out of town. Besides, we wouldn't have to cross any bridges."

Peters shook his head. "It would be midnight before we got back. I don't like to come home that late. Heather and Tracie still get upset if I'm not home before they go to bed."

After the divorce, Peters' two girls had spent some time in a flaky religious commune with their equally flaky mother. With the help of my attorney, Ralph Ames, we had managed to get them back home and in Peters' custody late the previous fall. Kids are pretty resilient, but the two girls still hadn't adjusted to all the abrupt changes that had disrupted their young lives. They were still basically insecure. So was Peters.

"Why don't I drive down by myself, then?" I suggested. "It's no big deal for me to come home late. Nobody's there waiting. Besides, it's important that we talk to Bambi before her dear old dad has any idea we know what's been going on."

"You've got yourself a deal," Peters told me. "You drive to Portland, and I'll handle the paperwork."

Talk about getting the best of the bargain! I headed for my apartment. No way was I going to drive one of the departmental crates to Portland when my bright red Porsche was longing for the open road.

By four, I was cruising down Interstate 5, headed south. Once I passed the worst of the Seattle/Tacoma traffic, I set the cruise control to a sedate sixty-two. Red Porsches draw radar guns like shit draws flies. Sergeant Watkins had given me a long lecture in community relations on the occasion of my second speeding ticket. I had slowed down some since then.

As I drove, I was conscious of springtime blossoming around me. Spindly blackberry clumps were green with a thin covering of new leaves. Here and there, hillsides were graced with farmhouses surrounded by blooming fruit trees.

Between Seattle and Portland, I-5 bypasses dozens of little western Washington towns—Lacy, Maytown, Tenino, Kelso—places travelers never see in actual life. They're nothing more than signs on the freeway and names and dots in a road atlas. Nevertheless, bits and pieces of small-town life leaked into my consciousness. There was the ever-present message from an eccentric Centralia dairy farmer whose private billboard still wanted to get us out of the UN, and the new chain-link fence surrounding the juvenile detention center in Chehalis that said we don't want our town contaminated by these kids. Further south, another billboard proclaimed the Winlock Egg Days.

I had never attended an egg festival. Or wanted to.

The day was flawlessly clear and bright. To the left across the freeway, Mount Rainier majestically reflected back fragile spring sunlight. It was too dark to catch sight of the shattered, still-steaming profile of Mount St. Helens.

I savored every moment of that drive south, from the thick papermill-flavored air of Longview to the cheerful lights on the grain elevator at Kalama. With every mile, the case receded into the far reaches of my mind. For those three quiet hours, I forgot about Darwin and Joanna Ridley, about Bambi Barker and her father, Wheeler-Dealer.

As a homicide cop, that's a luxury I don't give myself very often, but Candace Wynn and her mother had brought back memories of my own mother and her painful death. It had pulled me up short and forced me to recognize exactly how precious life is, had shocked me out of the trap of drifting through life without tasting or noticing.

I owed Candace Wynn a debt of gratitude. Sometime I'd have to call her up and thank her.

St. Agnes of the Hills School sits well back from the road in the middle of Beaverton. It boasts an expanse of beautifully manicured, discreetly lit grounds sandwiched between business parks and new and used car lots. It was late evening when I drove up the circular driveway and parked in front of the building. Spotlights showed off the golden bricks and arches of a graceful Spanish facade on the front of the building.

In the darkness, one front window of the building glowed industriously. I climbed the circular stairway and tried the heavy, double door. It opened into a highly polished, tiled vestibule. Directly ahead, the doors to a plain chapel stood open, but the room itself was deserted. To one side of the vestibule, the fluorescent glow of a light revealed a tiny receptionist's cubbyhole. There was, however, no receptionist in sight. From a room beyond that room, through a half-opened door, I heard the hollow clacking of an old manual typewriter.

I paused in the doorway of the second room. A woman in a prim white blouse with a short blue-and-white wimple on her head sat with her profile to the door, leaning over a typewriter in absolute concentration, her fingers flying. She was a bony woman with a hawkish nose. Wisps of gray hair strayed out from under her headpiece.

She was typing at a small, movable typing table. The large wooden desk beside her was polished to a high gloss and devoid of any clutter. An equally polished brass nameplate on the desk pronounced "Sister Marie Regina O'Dea" in a way that said the lady brooked no nonsense.

As the unchurched son of a fallen-away Presbyterian, what I knew about Catholic nuns could be stacked on the head of a proverbial pin. My previous knowledge was limited to the convent scenes in *The Sound of Music*, which was, for many years, my daughter's favorite movie. The sum of my stereotypes went little beyond the schoolboy rumors that roly-poly equals pleasant and angular equals mean, and ugly girls become nuns when nobody makes them a better offer.

Looking at Sister Marie Regina's narrow face, I wondered if anybody had ever made her an offer of any kind.

I stood quietly, watching her type. The woman had no idea I was there. She typed copy from a neat stack of handwritten pages. When she reached the bottom of a page, she stopped, moved the top sheet to the bottom of the stack, straightened the pile with a sharp, decisive thwack on the table, and put them down neatly again.

When she stopped to change pages the second time, I decided to go ahead and interrupt her. "Excuse me, but I'm looking for the lady in charge, Sister Marie Regina, I believe," I said, nodding toward the polished brass nameplate.

Startled, she jumped, her hand knocking the stack of papers to the floor. Without a word to me, she bent down, retrieved the papers, and straightened them completely before she ever officially acknowledged my existence.

"Yes," she replied crossly, eventually, her tone saying she welcomed me about as much as someone welcomes the twenty-four-hour flu. And that was before she knew who I was or what I wanted. "What can I do for you?"

"For starters, could you tell me where to find Sister Marie Regina?"

"I'm Sister Marie Regina."

"Good. My name is J. P. Beaumont. I'm a

detective with Seattle P.D. I'd like to speak to one of your students."

I held out my ID for her to look at, but her shrewd eyes never left my face, nor did she reach out to take the proffered identification.

"Which one?" she asked coldly. She knew which student I wanted, and I knew she knew. I went along with it, though, playing dumb just for the hell of it.

"A new student," I said innocuously. "One who's only been here a few days."

Sister Marie Regina O'Dea rose from the typing desk and walked to a tall, brown leather chair behind the polished wooden desk. With slow, deliberate movements, she picked up a blue blazer that was hanging there and put it on. She buttoned the front buttons with a flourish, like someone donning a full suit of Christian soldier armor.

When she spoke, her voice was crisp and peremptory. "Detective Beaumont, I'm sure you understand that the young woman you mentioned is here because she's undergone a severe emotional upheaval. Her family has no wish for her to be disturbed by you or by anyone else."

I matched my tone to hers. Two can play Winning by Intimidation. It's more fun that way.

"Sister Marie Regina, I'm here because I'm conducting a homicide investigation. Bambi

Barker is a material witness. I'm afraid her family's wishes have nothing whatsoever to do with it."

She smiled, a brittle smile calculated to be totally unnerving. I'm sure it struck terror in the hearts of recalcitrant fifteen-year-olds. "If you're from Seattle P.D., aren't you somewhat outside your jurisdiction?"

Unfortunately for Sister Marie Regina, I'm a hell of a long way past fifteen. "Concealing material evidence to a capital crime is somewhat out of yours as well, wouldn't you say, Sister?"

She sat down in the high-backed chair and leaned back, clasping her hands in front of her. She regarded me thoughtfully. I don't believe Sister Marie Regina was accustomed to counterattacks.

"Exactly what is it you want, Detective Beaumont?"

"I want to talk to Bambi Barker."

"That's impossible."

"Why?"

I refused to budge under the weight of her level stare. For several long moments we remained locked in visual combat before I took the offensive and attacked her sense of order. I took a straight-backed chair from its place near the wall, moved it to a position in front of her desk, turned it around so the back faced her, and sat astride it with my arms resting on the back of the chair.

"What kind of financial arrangements are necessary to get a girl transferred into St. Agnes over a weekend three months before she's supposed to graduate?"

Sister Marie Regina didn't answer. She didn't flinch, either, but I continued in the same vein.

"Enough to maybe buy a personal computer to replace that ancient typewriter?" I asked. "Or what about a new car? Didn't I see a new Ford Taurus sitting out front, a silver station wagon with temporary plates?"

She blinked then, and I rushed forward into the breach. "I could make a real case in the papers that the car was a bribe, you know. Payment in advance for keeping the girl away from our investigation."

"But that's not true," she blurted. "It was only to get her admitted . . ." Sister Marie Regina stopped abruptly, clenching her narrow jaws.

"You know that, Sister. And maybe I know that, but that's not how it's going to read in *The Oregonian*."

"You wouldn't."

"Oh yes I would. I wouldn't hesitate a minute. I want to talk to that girl, and I want to talk to her tonight. Now."

Sister Marie Regina wasn't used to being outmaneuvered. She stared wordlessly at me for a long time before she reached for a phone, picked it up, and dialed a two-digit number. She tapped her finger anxiously on the phone while she waited for it to be answered.

"Would you please have Sister Eunice bring the new student to my office?" There was a pause. "Yes, I mean now," she added crossly. "Tell her to get dressed."

She got up from her chair, smoothed her jacket, and walked to the door. Sister Marie Regina was a fairly tall woman in exceedingly sensible shoes whose crepe soles squeaked on the glossy surface of the tile floor. "Follow me, please."

With her stiff blue skirt rustling against her nylons, she led me out of her office and down a long hall with a series of unmarked doors lining either side. Toward the end, she stopped, opened a door, and showed me into a tiny room.

"These are our visiting rooms," she announced curtly. "Sister Eunice will bring Miss Barker here shortly." With that she went out, closing the door behind her.

The room was actually a sitting room in the old-fashioned-parlor sense of the word. The furnishings consisted of two dainty, ladylike chairs, a loveseat, and a couch—all of it suitably uncomfortable. A matched set of end tables and a coffee table completed the room's furnishings.

The only light came from an old hanging glass fixture that hung down in the middle of the room. Every flat surface was supplied with identical boxes of industrial strength tissue. Evidently, tears, lots of them, were not unexpected phenomena in St. Agnes' visiting rooms.

Having met Sister Marie Regina O'Dea, I could understand the need for tears, especially if the other nuns turned out to be anything like their stiff-backed leader.

I tried both chairs and the loveseat before I settled uneasily on the couch. It seemed to me the couch had been purposely designed to be unsuitable for human male anatomy. Despite the couch's discomfort, however, I nodded off briefly before the door opened again.

I sat up with a start. At first, in the dim light, I thought Sister Marie Regina had returned. Instead, a woman who looked very much like the headmistress ushered Bambi Barker into the room.

The sister held out her hand to me. Her grip was cool and firm. "I'm Sister Eunice," she said. "And this is Miss Barker."

From the moment I saw her, I could almost understand Tex Barker's desire to lock his daughter in a convent. Maybe even a bank vault. She was a voluptuous little twit. My mother would have called her a floozy. Even in the ill-fitting plaid schoolgirl uniform she wore, her well-built figure showed through plain as day. Her long blonde hair was cut short around her face in the latest heavy-metal style, and she wore plenty of makeup. I was a little surprised the nuns let her get away with that.

Bambi Barker had evidently been crying. Her eyes were red-rimmed, her nose was shiny, and enough mascara had run down her face to make two long, ink black rivulets.

Sister Eunice motioned Bambi Barker onto one of the dainty chairs and seated herself primly on the other.

"Excuse me, Sister," I said, "but I'd like to speak to Miss Barker alone."

"That's not possible," Sister Eunice replied firmly, folding her hands in her lap and settling in. "As senior proctor, I am required to be in attendance when any of my girls speak to an unaccompanied male."

"But, Sister . . ." I objected.

"Now see here, Detective Beaumont." She smiled evenly, showing a set of dentures. She straightened her skirt carefully. "I was instructed not to interfere, but this is the only way you'll be able to talk to her."

She turned to Bambi, reached out, and patted the girl's knee reassuringly. "It's all right, Bambi. I'll stay here with you. All you need to do is tell this man the truth."

Keeping her head ducked into her shoulders, Bambi Barker peered up at me, her full lips gathered in a sullen pout. It was difficult to know where to begin. I hadn't anticipated asking intimate questions of a randy teenager in the presence of a straitlaced, aging nun.

"Did they tell you why I wanted to talk to you, Miss Barker?" I asked.

She shook her head, keeping her eyes averted.

"You've heard about Coach Ridley, haven't you?"

Her head jerked up as if someone had pulled a string. "What about him?"

"He's dead," I answered. "He died sometime Saturday morning."

For a moment her eyes widened in horror, then she shook her head, her blonde mane shifting from side to side. "You're kidding, right?"

"No, Bambi. I'm not kidding. He's dead. I'm here investigating his murder."

With no warning, Bambi Barker slipped soundlessly from the chair to the floor like a marionette with severed strings. Sister Eunice reached out and succeeded in breaking her fall.

"Oh, no," Bambi sobbed over and over as

Sister Eunice caught her and rocked her against a flat, unyielding breast. "It can't be."

I slipped to the floor as well, lifting Bambi's chin so I could look into the shocked blue depths of her eyes. "What can't be, Bambi?" I asked. "Tell me."

She twisted away from my hand and once again buried her face against Sister Eunice. "Oh, Daddy," I heard her sob. "How could you!"

How could he indeed?

C H A P T E R
14

Sister Eunice spent the next half hour on her knees on the floor of that visiting room, pasting the pieces of Bambi Barker back together and forever putting an end to my lean/mean stereotyping of Catholic nuns. Sister Eunice may have been every bit as angular as Sister Marie Regina, but she was anything but heartless. She held Bambi close, rocking her gently like a baby and murmuring small words of comfort in her ear.

There was nothing for me to do but sit and wait for the storm of emotion to blow over. Sister Eunice must have gotten tired of my just hanging around, because finally she ordered me out of the room, sending me on a mission to bring back a glass of water. When I returned, Sister Eunice had engineered Bambi back onto a chair.

"Here now," she urged soothingly, taking the glass from my hand and holding it to Bambi's lips. "Try some of this."

Bambi took a small sip, choked, and pushed the glass away. "I'm all right."

"Are you sure?" Sister Eunice asked.

"I'm sure," Bambi mumbled.

It was time to start, but I approached Bambi warily. "I have to ask you some questions, Miss Barker."

She nodded numbly, without looking up. "So ask."

"Do you know anything about what happened to Darwin Ridley?"

Bambi Barker raised her head then and looked at me. "It was just a game," she said.

"A game?" I asked, not comprehending. "What do you mean, a game?"

"A game, a contest."

I felt really lost. "I don't understand what you're talking about. What was a contest?"

She shot a quick glance in the direction of Sister Eunice, who sat with her hands clasped in her lap, nodding encouragingly. "Don't pay any attention to me, Bambi," Sister Eunice said. "You go right ahead and tell the man what he needs to know."

Bambi took a deep breath and looked back at me. "Each year the cheerleaders have a contest to see . . ." She paused and looked at Sister Eunice again.

"To see what?" I urged impatiently.

"To see who can get one of the teachers in bed. It's, you know, a tradition."

My jaw must have dropped about three feet. At first I didn't think I'd heard her right. But I had. A tradition! The last time I had heard the word tradition, Bob Payson was telling me about the basketball team and Girl Scout cookies. So while the boys were worrying about nice little civilized traditions of the tea and crumpet variety, the cheerleaders were busy balling their favorite teacher. Jesus!

My mother once told me that girls are born knowing what it takes boys fifteen years to figure out. About then I figured fifteen years wasn't nearly long enough.

"The same teacher?" I asked, finding my voice. "Or a different one each year?"

She shrugged. "Sometimes the same. Usually not."

"Somebody keeps track from year to year?"

She nodded. "It's in one of the lockers in the girls' dressing room. Written on the ceiling. But it was just a game. Nothing like this ever . . ." She broke off and was quiet.

"Now let me get this straight. Each year somebody on the cheerleading squad seduces one of the teachers, and then you write his name down on a list?"

She nodded.

"Was there a prize for this game?"

"At the beginning of the year, everybody puts fifty dollars into a pot. When the winner brings proof, she gets the money."

"Proof? What do you mean, proof?"

"I mean, like you couldn't just say you did it, you know? You had to have proof. A picture, a tape, or something."

Fifteen years? Hell, forty-three years wasn't enough. I glanced at Sister Eunice. She continued sitting with her hands serenely clasped, her eyes never leaving Bambi's face. Maybe living in a convent with high school kids had taught Sister Eunice a whole lot more about the world than I had given her credit for.

It was all I could do to keep from grabbing Bambi Barker by the shoulders and shaking her until the braces flew off her teeth. "I take it you won this year?" I asked dryly.

"Yes." When she answered, her voice dropped almost to a whisper. My question had brought back the reality of the consequences of that nasty little game, as well as a little reticence.

"And the proof?"

"A picture. One of my friends took it."

"So how did your father get it?"

"I don't know, I swear to God."

"And who sent one to Joanna Ridley? Your father?"

"Maybe. I don't know. I've never seen him so mad. He was crazy."

"When did he find out?"

"Friday. Friday morning. He came to school to get me. I thought he was going to kill me right there in the car."

"He threatened you?"

"He hit me." One hand strayed to her lip as if in unconscious remembrance of that slap across the face. Tears appeared in the corners of her eyes. Deftly, Sister Eunice reached out and wiped them away with a lacy handkerchief.

"Did he threaten Mr. Ridley?"

"I think so."

"You think?"

"He said he was going to do something, but I didn't know what it was. It sounded bad."

"Do you remember what it was?"

She rubbed her eyes and more mascara flaked off and landed on her face. "It was something like ... It ended with *ate*. Something *ate*."

You don't have to work *The New York Times* crossword puzzle every day to be able to figure that one out.

"Castrate?" I asked. "Was that it?"

She nodded. "That's it. What does it mean?"

"Cut his balls off," I growled. I was in no mood to pull any punches or mince any words for Bambi Barker. She didn't deserve it, but I was aware of an uncomfortable shifting in Sister Eunice's otherwise tranquil presence.

Bambi Barker gulped and swallowed hard.

"That didn't happen," I added. "If that's what you're worried about. Somebody just strung Darwin Ridley up on the end of a rope."

Bambi dissolved into tears once again. When Sister Eunice reached out as if to comfort her, I stopped her hand. The nun looked me in the face for a long moment, then nodded in acquiescence and allowed her hand to drop back into her lap.

Suddenly, I realized Sister Eunice and I were coconspirators in the process. She wasn't merely observing. Sister Eunice was actively helping. What her motives were wasn't clear to me at the time, although it occurred to me that maybe she was bent on saving Bambi Barker's immortal soul.

We waited together until Bambi's sobbing quieted and eventually died away altogether. Only then did Sister Eunice reach out again, this time to take Bambi's hand. "Is it possible that your father did this terrible thing?" she asked.

You could have knocked me over with a feather. I don't suppose genteel Catholic nuns routinely conduct homicide interrogations, but Sister Eunice was a down-home killer at asking questions. She put the screws to Bambi directly, holding her eyes in an unblinking gaze, offering the girl no opportunity to look away or avoid the issue.

"He could have," Bambi whispered finally.

"All right, then," Sister Eunice said. Her voice was calm and firm. "You must tell Detective Beaumont here everything you know that could possibly be helpful."

"But I don't know for sure," Bambi protested.

"Tell us exactly what went on Friday," Sister Eunice urged quietly.

"After I left school?"

"Where did you go, home?"

Bambi nodded. "We went to the house. Mom was home, waiting."

That prompted a question from me. "Your mother knew about it, before you got there?"

"Everybody knew about it. There was a huge hassle, and Dad locked me in my room."

"How long were you there?"

"Until Saturday morning. Then they woke me up and told me to pack because I was coming here."

"They both brought you down?" I asked.

"We had to bring two cars. Mom drove one. They left it here." Bambi Barker's pout returned.

"For you?"

"No. It was, you know, like a gift to the school."

I get a little ego hit every time one of my

hunches turns out to be correct, even when it's not particularly important. It's good for my overall batting average. Sister Marie Regina O'Dea's shiny new Taurus station wagon bribe gave me a little rush of satisfaction.

I said, "How nice. So they drove you down and checked you in. I take it you weren't especially thrilled to come here."

Bambi glanced in Sister Eunice's direction. "I didn't have a choice."

"Why not?"

"He said he'd disown me."

"Would he?"

"He did Faline."

"Who's that?"

"She used to be my sister."

Faline. Bambi. Obviously somebody in the Barker family was a Walt Disney fan. "Used to be your sister?" I asked. "What do you mean by that?"

"He threw her out three years ago. No one's heard from her since."

"Why did they send you here? Why this school?"

"My mother's sister is a member of the Order of St. Agnes in Texas. She's the one who suggested it."

I changed the subject abruptly, hoping to throw her off guard. "Tell me about Coach Ridley."

"What about him?"

"How long had it been going on, between the two of you?"

"There was nothing going on, really. I, like, pretended, but it was just a game. I already told you."

"But when did it happen?"

"You mean when did we take the picture?" I nodded, and she shrugged. "Only last week."

"Where?"

"It's a place up on Aurora, in Seattle. A motel."

"How come he didn't see the flash?"

"Molly was outside, using her dad's camera. It doesn't need a flash."

I didn't have nerve enough to look at Sister Eunice right then. I probably could have, though. She deals with teenage kids all the time. She's probably used to it. Me, I'm just a homicide cop. Right then, homicide seemed a hell of a lot more straightforward. The whole scenario of Darwin Ridley being led like a lamb to the slaughter because of some stupid adolescent game shocked me, offended me.

And I thought I'd seen everything.

"Who's Molly?" I asked.

"A friend of mine. My best friend. Molly Blackburn."

"Also a cheerleader?"

Bambi nodded. "She lives right up the street from us. Will she get in trouble, too?"

I made a note of Molly Blackburn's name and address. Molly Blackburn, the budding photographer. Or maybe Molly Blackburn, the budding blackmailer—whichever.

"I can't say one way or the other," I told her.

It was almost midnight when Sister Eunice led Bambi Barker back to her room. Bambi had started down the hall when Sister Eunice poked her head back in the door of the visiting room and asked me to wait long enough for her to return.

When she did, she ushered me out of the visiting room and down the long, empty corridor to a tiny kitchen and lounge. There she poured me a cup of acrid coffee that tasted like it had been in the pot for three weeks.

"Will you be returning to Seattle tonight, Detective Beaumont?" she asked.

I scratched my head and glanced at the movable cat's-eye clock above an equally dated turquoise refrigerator. It was well after eleven. We had spent a long, long evening with Bambi Barker. "It's late, but I suppose so."

"And you're a man of honor?" she asked.

"What do you mean?"

"I mean, you won't be talking to *The Oregonian* before you leave Portland, will you?"

"I told Sister Marie Regina that as long as you helped me, I'd keep my mouth shut."

Sister Eunice looked enormously relieved. "Good," she said. "I'm very happy to hear it."

So much for Bambi Barker's immortal soul. Sister Eunice had become my ally for far more worldly reasons than to keep Bambi's soul safe from hell and damnation. She had done it to keep Sister Marie Regina's Taurus station wagon off the editorial page. Situational ethics in action.

I took the rest of the coffee to drink in the car, remembering the old Bible verse about judging not and being without sin and all that jazz. After all, I had fired the first shot. And I couldn't argue with the results. I had gotten what I wanted from Bambi Barker.

As I started the Porsche, I realized how hungry I was. When I reached downtown Portland, I stopped off at a little joint on S.W. First, a place called the Veritable Quandary. I remembered it from the mid-seventies as a little tavern where they made great roast beef sandwiches and you could play pickup chess while you ate. Unfortunately, the eighties had caught up with it. The easygoing tavern atmosphere had evolved into a full-scale bar scene. The chessboards and magazines had long since disappeared. The sandwich was good, though, and it helped counteract Sister Eunice's bitter coffee.

It was only as I sat there in solitary silence, chewing on my roast beef, that I realized I had never asked Bambi Barker how much her prize was for screwing Darwin Ridley. On second thought, I was probably better off not knowing.

Thinking about it spoiled my appetite. I didn't finish the sandwich.

CHAPTER
15

There was a lot to think about on the way home. Bambi Barker had shaken me. I couldn't help wondering how I would have felt if I had discovered that my own daughter, Kelly, had been pulling something like that when she was in high school. Would I have taken the time to find out that the girls had been playing the teacher for a fool, or would I have jumped to the opposite conclusion?

There could be little doubt of the answer to that one. J. P. Beaumont has been known to jump to conclusions on occasion. Somebody by the name of Wheeler-Dealer Barker could very well suffer from the same malady.

In fact, the more I thought about it, the more I figured there was a better-than-even-money chance that Bambi's old man had jumped to his own erroneous and lethal conclusions. We needed to know his whereabouts on Friday night and Saturday morning, while Bambi was locked in her room at home and her mother was standing guard.

Knowing of Molly Blackburn's existence helped answer one puzzling question. The idea that a father would have mailed out such a compromising picture of his own daughter had never made sense to me. I couldn't imagine any father doing such a thing, not even in the heat of anger. I had gone along with that suggestion when no other possibilities had presented themselves, but it made far more sense that the picture might have been part of a blackmail scheme, a complicated, two-sided deal aimed at wresting money from both families involved, the Barkers and the Ridleys.

It seemed likely that a copy of the picture had arrived at the Barker home sometime Friday morning. That was probably what had tipped off old Wheeler-Dealer. Joanna's had arrived days later. That was somewhat puzzling. Why the delay? If you're going to blackmail two different sets of people, why not do it simultaneously? Or maybe they had been mailed at the same time and the postal service had screwed up.

My questions defied any attempt to find answers, but they served to fill up the long straight stretches of interstate. There was hardly any traffic on the freeway at that time of night. Just me and a bunch of eighteen-wheelers tearing up the road. I made it back to Seattle in a good deal less time than the three hours it should have taken.

I dropped into bed the minute I got to my apartment. It was three A.M. when I turned out the light and fell asleep.

Fifteen minutes later the phone rang, jarring me out of a sound sleep. "Please stay on the line," a tinny, computerized female voice told me. Within moments, Ralph Ames' voice sputtered into the receiver. He sounded like somebody had just kicked him awake, too.

"What do you want?" he demanded in a groggy grumble.

"What do you mean, 'What do I want'? You called me, remember?"

"Oh, I must have forgotten to turn that damn thing off when I went to bed."

"What damn thing?" I wasn't playing with a full deck in this conversation.

"My automatic redialer."

An automatic redialer! Ralph Ames' ongoing love affair with gadgets was gradually becoming clear to me. If my phone had been ringing off and on all night, it was probably quite clear to Ida Newell, my next-door neighbor, as well.

"That's just great," I fumed. "I went to bed fifteen minutes ago, Ralph. What's so goddamned important that you woke us both up?"

"Your closing on Belltown Terrace. It's reset for Friday, three-thirty. Can you make it?"

I took a deep breath. "Sometimes you really piss me off. It's three o'clock in the morning. You expect me to have a calendar in my hand?"

"If you had an answering machine . . ."

"I don't want an answering machine." I rummaged through the nightstand drawer for pen and paper and wrote down the time and place for the real estate closing. "There," I said. "Is that all? Mind if I get some sleep now?"

"Be my guest," Ames replied, then hung up.

A scant three hours later, the phone rang again. Once more I shook the fog out of my head. Eventually, I recognized Al Lindstrom's voice. Big Al, as we call him, is another detective on the homicide squad. He generally works the night shift.

"What do you mean calling me at this hour?" I'm crabby when I don't get my beauty sleep.

"Don't get your sweat hot, Beau. I've got someone on the line. She wants to talk to you. Real bad."

"Look, Al. I've barely gotten into bed. Can't you take a message?"

"She wants to talk to you *now*."

"Jesus H. Christ. Who is it? Can't you get

her name and number? I'll call her back as soon as I get to the office."

"Just a minute. I'll ask." While he was off the line, I tried, with limited success, to rub my eyes open and unscramble my brain.

Eventually, Al returned to the line. "Says her name's Joanna Ridley. Says you can't call her. She wants to meet you in half an hour at the tennis courts in Seward Park."

"I'm still in bed, Al. I can't meet her in half an hour. Tell her I'll call her later."

"It's too late."

"Why?"

"She hung up."

"Shit!" I rolled out of bed. "Thanks a whole hell of a lot," I growled.

"Don't chew my ass," Al returned. "I'm just doing my job."

He slammed the phone down in my ear. I grabbed my nightstand telephone book and located Joanna's number, but when I finally dialed it, the line was busy. I tried several more times, but the line remained busy, leaving me to conclude that Joanna was serious about my not calling her back. She had evidently left the phone off the hook.

I gave my pillow a reluctant farewell pat and headed for the shower. Exactly eleven minutes later, the Porsche and I shot out through the building garage entrance onto Lenora.

Morning fog was thick as velvet as I drove up Boren and out Rainier Avenue. At six twenty-five traffic coming into the city was already picking up, but I was driving against it. I wondered as I drove why Joanna had refused to see me at her house, and why she had picked such an early hour in a deserted city park for our meeting.

Seward Park sits on a point that juts out into Lake Washington. On a clear day, Mount Rainier sits majestically above the water, framed on either side by the house-covered ridges of South Seattle and Mercer Island. That particular morning, however, there was no hint that a mountain lay hidden out there. Invisible behind the fog, it lurked in a blanket of silence that was broken only by the occasional huffing of an early morning jogger.

I saw Joanna Ridley's Mustang right away, tucked into a parking place against the tennis court fence. The driver of the Mustang, however, was nowhere in sight. Parking the Porsche next to Joanna's car, I set out looking for her.

Blooming dogwood and daffodils lined the park's entrance. I walked along a hedge of *Photinia*, its new growth crimson above the older green leaves. The startling spring colors stood out in sharp relief against the shifting gray fog. The grass was heavy with dew, sponging down beneath my feet as I walked along the breakwater.

The park seemed a lonely, desolate place for a new widow. The idea of suicide fleetingly crossed my mind. I wondered if Joanna had decided to end her own life. The thought had no more than entered my mind, however, when I spotted her near the water.

Wearing a huge sweater, she stood on the rock breakwater, profiled against the gray of both the fog and water behind her. A light breeze blowing off the lake pressed the sweater's soft material around the bulge in her middle, accentuating her pregnant figure. Unaware of my approach, she peered down from her perch at something in the water below her, something I couldn't see. When I finally got close enough to look below the breakwater, I found she was watching a flock of hungry ducks out bumming for handouts.

"You wanted to see me?" I asked.

Without warning, she whirled and sprang at me, clenching both fists as she did so. She moved so fast I was surprised she didn't lose her footing on the slippery, wet grass. Just in time I realized she was bringing a haymaker up from her knees, putting the full force of her body behind it. If she had landed that blow, it would have sent me flying.

My reflexes may not be what they used to be, but they were still good enough to save my bacon. I dodged back, away from her doubled fist, which whizzed past my face within an inch of my nose. She came scrambling after me, her face a mask of hard, cold fury.

I had seen a similar version of that look once, that night in the Dog House after we left the medical examiner's office. That look was mild compared to this. Right then, Joanna Ridley appeared to be entirely capable of murder.

"It's about time you got here, you son of a bitch!"

I had expected our encounter to begin on a somewhat more cordial note. After all, I wasn't even late. I stepped back again, just to be on the safe side, staying well out of reach.

"What the hell's going on, Joanna? What's wrong?"

Her right hand shot toward the pocket of the voluminous sweater. My first thought was that she was going for a gun.

Once burned, twice shy. The last time I got burned by a lady with a gun, I came within inches of checking out for good.

With adrenaline pumping from every pore, I bounded forward and grabbed her wrists, pinning them to her sides before she had a chance to draw. Like a desperate, captive bird she struggled to escape my grasp. We must have stood like that for half a minute or so before I realized that what she had in the pocket of her sweater was nothing more than a rolled-up section of newspaper.

She was still pulling against me with all her might when I let go of her wrists. She fell away from me toward the breakwater and would have fallen backward into the lake if I hadn't caught her. We fell to the ground together in a tumbled heap.

The fall knocked the wind out of her. For a moment she was silent, her dark eyes staring up at me in mute rage. When she caught her breath, she screamed. "Get away from me, you bastard. Get away!"

"Are you all right? Are you hurt?" I tried to break through her anger, but she didn't hear me. She kept right on screaming.

Suddenly, I was lifted off the ground. Someone grabbed me by the back of my shirt the way a mother dog grabs a puppy to carry it. Except puppies don't wear ties with knots that block their windpipes. I dangled in midair, coughing and choking.

From behind me, I heard someone say, "Hey, lady. This guy botherin' you?"

Joanna Ridley didn't answer him. I swung around, trying to break his hold, but the guy had arms like a gorilla. I couldn't lay a hand on him. I was about to black out when he dropped me to the ground like a sack of potatoes. I lay there for a moment, stunned and gasping, trying to force air back into my lungs.

When I looked up, a giant of a man was gently helping Joanna to her feet.

"I'm a police officer," I sputtered. I reached for my ID, but my pocket was empty. The leather case had evidently fallen out in the course of the struggle.

"Yeah, and I'm Sylvester Stallone," he returned. Joanna Ridley was on her feet and mercifully quiet. "You all right, lady?" he asked. "You want somebody to take you home?"

I crawled around on my hands and knees in the grass, searching for my ID. Finally, I located it, resting against a rock, just below where Joanna and I had fallen. I clambered to my feet and staggered over to where they stood. At six three, I'm no piker when it comes to size, but this guy made me look like a midget. Muscles bulged under his oversized T-shirt and rippled down his legs from under the skimpy running shorts he wore.

I tried to show him my ID, but he brushed me aside. "Get away from her before I call the cops."

"Goddamn it, I *am* a cop. Detective J. P. Beaumont, Seattle P.D. Homicide."

"No shit? Since when do cops go around beating up pregnant ladies in parks?"

I wouldn't have convinced him, not in a million years, but right then Joanna Ridley stopped her silent sobbing and, surprisingly, spoke in my defense. "It's all right. I fell down. He caught me."

The man bent down and looked her full in the face. "You sure, now? I can throw his ass in the water if you want. You say the word and I'll drown this sucker."

"No. Really. It's all right."

He stepped away then, reluctantly, looking from one of us to the other as if trying to figure out what was really going on. "Okay, then, if you say so." Without another word, he turned on his heel and jogged away from us, running shoes squeaking on the wet grass.

Warily, I approached Joanna. "What's wrong? Tell me."

Once again, she reached into the pocket. When her hand emerged, she was holding the newspaper. She was under control now, but her eyes still struck sparks of fury as she slapped the newspaper into my outstretched hand.

"I thought you said you'd keep it quiet."

"Keep what quiet?"

"About what happened. I thought I could trust you, but you took it straight to the newspaper."

"Joanna, what are you talking about?"

"The picture."

"My God, is the picture in here?" Dismayed, I unrolled the newspaper.

"It just as well could be," Joanna replied grimly.

I scanned down the page, the front page of the last section of the newspaper. The local news section. There on the bottom four columns wide, was Maxwell Cole's crime column, "City Beat." The headline said it all:

"Sex Plus Race Equals Murder."

I scanned through the article quickly, while Joanna Ridley watched my face. When I finished reading, I looked up at her. I was sickened. There could be no doubt from the article that Maxwell Cole had indeed seen the photograph of Darwin Ridley and Bambi Barker. All of Seattle could just as well have seen it. The article left little to the imagination. The only thing it didn't mention was Bambi Barker's name. Knowing Maxwell Cole, I figured Wheeler-Dealer's money and position in the community had something to do with that.

I took Joanna Ridley by the arm and led her to her car.

"Where are you going?" she asked as she half-trotted to keep up with me.

"To find Maxwell Cole," I told her. "If I don't kill him first, you can have a crack at him."

CHAPTER
16

I put Joanna Ridley in her car and told her to go on home, that I'd call her as soon as I knew anything.

As she started the Mustang, I motioned for her to roll down the window. "Don't forget to put your phone back on the hook," I told her. She gave me a half-hearted wave and drove away.

I started the Porsche and rammed it into gear. My first instinct was to find Maxwell Cole, beat the crap out of him, and find out who the big mouth was, either in the crime lab or in Seattle P.D. Somebody had leaked the information.

I drove straight to the *Post-Intelligencer*'s new digs down on Elliott, overlooking Puget Sound. Eight o'clock found me standing in front of a needle-nosed receptionist who told me Maxwell Cole wasn't expected in before ten. I should have known a slug like Cole wouldn't be up at the crack of dawn.

Rather than hang around the newspaper and cool my heels, I went down to the Public Safety Building. I stopped at the second floor and stormed into the crime lab.

Don Yamamoto, head of the Washington State Patrol's crime lab, is a criminalist of the first water. He's one of those second-generation Japanese who, as a kid, was incarcerated along with his parents in a relocation camp during World War II. He spent all his spare time during the years they were locked up reading the only book available to him—a Webster's unabridged dictionary—and he came out of the camp with a far better education than he probably would have gotten otherwise.

He's a smart guy, smart and personable both, well respected by those who work for and with him. The receptionist waved me past without bothering to give me an official escort. As usual, the door to Yamamoto's office stood open. I knocked on the frame.

"Hey, Beau, how's it going?" he asked, looking up from a stack of paperwork on his desk.

"Not well," I answered. "We've got troubles." I laid it on the line to him. He listened without comment. When I finished, he sat back in his chair, folding his arms behind his head.

"I think you're wrong, Beau. That story didn't come from this office. None of my people go running off at the mouth."

He got up and led the way to the evidence room. He stopped at the doorway long enough to examine the log. "Only two people actually handled that photograph," he said. "One was Janice Morraine, and the other is Tom Welch. Either of those sound like people who'd be messing around with the likes of Maxwell Cole?"

I shook my head. I knew them both fairly well. I had to agree with their chief's assessment.

"So how did Max get the story?"

"Why don't you go straight to the horse's mouth and ask him that question?" Don suggested.

"I tried that. He wasn't in."

"So try again."

I turned on my heels and walked out of his office. Standing in the elevator lobby waiting for the door to open, I was surprised when the door *behind* me opened. Don Yamamoto followed me into the corridor. "But you'll let me know if you find out something I need to know, right?" he asked.

Don Yamamoto trusted his people implicitly. Up to a point.

I chuckled. "Yes," I answered. "I'll let you know."

It was eight-forty when I reached Peters' and my cubicle on the fifth floor. Peters glanced meaningfully at his watch. Having a partner can be worse than having to punch a time clock. Time clocks don't expect explanations.

"Get off it," I told him before he had a chance to open his mouth. "I got back from Portland at three this morning, and I've been up working since six, so don't give me any shit."

"My, my, we are touchy this morning," Peters said with a grin. "So tell me what you learned in Portland."

I did. All of it. By the time I finished telling him about the cheerleading squad's nasty little rite of passage, he wasn't nearly as cheerful as he had been. In fact, he was probably wondering about the advisability of having daughters.

"I talked to all those girls," he said. "They seemed like nice, straight, clean-cut kids."

"You can't tell a book by its cover, remember?"

"Right, so what do we do? Tackle Wheeler-Dealer? Go have a heart-to-heart talk with Molly Blackburn? Read the writing in the locker?"

I got up and glanced over the top of the cubicle walls to the clock at the end of the room. It was five to ten. "All of the above," I told him, "but not necessarily in that order. We're starting with Maxwell Cole, bless his pointed little head."

We dropped the Porsche off at my place and took a departmental crate to the *P.I.* It turned out Maxwell Cole's pointed head was nowhere within striking distance. The same scrawny receptionist gave me an icy smile and told me Mr. Cole was out on an assignment. She had no idea when he'd be back. Lucky for him.

We left there and drove to Mercer Island, figuring we'd make a brief visit to Wheeler-Dealer Barker's home on our way to his dealership in Bellevue. The address jotted in Peters' notebook led us to a stately white colonial on a lot that seemed to be several sizes too small. A multinote chime playing "The Yellow Rose of Texas" announced our arrival. A plain, small-boned woman wearing a long honey-colored robe came to the door.

Her mousy blonde hair was still damp from a shower, and her face was devoid of makeup. Her nose was shiny, her eyes red-rimmed. This was a lady who had been having a good cry in the privacy of her own home. She looked up at us anxiously.

"Are you Mrs. Barker?" I asked. "Mrs. Tex

Barker?" I held out my identification so she could read it.

"I'm Madeline Barker," she returned.

"May we come in?"

She stepped away from the door uncertainly before finally motioning us inside. We entered a large, well-appointed vestibule, complete with a huge bouquet of fragrant spring flowers.

"What is it?" she asked.

I think I had expected Mrs. Wheeler-Dealer Barker to speak with a thick southern drawl. I would have thought she'd offer us coffee with chicory and maybe a mess of grits or black-eyed peas. I was dismayed to discover that all trace of her origins had been eradicated from Madeline's manner of speech. Grits and chicory were nowhere in evidence.

"It's about your husband," I told her. "Your husband and your daughter."

I said nothing more. A mixture of distress and confusion washed over Madeline Barker's face. Reflexively, she clenched her fists tightly and shoved them deep into the pockets of her robe.

"What about them?" she asked, her voice cracking as she struggled to maintain an outward show of calm.

"Would you mind telling us exactly what went on here Friday afternoon?"

She turned her back on us then and walked

as far as the doorway into the next room. Stopping abruptly, she leaned against the wall for support, her breath coming in short panicky gasps.

Peters moved toward her. He spoke in a gently reassuring manner. "We're trying to resolve a homicide, Mrs. Barker. Darwin Ridley's. As I'm sure you know, your daughter was involved to some degree. We need to find out exactly . . ."

Madeline Barker suddenly found her voice and swung around to face us. "You don't think . . . Bambi couldn't have done it. She was here, in her room, all night. She never went out."

"We're aware of that. You see, we've already talked to your daughter."

"Oh," she said. "Then what are you doing here? Why are you still asking questions?"

"Was your husband here all night, too?" I asked.

She paled suddenly and retreated farther into the living room, instantly creating a larger physical buffer zone between my question and her.

"What do you mean?" she demanded. "You think Tex had something to do with it?"

"If you'd just answer the question, Mrs. Barker. Was your husband here in the house with you all night or was he gone part of the time?"

Madeline Barker pulled herself stiffly erect.

"I won't answer that," she said. "I don't have to."

There are times when no answer speaks volumes. This was one of those times. Tex "Wheeler-Dealer" Barker had not been home all night the night Darwin Ridley died, of that we could be certain. That gave Barker two of the necessary ingredients for murder—motive and opportunity. When had he left the house and what time had he returned? Those were questions in need of answering. For right then we seemed to have taken a giant step toward getting some answers.

Peters did what he could to soothe Madeline Barker's ruffled feathers. "You're absolutely right, Mrs. Barker. You don't have to answer that question if you don't want to," he told her reassuringly.

The questioning process, conducted in pairs, is a subtle game. Peters and I had learned to play it well, using one another as foils or fall guys with equal ease. The slight nod he gave me said we were shifting to Good Cop/Bad Cop, and I was the bad guy.

"Could you tell us about the picture, then, Mrs. Barker?" I asked.

"Picture?"

"You know which picture, Mrs. Barker. We've seen it, and I'm sure you have, too."

I've learned over the years that if someone doesn't want to talk about one thing, you give them an opportunity to talk about something else. They fall all over themselves spilling their guts. Madeline Barker was happy to oblige.

She made no further attempt to pretend she didn't know what we were talking about. "It came in the mail," she admitted. "About ten o'clock that morning."

"Here? To the house?"

She nodded. "It was addressed to both of us, so I opened it. I couldn't believe my eyes. Bambi's always been such a good girl."

"Was there anything else in the envelope besides the picture?" I asked. "A note maybe? A demand for money?"

"No. Nothing. Just the picture. That awful picture."

"Where is it now?" Peters inquired.

"It's gone," she replied.

"Gone?"

'Tex told me to get rid of it. I burned it."

"And the envelope?"

"That, too. In the kitchen sink. I ran the ashes down the garbage disposal. That's what it was," she added. "Garbage."

"Let's go back to when you opened the envelope," I put in. "What happened then?"

Madeline Barker took a deep breath. "I was so upset, I didn't know what to do. So I called Tex. At work."

"And what did he do?"

"He came right home."

"To look at the picture?"

"Yes."

"And then what?"

"He went to school to get Bambi. To bring her home."

"He was angry?"

"Angry! He was crazy. Bambi wasn't like Faline. Bambi was never a problem. She was always a good student, always popular, easy to get along with. And then this. I was afraid Tex would have a heart attack over it. He already has high blood pressure, you know."

"What happened when he brought her here?"

"There was a fight, a terrible fight. She said she was going to the game no matter what we said, that we couldn't stop her."

"And that's when he locked her in her room?"

Madeline nodded, then turned an appraising look on me. For the first time I think she realized that we had already heard the story once from Bambi, that we were simply verifying information we already knew.

"Who came up with the idea of sending her to Portland?" I asked.

"I did," Madeline answered firmly. "We've fallen away from the church, but I wanted her away from that man. I wanted her out of town. I called my sister. She's in a convent in Texas. She helped us arrange it."

We didn't stay much longer after that. Madeline Barker had told us as much as she could, or at least as much as she would. There was no need to pressure her any more than we already had.

Once back in the car, Peters turned on the engine, then paused with his hand on the gearshift. "She still thinks Darwin Ridley seduced her daughter." Neither one of us had bothered to mention that it was the other way around.

I shrugged. "It won't be long before she finds out differently, especially with the likes of Maxwell Cole hanging around."

Peters drove us away from the Barker house. "That raises another question, doesn't it?"

"What does?"

"The picture. Why wasn't there a note? That bothers me. Blackmail requires communication—two-way communication. According to what Joanna Ridley told us, there wasn't a note with her picture, either. How can it be blackmail?"

"How should I know? These are a bunch of school kids. Maybe they don't know all the ropes yet. They're just talented amateurs trying to break into the big time."

"They've broken into it, all right," Peters commented grimly. "Murder's pretty big time."

I allowed as how that was true.

CHAPTER
17

Peters drove us to Wheeler-Dealer Barker's Bellevue Ford, which sits on a sprawling piece of real estate smack in the middle of Bellevue's auto row. The place was actually a total contradiction, a state-of-the-art auto dealership made up to look like an old-time, flagstone ranch house. The lot was lined with log-rail fences, and the salespeople were all decked out in cowboy boots and ten-gallon hats.

Obviously, Tex Barker had brought along the spirit of the Lone Star state as well as his name when he migrated to Washington.

The lady at the receptionist's desk wore a blue gingham outfit that would have been a lot more at home in a square dance convention than in an office. "Can I help you find someone?" she asked in the thick drawl I had expected from Madeline Barker.

"We're looking for Mr. Barker."

"He's on the phone just now, if you care to wait. Can I get you coffee, tea?"

"No, nothing. We're fine."

The waiting area had two genuine brown leather sofas with wheel spokes in the armrests. I hadn't seen one of those since the mid-fifties. I didn't know anybody still made them. The ashtray had a dead scorpion encased in it. I thought those were museum pieces as well.

"You've never seen any of his commercials?" Peters asked as we waited in the showroom full of cars.

"Never," I replied.

"It's interesting," Peters added.

"What is?"

"Now that I've met his wife. He's always offering to throw her in with the deal, if what they've got isn't good enough."

"Are you serious?" I thought about Madeline Barker. She didn't seem like someone who would enjoy that sort of thing, especially living among some of the more rarefied Mercer Island types. With a husband and a father like that, she and Bambi both must have had a lot to live down.

Not one but three hungry salesmen came by to pitch cars to us while we sat there. It was clear this was the good-ol'-boy, let's-go-out-and-kick-tires school of automobile salesmanship. They were particularly interested in pitching a T-bird Turbo Coupe that they all insisted was a "hot little number." I couldn't help wishing we had been driving my Porsche instead of the department's lukewarm Dodge.

Eventually, a door opened and Old Wheeler-Dealer himself sauntered out of his private office onto the showroom floor. He was a tall, handsome man in an aging cowboy way. He wore a dove gray western-style Ul-trasuede jacket with a complex pattern embroidered on the front of the shoulders in flashy silver thread and a silver and turquoise bolo tie. His huge ten-gallon hat with its snakeskin band was tipped back on his head. I'm no fashion expert, but I guessed the alligator boots were of the real, rather than imitation, variety.

"How'do, boys. Understand y'all are waitin' for me?" Peters and I nodded. "Interested in one of our fine automobiles, here? We've got some sweet deals, I'll tell you, some really sweet deals."

"We're with Seattle P.D.," I said, handing him my identification. "Homicide. We're investigating Darwin Ridley's murder."

"What's that got to do with me?" Barker stuck out his chin and thrust my ID back into my hand.

"Plenty," I told him. "Do you mind if we ask you a few questions?"

"Mind? I most certainly do. I got a business

to run here. I can't waste my time answerin' no-account questions." He turned and started back into his office. I reached out and grasped the sleeve of his jacket.

"We've talked to Bambi," I said.

He turned and swung around toward me. "You what?"

"I said, we talked to Bambi. Down in Port-land."

"Why, you worthless creep. I'll beat the holy shit out of you." He took a wild swing at me, but Peters caught his fist while it was still in transit. It was the second time that day some-one had swung at me and missed. My nose was grateful. So were my front teeth.

"I think we'd be better off discussing this privately, Mr. Barker," Peters suggested.

Barker shook Peters' restraining hand off his arm. "Oh you do, do you? What makes you think I want to talk to you in private or oth-erwise?"

"It's not a matter of wanting," I told him evenly. "We've seen the picture," I added.

A look of barely controlled fury crossed Tex Barker's face. "Oh" was all he said. He turned away and stalked into his office. Peters and I exchanged glances before we followed him. He stopped at the door, let us into the room, then snarled at the gingham-clad receptionist outside, "I'm not to be disturbed!"

He slammed the door and pushed his way past us into his small but sumptuous office, taking a seat behind a large, imposing desk. He made no suggestion that we be seated. We sat uninvited.

"Bambi had nothin' to do with that man's death," he declared, speaking slowly, attempting to keep his voice carefully modulated, making a visible effort to maintain control. Despite his efforts, the words virtually exploded into the room as they left his lips.

"Did you see Darwin Ridley last Friday?" I asked. "Did you talk to him after you saw the picture that came in the mail that morning?"

He glared at me. "I did not!"

I knew he was lying. I can't say for sure how I knew. I just did. Maybe it was the momentary flicker in his eyes. "Where were you Friday night, Mr. Barker?"

"Home."

I shook my head. "No. Not all night. Someone came to the Coliseum and spoke to Darwin Ridley just at the end of halftime. Were you that person?"

Tex Barker's eyes narrowed ever so slightly. "And what if I was?" he demanded. "What if I stopped by long enough to tell that son of a bitch that if I ever caught him near my daughter again I'd cut his black balls off?"

"Did you?" I asked.

He slammed his fist on the desk, sending a

coffee cup skittering dangerously close to the edge. "No, sir, God damn it! I didn't. Never got a chance. Some SOB beat me to it. It ain't often somebody catches Wheeler-Dealer flat-footed, but someone sure as hell outdrew me on this one."

"So you're saying you'd have killed him yourself if you'd had the chance?"

"Damn right."

Peters had been observing this exchange from the sidelines. "What did you say to him when you saw him?"

"That he was a dead mother if I ever caught him within fifty miles of Bambi."

"I'd be willing to bet that wasn't news to him."

A self-satisfied grimace touched the corners of Barker's mouth. "No it wasn't. He'd gotten my message."

"What message? From his wife?"

Barker nodded. "That's right."

"And when did you tell him that?"

"Just at the end of halftime. I caught up with him after the team went on the floor."

"Let me get this straight," I said. "You came to the Coliseum, tracked him down during halftime, and told him that if he ever came near your daughter again, you'd kill him. Where'd you go after that?"

"Home."

"Straight home?"

Barker shrugged noncommittally.

"What time did you get there?"

"Ten. Eleven. I don't know, don't remember. I didn't look at the clock."

"I'd suggest you try to remember, Mr. Barker," I warned him. "We're dealing with homicide here. You have motive and you have opportunity. Within hours of the time of the victim's death you threatened to kill him. If I were you, I'd go looking for an alibi. Someone besides your wife," I added.

Barker glared back at me. "I don't need no fuckin' alibi. If I'd killed the son of a bitch, I'd be down at police headquarters braggin' about it."

That could have been the truth. Wheeler-Dealer didn't strike me as a man who would hide his light under a bushel, even if that light happened to be murder.

We were there a while longer. When we left and were making our way back to the car, Peters asked, "What do you think?"

"I don't think it was him."

Peters sounded shocked. "You don't? Why not?"

"His ego's all bound up in this. He's pissed because someone beat him out of getting even. Believe me, had he done it, he'd be yelling it to high heaven."

"Beau, he's suckering you. That's exactly what he wants us to believe."

"We'll see," I said. "What say we drive over to the school and check out the names in the locker?"

"Sure? Why not?"

It was early afternoon when we got to Mercer Island High School. The clerk told us that the principal, Ned Browning, was busy. We asked for Candace Wynn instead. She was sitting at a desk in the counseling office, poring over a yellow sheet covered with writing. She stood up as we entered.

"Are you here about the memorial service?" she asked.

"Memorial service?"

"For Darwin. Tomorrow evening, after the funeral. Mr. Browning asked me to be in charge of planning it. The funeral is going to be small and private. We thought there should be something here at school for the kids. Something official."

"I'm sure that's a good idea, Mrs. Wynn, but that's not why we're here."

"What, then?"

"Do you have keys to the lockers in the girls' locker room?"

"Pardon me?"

"I had a long talk with Bambi Barker in Portland last night," I said. "There's something on one of the locker ceilings we need to see."

Andi Wynn frowned. "I could probably get a master key," she said doubtfully, "but I'm not sure I should. Did you talk to Mr. Browning about this? Shouldn't you have a search warrant or something?"

Peters sighed. "We probably should, but we're not searching for evidence per se. It's a matter of our simply corroborating something Bambi told us. I can assure you, we won't be looking for anything but that one thing."

Andi Wynn sat quietly, considering what Peters had said. Finally, she shrugged. "I don't suppose it would matter that much."

The three of us waited in her office chatting about inconsequentials until the final bell rang and school was dismissed. Then Andi left us to go to the office for the key. When she returned, she led us to the girls' locker room. While Andi stood to one side and waited, Peters and I spent twenty minutes opening lockers, glancing up at the top to see if anything was written there, and then closing them again, being careful to disturb nothing else in the process. We were almost finished when we opened locker number 211.

Peters was the one who saw the names written there. "Bingo! Holy shit! Look at this."

Peters isn't the excitable type. He stepped aside, and I moved quickly to the locker, craning my neck to see what was written there, scratched with a sharp object into the gray paint on the locker's metal top.

Just as Bambi had said, Darwin Ridley's name was the last one on the list, printed in awkwardly scrawled letters.

The name that caught my eye, though, was that of Ned Browning. The principal.

His name was on the list, too.

Twice.

When I stepped away from the locker, Andi Wynn was looking uncertainly from Peters to me. "What is it?" she asked. "What did you find?"

"Look for yourself," I said.

She did. I watched her expression when she turned back to face us. "I don't understand."

"It's a trophy case," I told her. "The cheerleaders' trophy case."

"What does it mean?"

"It doesn't matter. Let's get out of here, Peters."

I welcomed the fresh air when we stepped back outside. I felt sick. Ned Browning, too. The one who had been so protective of his "young people." He, too, had fallen victim to the cheerleaders' hit list. More than once.

We were nearing the office when I rounded

a corner and ran full tilt into Ned Browning himself. Ned Browning and Joanna Ridley.

Joanna looked surprised to see me. "What are you doing here?" she asked.

"Working. What about you?"

She nodded toward Ned Browning, who was carrying a large cardboard box. "Mr. Browning asked me to come get Darwin's things. They're hiring a replacement and he needs to use the desk."

Ned nodded. "It was most awkward, having to call, even before the funeral, but the board has moved forward and hired a replacement. He'll be here at school tomorrow. I felt Mrs. Ridley was the only one who should handle her husband's things."

"Did you find out anything?" Joanna asked.

More than we expected, I wanted to say, but I didn't. Instead, I reached for the box Ned had in his hands. "Would you like me to carry this to your car?"

She nodded, and Ned handed it over. It was fairly heavy. "I'll be getting back to my office," he said. He turned to Joanna and took her hand. "Thank you so much for stopping by. Will you be attending the memorial service tomorrow night?" he asked. "Mrs. Wynn here is in charge of planning it."

Joanna glanced in Andi's direction and shook her head. "I don't know. I doubt it. It'll depend on how I feel after the funeral. I appreciate what you're doing, but I may be too tired."

Ned nodded sympathetically. "I understand completely. It would be nice if you could. It would mean a great deal to the students, but of course your physical well-being must come first."

He took Joanna's hand and pressed it firmly. "You take care now, Mrs. Ridley. We'll hope to see you tomorrow. Let me know if there's anything else I can do."

Ned Browning scurried away toward his office, the little shit. I wanted him out of my sight. I turned to Peters. "I'll help get this loaded into Joanna's car and be right back."

We left Andi Wynn and Peters standing together in the breezeway. "Where did it come from?" Joanna asked.

"What?"

"The picture. I thought you were going to find out how the man at the newspaper got it."

"Oh, that." Maxwell Cole's column seemed eons away. "No," I told her. "I haven't been able to locate him yet."

"Oh," Joanna said. She sounded disappointed.

Her Mustang was parked in the school lot. She led the way to the trunk and unlocked it. The cover bounced open. A large tin-plated container, the kind restaurants use to hold fifty pounds of lard, sat in the middle of an otherwise empty trunk.

Joanna looked at it and frowned. "What's that doing here?" she asked.

"What is it?"

"It looks like my flour container. But what would it be doing in my car?"

I put down the box. "I don't know," I said. "Let me take a look."

As soon as I cracked the lid on the container, before I even looked inside, I was sorry. The stench was overpowering. Fools rush in where angels fear to tread. I lifted the lid anyway.

Coiled at the top was a length of rope. Under it, through the center of the rope was what appeared to be a man's shirt. A maroon man's shirt, dusted with flour.

For a moment, Joanna had recoiled, driven away by the overwhelming odor of human excrement. Despite the smell, she came forward again to peer warily inside the container. She saw the shirt at the same time I did.

"That's his shirt," she whispered.

I shoved the lid back shut. "Are you sure?"

She nodded, holding her hand to her mouth. "That was his favorite, his game shirt. He always wore it."

"That day, too?"

She nodded. "It's either his shirt or one just like it."

I examined the outside of the container. A

fine film of white powder lingered on the outside and on the top. I took a tiny swipe at the
bottom edge with my finger and touched it to
my tongue. It was indeed flour.

"And this looks like your flour container?"

"I'm sure of it. I keep it in the storeroom out
in the carport. There's a smaller one, a canister
in the house. When I need to refill it, I get the
flour from this one."

"And you have no idea how long this has
been in your trunk?"

"No."

I closed the lid of the trunk. "Open the car
door," I ordered. "We'll put the box in the
back."

Unquestioningly, Joanna did as she was bid-
den. She unlocked the rider's door and held
up the front seat while I shoved the box in.
When I turned back toward her, she was trem-
bling visibly, despite the fact that a warm afternoon sun was shining on her.

"Wait here," I said. "We'll go somewhere
we can talk."

I left her there and went in search of Peters.
I found him and Candace Wynn standing
right where we'd left them. They were laughing and talking.

"I'm going to be gone for a while," I told
Peters abruptly.

Puzzled, he looked at me. "Want me to go
along?" he asked.

I shook my head. "No need. I'll be back in half an hour or so."

To this day, I'm not sure why I didn't have Peters come along with us. Joanna's Mustang was small, but there would have been room enough for the three of us.

Peters shrugged. "Okay. Suit yourself. I'll wait here. Besides, I should get the camera from the car and take some pictures of that list. Even if it's not admissible, doesn't mean it isn't usable."

I nodded in agreement. Leaving them, I hustled back to Joanna Ridley. She was still standing beside the Mustang, where I'd left her, as if glued to the spot. She jumped like a startled deer when I returned.

"Would you like me to drive?"

Wordlessly, she handed me her keys. I helped her into the car and shut the door. I got in and put the key in the ignition.

Joanna seemed dazed, unable to grasp what had happened. "Why are those things in my trunk?"

"That's what we're going to find out," I told her. I started the car and backed it out of the parking place. The only restaurant I knew on Mercer Island was a Denny's down near I-90. I fought my way through the maze of highway construction and found the restaurant on only the second try. For most of the drive, Joanna sat next to me in stricken silence.

Once in Denny's, we went to a booth in the far corner of the room and ordered coffee. "Tell me again where you kept the flour container," I demanded.

"In the storeroom at the end of the carport."

"Locked or unlocked?"

"Locked. Always."

"When was the last you saw it?"

"I don't know. A couple of weeks, I guess. I don't keep track."

"And you haven't noticed if the storeroom has been unlocked at any time?"

"No."

"When were you out there last?"

She shrugged. "Sometime last week."

"And the flour container was there?"

"As far as I know, but I don't remember for sure." She paused. "What are you going to do?"

"Take the container to the crime lab. See what they can find out."

"Why was it there?"

"In your car?"

She nodded.

"Someone wanted it found there."

"So you'd think I killed him?"

"Yes."

"Do you?"

"No."

There was another long pause. The waitress came and refilled both our coffee cups. While she did it, Joanna's eyes never left my face.

"Is that smart?"

"For me not to suspect you? Probably not, but I don't just the same."

"Thank you."

I was sitting looking at her, but my random access memory went straying back to Monday night, the first night I had seen her, when I brought her back from the medical examiner's office. The light in the carport had been turned off. Was that when the flour container disappeared?

I leaned forward in my chair. "Joanna, do you remember when we left your house that night to go to the medical examiner's office? Do you remember if you turned off the light in the carport before we drove away?"

She frowned and shook her head. "I don't remember at all. I might have, but I doubt it."

"Did you notice that when we came back the light wasn't on?"

"No."

"Where's the switch for the light in the carport?"

"There are two of them. One by the back door and one by the front."

"Both inside?"

"Yes."

I downed the rest of my coffee and stood up. "Come on."

"Where are we going?"

"We're going to drop the container off at the crime lab and make arrangements for them to send someone out to your house to dust it for prints."

"You think the killer was there, in my house?"

"I'm willing to bet on it."

"But how did he get in? How did he open my car without my knowing it?"

"Your husband had keys to your car, didn't he?"

She nodded.

"And the killer had Darwin's keys."

She stood up, too. "All right," she said.

"I'm making arrangements for someone to put new locks on all your doors, both on the house and the car."

Joanna looked puzzled. "Why?"

"If he got in once," I said grimly, "he could do it again."

I had no intention of unloading the container from Joanna's car into ours to take it to the crime lab. Janice Morraine, my friend at the crime lab, tells me evidence is like pie dough—fragile. The less handling the better.

It was rush hour by the time we were back in traffic. I-90 westbound was reduced to a single lane going into the city. It took us twenty minutes to get off the access road and onto the freeway. Rush hour is a helluva funny word for it. We spent most of the next hour parked on the bridge. I would make a poor commuter. I don't have the patience for it anymore.

Joanna was subdued as we drove. "The funeral's tomorrow," she said finally. "Will you be there?"

"What time?"

"Four," she replied.

"I don't know if I'll make it," I said. "What about the memorial service at school. Will you be going to that?"

"No. I don't think I could face those kids. Not after what happened."

I didn't blame her for that. I would have felt the same way. "If I were you, I don't think I could, either," I told her.

The entire cheerleading squad would probably be there.

Except for one. Bambi Barker.

CHAPTER
19

Joanna Ridley dropped me back at Mercer Island High School a little after seven. It wasn't quite dusk. The only car visible in the school lot was our departmental Dodge. A note from Peters was stuck under the windshield wiper. "See the custodian."

I went looking for one. It took a while, but I finally found him polishing a long hallway with a machine that sounded like a Boeing 747 preparing for takeoff. I shouted to him a couple of times before he heard me and shut off the noise.

"I'm supposed to talk to you."

"Your name Beaumont?" he asked. I nodded, and he reached in his pocket and extracted the keys to the car in the parking lot. "Your partner said you should pick him up at the Roanoke."

It didn't make sense to me. If Peters had gotten a ride all the way to the Roanoke in Seattle, why hadn't he asked Andi Wynn to drop him off at the department so he could have picked up his own car? I was operating on too little sleep to want to play cab driver, but I grudgingly convinced myself it had been thoughtful of him to leave the car. At least that way I'd have access to transportation back downtown.

None too graciously, I thanked the custodian for his help and set off for Seattle. Something big must have been happening at Seattle Center that night. Traffic was backed up on both the bridge and I-5. I finally got to the Roanoke Exit on the freeway and made my way to the restaurant by the same name on Eastlake at the bottom of the hill.

Andi Wynn's red pickup wasn't outside, and when I went into the bar, there was no trace of Peters and Andi inside, either.

"Can I help you?" the bartender asked.

"I'm looking for some friends of mine. Both of them have red hair. A man, thirty-five, six two. A woman about the same age. Both pretty good-looking. They were driving a red pickup."

"Nobody like that's been in here tonight," the bartender reported. "Been pretty slow as a matter of fact."

"How long have you been here? Maybe they left before you came on duty."

The bartender shook his head. "I came to work at three o'clock this afternoon."

I scratched my head. "I'm sure he said the Roanoke," I mumbled aloud to myself.

"Which one?" the bartender asked.

"Which one? You mean there's more than one?"

"Sure. This is the Roanoke Exit. There's the Roanoke Inn over on Mercer Island."

"I'll be a son of a bitch! You got a phone I can use?"

He pointed to a pay phone by the rest room. "Don't feel like the Lone Ranger," he said. "The number's written on the top of the phone, right under the coin deposit. It happens all the time."

Sure enough, the name Roanoke Inn and its number were taped just under the coin deposit. Knowing that I had lots of company didn't make me feel any better. I shoved a quarter into the phone and dialed the number. When someone answered, I had to shout to be heard over the background racket.

"I'm looking for someone named Peters," I repeated for the fourth time.

"You say Peters? Okay, hang on." My ear rattled as the telephone receiver was tossed onto some hard surface. The paging system at the Roanoke was hardly upscale. "Hey," whoever had answered the phone shouted above the din, "anybody here named Peters? You got a phone call."

I waited. Eventually, the phone was picked back up. "He's coming," someone said, then promptly dropped the receiver again.

"Hey, Beau!" Peters' voice came across like Cheerful Charlie. "Where you been? We've been waitin'."

It didn't sound like Peters. "Andi and I just had spaghetti. It's great. Want us to order you some?"

Spaghetti? Vegetarian, no-red-meat Peters pushing spaghetti? I figured I was hearing things. "Are you feeling all right?" I asked.

"Me?" Peters laughed. "Never better. Where the hell are you, buddy? It's late."

Peters is always accusing me of being a downtown isolationist, of not knowing anything about what's on the other side of I-5, of regarding the suburbs as a vast wasteland. I wasn't about to 'fess up to my mistake.

"I've been delayed," I muttered. "I'll be there in a little while."

It was actually quite a bit longer than a little while. I drove and cussed and took one wrong turn after another. The thing I've learned about Mercer Island is that no address is straightforward. The Roanoke Inn is an in-crowd joke, set off in the dingleberries at the end of a road that winds through a seemingly residential area. By the time I got there, it was almost nine o'clock. I was ready to wring Peters' neck.

The building itself is actually an old house, complete with a white-railed front porch. Inside, it was wall-to-wall people. The decorations, from the plastic scenic lamp shades with holes burned in them to the ancient jukebox blaring modern, incomprehensible rock, were straight out of the forties and fifties. I had the feeling this wasn't stuff assembled by some yuppies trying to make a "fifties statement." This place was authentic. It had always been like that.

In one corner came a steady jackhammer racket that was actually a low-tech popcorn popper. I finally spotted Peters and Andi Wynn, seated cozily on one side of a booth at the far end of the room. A pitcher of beer and two glasses sat in front of them. Peters, with his arm draped casually around Andi's shoulder, was laughing uproariously.

I had known Peters for almost two years. I had never heard him laugh like that, with his head thrown back and mirth shaking his whole body. He had always kept himself on a tight rein. It was so good to see him having a good time that I forgot about being pissed, about it being late, and about my getting lost.

I walked up to the booth and slid into the seat across from them. "All right, you two. What's so funny?"

Peters managed to pull himself together. He wiped tears from his eyes. "Hi, Beau. She is." He ruffled Andi Wynn's short auburn hair. "I swear to God, this is the funniest woman I ever met."

Andi Wynn ducked her head and gave me a shy smile. "He's lying," she said. "I'm perfectly serious."

That set him off again. While he was convulsed once more, Andi signaled for the bartender. "Want a beer?"

I looked at Peters, trying to assess if he was smashed or just having one hell of a good time. "No thanks," I said. "Somebody in this crowd better stay sober enough to drive."

The bartender fought his way over to us. I ordered coffee and, at Peters' insistence, a plate of the special Thursday night Roanoke spaghetti. The spaghetti was all right, but not great enough to justify Peters' rave review. I wondered once more exactly how much beer he had swallowed.

"What's going on?" Peters asked, getting serious finally. "It took you long enough."

"We found something in Joanna's car," I said. "I took it down to the crime lab."

Peters frowned. "What was it?"

I didn't feel comfortable discussing the case in front of Andi Wynn. "Just some stuff," I told him offhandedly. "Maybe it's important, maybe not."

Peters reached for the pitcher, glanced at me, and saw me watching him. "I went off duty at five o'clock," he said in answer to my unspoken comment. Leaning back, he refilled both his and Andi's glasses from the pitcher.

"We waited a long time. It got late and hungry out. We finally decided to come here. What do you think? It's a great place, isn't it?"

I wouldn't have called it great. It was nothing but a local tavern in the "Cheers" tradition, with its share of run-down booths, dingy posters, peeling paint, and loyal customers planted on concave barstools.

"I was telling Ron that we used to come here after school," Andi said. "Darwin, me, and some of the others."

When she called him Ron, it threw me for a minute. I tended to forget that Peters had a first name. And it surprised me, too, that in the time since I'd left them to go with Joanna Ridley, Peters and Andi had moved from formal address to a first-name basis. I felt like I'd missed out on something important.

"Is that right? When was that?" I asked, practically shouting over the noise of a new song blaring from the jukebox.

"Last year," she answered.

I swallowed the food without chewing it, gulped down the coffee, and rushed them out the door. Andi's pickup was parked outside. I got in to drive the Dodge while Peters walked

Andi to her truck, opened the door for her, and gave her a quick goodnight kiss. Andi started her engine and drove away. Peters returned to our car looking lighter than air.

That kiss bugged me. I distinctly remembered Ned Browning calling her Mrs. Wynn, not Miss Wynn. What the hell was Peters thinking of?

I climbed Peters' frame about it as soon as he got in the car. "Isn't she Sadie, Sadie married lady?" I asked.

"Divorced," Peters said. And that was all he said. No explanation. Not even a lame excuse.

I stewed in my own juices over that for a while before I tackled him on the larger issue of the Roanoke Inn. "It's a good thing you left the car where it was when you decided to go drinking. We'd have one hell of a time explaining what we were doing hanging out in a tavern in a departmental vehicle at this time of night."

"Wait a minute. Who's the guy who was telling me just the other day that I needed to lighten up a little, to stop being such a stickler for going by the book?"

"I didn't mean you should overreact," I told him.

I took Peters to his own place in Kirkland rather than dropping him downtown to drive his Datsun back to the east side. I didn't know how much beer he had drunk, and I wasn't willing to risk it.

When I told him I was taking him home, he gave a noncommittal shrug. "I'm not drunk, Beau, but if it'll make you feel better, do it."

On the way to his house I told him about the contents of Joanna Ridley's trunk. "The rope was coiled on top?" he asked.

"Yes."

"And she could tell looking through the rope that those were the clothes he wore the day he died?"

"That's right."

"Doesn't it strike you as odd?"

"Why should it?"

"It seems to me that one way of knowing what's inside a closed container is to be the one who put it there."

"Joanna Ridley didn't do it," I replied.

He didn't talk to me much after that. I couldn't tell what was going on, if he was mad because I thought he was too smashed to drive home or if he was pissed because I wasn't buying his suspicions about Joanna Ridley.

As we drove into his driveway, I said, "I'll come get you in the morning if you like."

"Don't bother." His tone was gruff. "I'll catch a bus downtown. This is only the suburbs, Beau. Despite what some people think, it isn't the end of the earth."

He got out and slammed his door without

bothering to thank me for the ride. I was too tired to worry about what ailed Peters. My three hours of sleep had long since fallen by the wayside. I needed to fall into bed and get some sleep.

It's hell getting old.

C H A P T E R
20

My alarm went off at seven, and the phone went off exactly one minute later. It was Ames, chipper and cheerful Ames, calling me from Arizona and wondering whether or not I would pick him up at the airport at one that afternoon. I blundered my way halfway through the conversation before I remembered the real estate closing for Belltown Terrace was scheduled for three-thirty.

"Shit! I never wrote it down in my calendar."

"Wrote what down? What's the matter, Beau?"

"The closing. It's scheduled for the same time as Darwin Ridley's funeral."

"Do you have to go?"

"I ought to, but maybe I could ask Peters. He shouldn't mind."

"Good. After the closing, we need to go see the decorator, too. He's been calling me here in Phoenix. Says he can never catch you."

"Look, Ralph, I don't spend my time sitting around waiting for the phone to ring."

"You should get a machine, an answering machine with remote capability."

"Will you lay off that answering machine stuff? I'm not buying one, and that's final."

"Okay, okay. See you at one."

Even riding the bus from Kirkland, Peters beat me to the office. His unvarying promptness bugged the hell out of me at times, particularly since, no matter what, I was always running behind schedule. He was seated at his desk with his nose buried in a file folder. He was obviously scanning through the material, looking for one particular item.

"What are you up to?" I asked, walking past him to get to my desk.

"Here it is," he said. He dropped the file folder, grabbed his pen, and copied some bit of information from the folder into his pocket notebook.

"Here's what?" I asked. I confess I was less interested in what he was looking for than I was with whether or not there was coffee in the pot on the table behind Margie's desk. There was—a full, freshly made pot.

"Rimbaugh. That's his name."

"Whose name? Peters, for godsake, will you

tell me what you're talking about?"

"Remember Monday afternoon? We talked to all those old duffers who are part-time security guards down at Seattle Center? Dave Rimbaugh is one of them. He was assigned to the locker rooms."

"So?"

"So I've got this next-door neighbor who works for Channel Thirteen. In the advertising department. I called him last night after I got home and asked him if he could locate a picture of Wheeler-Dealer Barker for us. He called just a few minutes ago. Said he'd found one and when did we want to come by to pick it up."

"Why go to the trouble? What's the point? We already know Barker was there. He told us so."

"Sure he did. He said he was there at half-time, but what if he was there later, too? Maybe he came back or, better yet, maybe he never left."

Picking up my empty coffee cup, I sauntered over to the coffee table mulling Peters' hypothesis. It was possible, I supposed, but it didn't seem plausible. I came back with coffee and set my cup down on the desk.

"Well?" Peters asked.

I shook my head. "I don't think so. Barker isn't our man."

"Why not?"

"Gut instinct."

Just that quick, Peters got his back up. "Right. Sure it is. You know, Beau, sometimes I get tired of working with the Grand Old Man of Homicide. You're not always on the money. I think Barker's it, and I'm willing to invest some shoe leather in proving it. You coming or not?"

He didn't leave a whole lot of room for discussion. We got a car from the garage, a tired Chevette without as much zing to it as the Dodge we'd driven the day before—no zip and a hell of a lot less legroom. I wonder sometimes if the ratings would be the same if the guys on "Miami Vice" drove Chevettes.

We stopped by Channel 13's downtown office. The receptionist cheerfully handed over a manila envelope with Peters' name scrawled on the front. Inside was an eight-by-ten glossy of Tex Barker himself, without the cowboy hat and grinning from ear to ear. There were several other pictures as well, eight-by-tens of people I didn't recognize.

Peters shuffled through them, looked at me, and grinned. "See there? What we've got here is an instant montage."

One of the realities of police work these days is that you never get to show witnesses just the person you want them to see. You always have to show a group of pictures and hope they pick out the right one. Going by the

book can be a royal pain in the ass. I gave
Peters credit for taking care of it in advance.

Dave Rimbaugh's address was off in the
wilds of Lake City, about a twenty-minute
drive from downtown Seattle. Peters drove. As
we made our way up the freeway, Peters
glanced in my direction. "Tell me again about
the stuff you found in the back of Joanna Ridley's car. You said it was her flour container?"

"That's right. Out of the storeroom at the
end of her carport."

"They're dusting it for prints?"

"The container and the trunk for certain.
They said yesterday they're going to try to
work out a deal with the county to run the
contents past the county's YAG to see if they
can raise anything there."

"YAG? What the hell's a YAG?"

"Their new laser printfinder. Janice Morraine was telling me about it. They use it to
raise prints on all kinds of unlikely surfaces—
cement, rumpled tinfoil."

"Off rope and clothing, too?"

"Not too likely, but possible. She said
there's a remote chance. I've also called for a
tech to go over Joanna Ridley's house for
prints."

"Any idea when the container was placed
in the car or any sign of forced entry?"

I shook my head. "The killer had Darwin's

keys, remember? House keys and car keys, both."

"I had forgotten," Peters said thoughtfully.

"She's going to have all her locks changed today, just in case."

Peters nodded. "That's probably wise."

We were both quiet for a moment. It was as good a time as any to bring up my scheduling conflict between the real estate closing and Darwin Ridley's funeral.

"By the way," I said casually, "Ralph Ames is flying in this afternoon. I pick him up at the airport at one. We're supposed to close on Belltown Terrace at three-thirty this afternoon. Do you think you could handle Ridley's funeral by yourself?"

I more than half-expected an objection, for Peters to say that he needed to be home with his kids. It's an excuse that packs a whole lot of weight with me. Had he used it, I probably would have knuckled under, given Ames my power of attorney, and had him stand in for me at the closing.

Instead, Peters surprised me. "Sure, no problem. What about the memorial service after the funeral? Want me to handle that, too?"

"That would be great."

Dave Rimbaugh's house was a snug nineteen-thirties bungalow dwarfed by the evergreen trees that had grown up around it. The woman who came to the door was almost as

wide as the door itself. Her pug nose and the
rolling jowls of her face made her look like a
bulldog. A nearsighted bulldog wearing thick
glasses.

"Davey," she called over her shoulder.
"Hon, there's somebody here to see you."

"Davey" wasn't a day under seventy. He
was a spry old man, as lean as his wife was
fat. They were a living rendition of the old
Jack Sprat routine. His face lit up all over
when Peters showed his ID and told him who
we were and what we wanted.

"See there, Francie. I told you I talked to a
real detective on the phone, and you thought
I was pulling your leg." He led us into the
living room. Every available flat surface in the
room was full of glass and ceramic elephants
of every size and description. Dave Rimbaugh
noticed me looking at them.

"We've been collecting them for fifty-six
years now," he said proudly. "There's more in
the dining room. Would you like to see
those?"

"No, thanks," I told him quickly, stopping
him before he could hurry into the next room.
"I can see you've got an outstanding collection, but we'd better get to work. Business before pleasure, you know."

"Good." Rimbaugh nodded appreciatively.
"Don't like to waste the taxpayer's money,
right?"

"Right," I said, sitting down on the wing-backed chair he offered me, while Peters sank into the old-fashioned, flower-patterned couch.

Rimbaugh rubbed his hands together in anticipation. "Now then, what can I do for you boys?"

Peters grimaced visibly at the term "boys." It was clear "Davey" Rimbaugh regarded us as a couple of young whippersnappers. Doing his best to conceal his annoyance, Peters reached into a file folder and pulled out the fanfold of photographs. He offered them to our host.

"Take a look at these, Mr. Rimbaugh. See if there's anyone here you recognize, anyone you may have seen at the Coliseum last Friday night."

Dave Rimbaugh only had to glance through the pictures once before he pounced on Wheeler-Dealer's smiling countenance. "Him," he said decisively. "That's him. He was there."

Unable to contain her curiosity, Francie Rimbaugh got up from the couch and came over to her husband's chair. She stood behind him like she'd been planted there, leaning over his shoulder so she, too, could look at the picture in his hand.

"Why, forevermore!" she exclaimed. "I know him. Isn't that the man on the television, the one on the late movies? I think he sells cars. Or maybe furniture."

Dave Rimbaugh held the picture up to the light. "Why, Francie, I do believe you're right. He looked familiar at the time, but I just couldn't place him."

He patted his wife's rump affectionately and pulled her close to him. "Francie here, now she's the one with the memory for faces," he said. "Faces and names both."

"Do you remember when you saw this man?" Peters asked. "It's important that we know exactly when he was there."

Dave Rimbaugh leaned back in his chair and closed his eyes, frowning with the effort of concentration. "All I remember is, I was drinking a cup of coffee at the time. Almost spilled it all over me when he rushed past. Said there was an emergency of some kind. Didn't ask him what, just let him go through."

"So what time was it?" Peters prodded. "Halftime? Later than that?"

"I don't know if it was halftime or not. They play a whole bunch of games each day during the tournament. Let's see. Wait a minute, I had only two cups of coffee that night. That was all that was left in the pot when I filled the thermos. When he almost knocked me down, I remember thinking it's a good thing it's almost time to go home, 'cause there isn't any coffee left."

I could see Peters was losing patience with trying to pull usable information out of the old man's ramblings. "What time did you get off work?" I asked.

"Nine o'clock," he said. "Isn't that right, Francie? I was home by ten, wasn't I?"

She nodded. "That's right. We watched the early late movie together before we went to bed. The old one with Gary Cooper in it."

"And how close was that second cup of coffee to the time you came home?"

"It was just before. Sure, that's right. Must have been right around eight." Rimbaugh looked at us triumphantly.

"You're sure you didn't see him after that?" Peters asked.

"Nope. Not that I remember."

Peters sighed and rose. I followed.

"Does that help?" Rimbaugh asked.

"I hope so," Peters replied. "We'll be back in touch."

Once outside, we held a quick conference. "What do you think?" Peters asked.

I shrugged. "Eight o'clock sounds like half-time to me."

"But he could have come back later, without Rimbaugh seeing him."

That, too, was a distinct possibility. As distinct a possibility as anything I'd come up with. There was no way to tell for sure.

So much for being the Grand Old Man of Homicide.

C H A P T E R
21

Peters went back to the Public Safety Building. During my lunch hour, I took the Porsche
and drove down to Sea-Tac to pick up Ralph
Ames.

Ralph was a dapper-looking guy, an attorney's attorney. He had a low-key look about
him that said he knew what he was doing. I
probably never would have gotten to know
him if I hadn't inherited him from Anne Corley. It took a while to get to know the man
under his air of quiet reserve, but once I did,
he turned out to be one hell of a nice guy.

At the airport that day, when I went to pick
him up, he had an uncharacteristic shit-eating
grin on his face that worried me some, but not
enough for me to do anything about it.

There was just time to grab him from the
arriving-passenger level, hightail it back to

town, and have him drop me at the department. He took my Porsche back to my place while Peters and I drove to Mercer Island High School, where we planned to have a chat with Molly Blackburn.

Ned Browning was most reluctant to call Molly out of class so we could talk to her. I have to admit that knowing the principal's name appeared not once but twice in the trophy list in the girls' locker room gave me a whole new perspective on his outward show of high principles and middle-class morality.

"Detective Beaumont, I'm not at all sure I should let you talk to one of my students without her parents' express knowledge and permission."

I wasn't feeling particularly tolerant toward that officious little worm. In fact, I became downright belligerent. "We don't have time to screw around, Mr. Browning. We need to see that girl today. Now."

"Certainly, you don't think one of my students had something to do with the murder!" There was just the right tone of shocked consternation in Ned Browning's voice. He should have been an actor instead of a high school principal. He gave an award-winning performance.

"Your students know a hell of a lot about a lot of things they shouldn't."

I let it go at that. There was no outward,

visible sign that he understood the ramifications of what I said, yet I knew my seemingly casual remark had hit home. Finally, he reached for his phone and called for a student page to bring Molly Blackburn to his office.

Molly waltzed into the room like she owned the place. I recognized her as the blonde who had been pitching such a fit, literally bawling her eyes out, the day Peters and I had interviewed all those kids. Talk about acting!

"You wanted to see me, Mr. Browning?" she asked brightly.

"These gentlemen do," he replied. "You remember them, don't you, Molly?"

Molly looked at Peters and me. When she recognized us, she stepped back a full step. "Y-yes," she stammered uncertainly.

"Good. They've asked to speak to you. Mr. Howell is out today, so you may use his office. I have scheduled a parent conference in just a few minutes. Unfortunately, I won't be able to join you. This way, please."

Unfortunately? Hell! It was a good thing he had another meeting. No way would I have let that son of a bitch join us for Molly Blackburn's interview.

He led us to an adjoining office. Molly's entrance into that room was far different from the one she had made into the principal's office. She lagged behind us like an errant puppy who's just crapped all over the new rug and who knows he's going to get it.

We knew, and she knew we knew. As soon as the door closed behind Ned Browning, I whirled on her and let Molly Blackburn have it with both barrels.

"What's the matter? Did Bambi call to warn you?"

Her eyes widened. She was still standing in the doorway. She groped blindly for a chair and eased her way into it. "Yes," she whispered.

"So you know why we're here?"

She shook her head. "No, not really." Her face was white. She was scared to death, and I wanted her to stay that way.

"Are you the one who was trying to blackmail the Ridley's and the Barkers?"

"Wh-what?" she stammered. Under pressure, she seemed to be having a great deal of trouble making her voice and mouth work in unison.

"You're the one with the fancy camera, aren't you? The one who took the "proof" shot of your friend Bambi and Darwin Ridley?"

She licked her lip nervously, swallowed, and nodded. Barely. Almost imperceptibly.

"So where's the negative?"

"I don't know," she whispered.

"Don't know! What do you mean, you don't know?"

"It's gone. Someone took it."

"When?" I demanded. "Where was it?"

"I had it with me. I had all the negatives from that roll of film in my book bag. I didn't dare leave them at home. Sometimes my parents go through my things."

"So you carried them around with you. When did you notice they were gone?"

"Friday afternoon. After Mr. Barker came to school to get Bambi. I looked for them then, but they weren't there."

"And how long had the negatives been in your purse?"

"Not my purse. My book bag. I brought the picture to school on Monday. That was the day . . ." She broke off.

"Let me guess. That's the day you scratched Darwin Ridley's name in the locker."

"How did you know that?"

"It doesn't take a Philadelphia lawyer to figure it out," I told her. "So sometime between Monday and Friday, the negatives disappeared," I continued. "What happened to the original picture? Where is it?"

"It's gone, too. We burned it when we wrote down the name."

"Too bad you didn't burn the negative as well."

"Why? I don't understand."

I wanted her to understand. I wanted her to feel the responsibility for Darwin Ridley's death right down to the soles of her feet. "Because," I growled, "it found its way into the wrong hands. That's why Darwin Ridley was murdered."

Molly's eyes flooded with tears. "No! It's not true. It can't be!" She glanced in Peters' direction as if seeking help, reassurance. None was forthcoming. Peters had remained absolutely silent throughout the proceedings.

Now he folded his arms uncompromisingly across his chest. "It's true," he said quietly.

Molly doubled over, sobbing hysterically into her lap. Neither Peters nor I offered her the smallest bit of comfort. I felt nothing but profound disgust. Finally, she quit crying on her own.

"What's going to happen to me?" she asked, looking up red-eyed and frightened.

"That depends on you, doesn't it. Are you going to help us or not?"

She nodded. "I'll help."

"All right. Try to think back to when the negatives could have disappeared. Can you remember any times when the bag was left unattended?"

"No. I always have it with me." She motioned toward a shiny green bag on the floor. "See?"

"Did anyone else know the negatives were there? Did you tell any of your friends?"

"No. Not even Bambi. Nobody knew."

"And what were the negatives in? One of

those envelopes from a fast photo-developing place?"

"No. A plain white envelope. I developed them myself. At home."

"It must be nice to be so talented," I commented sarcastically. "Do your parents have any idea what you've been doing?"

"Don't tell them. Please. They'd kill me."

I had been sitting behind the assistant principal's desk. I got up then and walked to the window. "They probably wouldn't," I said. "But I don't think I'd blame them if they did." I turned to Peters. "Do you have any other questions?"

He shook his head. "Not right now. You've pretty well covered it."

I looked back at Molly. She was staring at me, eyes wide and frightened. "Get out of here," I ordered. "You make me sick." She scurried out of the room as fast as she could go.

"You were pretty tough on her," Peters remarked after the door closed.

"Not nearly as tough as I should have been."

Glancing down at my watch, I realized it was after two, and I didn't have the location for my closing. "I'd better call Ames and find out where I'm supposed to be and when. If we're going to be stuck in traffic, it might be nice if we were at least going in the right direction."

I picked up the assistant principal's phone and dialed my own number. It rang twice. When a woman's voice answered, I hung up, convinced I had dialed a wrong number. I tried again. That time my line was busy.

Peters stood up. "While you're playing with the phone, I need to go check on something." He walked out of the office, and I tried dialing one more time. This time, when the woman's voice answered, I stayed on the line to listen. The recorded voice was soft and sultry.

"Hello, my name is Susan. Beau is unable to come to the phone right now, but he doesn't want to miss your call. Please leave your name, number, time of day, and a brief message at the sound of the tone, and Beau will call you back just as soon as he can. Thanks for calling. Bye-bye." Then there was a beep.

"What the fuck!"

I held the receiver away from my mouth and ear and looked at it like it was some strange apparition I'd never seen before. I felt like somebody had just clunked me over the head with a baseball bat. What the hell was an answering machine doing on my phone?

Just then, I heard Ames' voice, shouting at me from the receiver. "Hey, Beau. Is that you? Are you there? What do you think? Do you like it?"

"Ralph Ames, you son of a bitch. No, I don't like it. I told you before, I don't want an answering machine."

"Come on, Beau. It's great. In three days you'll love it. It's a present, an early housewarming present."

"You jerk! When I get home, I'll tear it out of the wall and wrap it around your neck!" I slammed down the phone just as Peters came back into the room. He was grinning, but he wiped the look off his face the minute he saw me.

"Hey, Beau. What's up?"

"That damn Ames went and installed a stupid answering machine in my house while my back was turned, without even asking me."

"So? It's probably a good idea. You're not the easiest person in the world to catch. Where's the closing? Did you find out?"

I had been so disturbed by the answering machine that I had forgotten the reason I had called. Chagrined, I picked up the phone and redialed. The answering machine clicked on after the second ring. "Hello. My name is Susan . . ."

"Damn it, Ames!" I shouted into the phone. "I know you're there. If you can hear me, turn this goddamned thing off and talk to me."

The woman's voice was stifled. Ames' voice came on the line.

"Here I am, Beau. What do you need?"

"The closing. I know when it is, but I don't know where."

"Downtown in Columbia Center. Up on the seventieth floor. Ellis and Wheeler. It's getting pretty late. Want to meet me there? I can bring your car."

"Fine," I answered curtly. "See you there." I hung up again.

"You don't have to be such a hard-ass about it," Peters chided me as I stood up to leave. "I'm sure Ames thought he was helping you out. There are times I'd like to have one of those gadgets myself."

"Great," I grumbled. "I've got a terrific idea. We'll unplug it from my house and plug it back in in yours."

Peters smiled. "When are you going to give up and accept the inevitable? Automation and microchips are here to stay."

"Not in my house they aren't," I replied, then stalked from the room with Peters right behind me.

I'm one of those people they'll have to pull kicking and screaming into the twenty-first century, if I live to be that old.

I have no intention of going quietly.

C H A P T E R
22

On Friday afternoon, traffic in Seattle is a nightmare. We made it back across the bridge with barely enough time for Peters to make it to Darwin Ridley's funeral at the Mount Baker Baptist Church. Peters dropped me off at a bus stop on Rainier Avenue South. I grabbed a Metro bus jammed with rowdy schoolkids for a snail's-pace ride downtown. If I were into jogging and physical fitness, I probably could have beaten the bus on foot.

Once downtown however, Columbia Center isn't hard to find. It's the tallest building west of the Mississippi, to say nothing of being the tallest building in Seattle. The lobby is a maze, however, and it took a while to locate the proper bank of elevators for an ear-popping ride to the seventieth floor.

Stepping out of the elevator, the carpet beneath my feet was so new and thick that it caught the soles of my shoes and sent me flying. I came within inches of tumbling into the lap of a startled, brunette receptionist, who managed to scramble out of the way.

There's nothing like making a suave and elegant grand entrance.

"J. P. Beaumont," I said archly, once I was upright again, hoping somehow to regain my shattered dignity. "I'm supposed to meet Ralph Ames here."

It didn't work. Dignity was irretrievable. The receptionist had to stifle a giggle before she answered me. "Mr. Ames is already inside," she said. "This way, please."

Rising, she turned and led me down a short, book-lined hallway. As she looked away, the corners of her mouth continued to crinkle in a vain attempt to keep a straight face.

At the end of the hallway we came to another desk. There, the receptionist handed me off to another sweet young thing, a blonde with incredibly long eyelashes and matching legs. It was clear the personnel manager in that office had an eye for beauty. I wondered if these ladies had any office skills, or if good looks constituted their sole qualification for employment.

"Mr. Rogers told me to show you right in," the blonde said. She opened a door into a spacious office with a spectacular view of Seattle's humming waterfront on Elliot Bay. In one corner of the room sat Ralph Ames and another man hunched over a conference table piled high with a formidable stack of legal documents.

"So there you are," Ames said, glancing up as I entered the room. "It's about time you got here. I'd like to introduce Dale Rogers. He's representing the syndicate. This whole transaction is complicated by the fact that you're both buyer and seller."

Ames has a penchant for understatment. The process of buying my new condominium was actually far more than complicated. It was downright mystifying.

Months before, acting on Ames' suggestion that I'd best do some investing with my recent inheritance, I had joined with a group of other investors to syndicate the purchase of a new, luxury condominium high-rise in downtown Seattle. Now, operating as an individual, I was purchasing an individual condominium unit from the syndicate.

Ames and the other attorney busily passed papers back and forth, both of them telling me where and when to sign. Between times, when my signature was not required, I sat and examined the contrast between the panoramic view of water and mountains through the window and the impossibly ugly but obviously original oil painting on the opposite wall. I couldn't help but speculate about how much this exercise in penmanship was costing me on a per-minute basis, and how many square inches of that painting I personally had paid for.

In less time and for more money than I had thought possible, I was signed, sealed, and delivered as the legal owner of my new home at Second and Broad. Ralph Ames literally beamed as I scrawled one final signature on the dotted line.

"Good for you, Beau. It's a great move."

Dale Rogers nodded in agreement. "That's right, Mr. Beaumont. As soon as the weather turns good, you'll have to have us all over for a barbecue. I understand there's a terrific barbecue on the recreation floor. My wife is dying to see the inside of that building."

"Sure thing," I said. My enthusiasm hardly matched theirs, however. I didn't feel much like a proud new home owner. I felt a lot more like a frustrated detective battling a case that was going nowhere fast, fighting the war of too much work and not enough sleep.

It was ten after five when we walked out of Columbia Center onto Fourth Avenue with a crush of nine-to-fivers eagerly abandoning work.

"Where's the car?" I asked.

"In the Four Seasons' parking garage," Ames answered. "But we've got one more appointment before we can pick it up."

I sighed and shook my head. I wanted to go home, have a drink, and put my feet up. "Who with now?"

"Michael Browder, the interior designer, remember? I told you about it on the phone. He's meeting us in the bar of the Four Seasons at five-thirty. Now that you've closed on the deal, he needs a go-ahead for the work. He told me the other day that you still haven't even looked at his preliminary drawings."

Bull's-eye! I had to admit Ames had me dead to rights. I had been actively avoiding Michael Browder, but I didn't care to confide in Ames that the main reason was that Michael Browder was gay. Ames had dropped that bit of information in passing one day. It didn't seem to make any difference to Ames, but it did to me.

I'm not homophobic, exactly, but I confess to being prejudiced. I don't like gays. I had never met one I liked. Or at least hadn't *knowingly* met one I liked.

Ames and I found a small corner table and ordered drinks. I sat back in my chair to watch the traffic, convinced I'd be able to pick out a wimp like Michael Browder the instant he sashayed into the room.

Wrong.

The man who, a few minutes later, stopped in front of our table and held out his hand was almost as tall as I am. Broad shoulders filled out a well-cut, immaculate, three-piece gray suit. He had neatly trimmed short brown hair. The solid handshake he offered me was accompanied by a ready smile.

"Mr. Beaumont?" he said to me with a polite nod in Ralph Ames' direction. "Michael Browder. Glad to meet you, finally."

No limp wrist. No lisp. No earrings.

Old prejudices die hard.

Settling comfortably back into a chair, Browder ordered a glass of Perrier. "Mr. Ames has been a big help," he continued. "He's given me as much information about you as he could, but it's very difficult to design a home for someone I don't know personally, Mr. Beaumont. I've been told, for instance, that you're sentimentally attached to an old recliner, but that's secondhand information. I told Mr. Ames that unless I talked to you, in person, I was leaving the project."

That didn't sound to me like much of a threat. I didn't care much one way or the other, and Michael Browder's speech didn't particularly endear him to me. In fact, I was downright insulted. On the one hand, he accused me of sentimentality. On the other, I was offended by what I viewed as his personal attack on my old recliner.

What he had said was true, as far as it went. I had indeed sent word through Ames that my recliner was going with me no matter what, and that it was moving to the new place as active-duty furniture, not as a relic destined for the storage unit in the basement.

"So do you have drawings along to show me or not?" I demanded impatiently.

Browder leaned down and opened a large leather portfolio he had placed beside his feet. By the time he had finished showing me the sketch of the living room, he had my undivided attention. By the second drawing, he had me in the palm of his hand. My previous experience with an interior designer had achieved somewhat mixed results. Michael Browder, however, without our ever having met in person, seemed to know me like a book.

The furnishings, the swatches of material, the colors, were all straightforward and attractive, functional and practical. They were the kinds of things I would have picked for myself, if I'd had either the brains or the time to do it. Throughout his presentation, Browder kept asking me pointed questions and making brief notes about color preferences, wood grains, and stains. His enthusiasm was contagious. By the time he was finished, I was pretty excited myself.

"So when do you start?" I asked.

"As soon as you say so," Browder replied.

"So start," I told him. "ASAP."

"And when can I pick up the recliner to have it recovered?"

I had been happy to see that he had included my recliner in his drawings for the den, but Browder had negotiated my consent to have the old warhorse reupholstered. It was a small concession on my part.

"You can pick it up whenever you want," I answered.

He nodded. "Good. What about now? I have my van along. We might as well get started."

Which is how we ended up caravanning over to the Royal Crest, all three of us. We went up to my apartment and straight into the living room, picked up the recliner, and hauled it downstairs in the elevator.

By then my opinion of Michael Browder had come a long way from my preconceived notion of what he'd be like, but once the recliner was loaded, he declined an invitation to come back up to the apartment for a drink.

"I've got to get home," he said.

It was a good thing. I was out of booze. Ames and I had to walk over to the liquor store at Sixth and Lenora for provisions before we could make drinks.

When I went into the kitchen to serve as bartender, I discovered the answering machine in a place of honor, sitting in state on the kitchen counter. In the intervening hours of paper signing and apartment designing, I had forgotten about the answering machine and how I had fully intended to wrap the electrical cord around Ralph Ames' neck.

Next to it on the counter sat not one, but two boxes of Girl Scout cookies. Mints.

Ames, from the doorway, saw me encounter the cookies and the machine. My dismay he read as a combination of pleasure and surprise. "I figured living in a secured high-rise there's no way you'd have a chance to buy any Girl Scout cookies on your own," Ames said proudly. "I bought some at the airport and brought them along on the plane."

I didn't have the heart to tell him I had already single-handedly bought and given away a whole mountain of Girl Scout cookies. As far as the answering machine was concerned, it was easier to accept it with good grace than to be a pinhead about it.

Ames eagerly explained all the little bells and whistles on the machine, including the blinking light that both signaled and counted waiting messages and the battery-operated remote device that would allow me to retrieve my messages from all over the world. Great! I gritted my teeth into a semblance of a smile and kept my mouth shut.

We had one drink in my apartment, then walked over to Mama's Mexican Kitchen on Second and Bell for dinner. Despite the fact that he lives in Phoenix, Ames claims Mama's taquitos are the best he can get anywhere.

Myself, I'm partial to margaritas.

Mama's has those, too.

C H A P T E R
23

I don't know why I bother having a clock in my bedroom. It isn't necessary. The phone usually wakes me up, even when I don't need to be up.

That's what happened that Saturday morning, a Saturday when I had planned to sleep late, stay home, and do nothing but work a week's worth of crossword puzzles. The best laid plans, someone once said. The phone rang at five after seven.

"Detective Beaumont?"

"Yes," I responded, fighting the surplus of tequila cobwebs in my brain and trying to place the woman's voice. No luck.

"This is Maxine. Maxine Edwards."

Maxine? I could have sworn I didn't know a single Maxine in the world. I still didn't have the foggiest idea who owned the insistent voice on the phone demanding that I wake up.

"Have you heard from Ron?"

I started to ask "Ron who?" when my brain finally kicked into gear. Maxine Edwards, the older woman Ames had hired to be Ron Peters' live-in housekeeper/babysitter.

"Not since yesterday. Why? Isn't he home?"

"No, he's not. He never came home at all. Heather and Tracie are upset." From her tone of voice, it was clear Peters' girls weren't the only ones who were upset. So was Maxine Edwards. "He called yesterday afternoon," she continued. "He said he was going to a funeral, that he'd be home late. That's the last I've heard from him."

I sat up in bed. The headache started pounding the moment I lifted my head off the pillow. "That doesn't sound like him."

"I know. That's what's got me worried."

"Where are the girls?"

"They're in watching cartoons. I didn't want them to know I was calling you. I told them you two were probably busy working and just didn't have time to call."

"We're not working," I said.

"I can't imagine him not calling," Mrs. Edwards continued. "For as long as I've been here, he's never done anything like this."

I had to agree it didn't sound like something Peters would pull, but then eating spaghetti didn't sound like him, either. My first thought was that Candace Wynn had something to do with Peters being AWOL, but I didn't mention that to Mrs. Edwards.

"Did he say if he was going anywhere after the funeral?" I asked.

"He said something about a memorial service afterward."

"That would be at the school. Don't worry. Let me do some checking. I'll call you with whatever I find out."

Bringing the bottle of aspirin from the bathroom with me, I ventured out into the living room. Ames was still on the Hide-A-Bed. He wasn't in any better shape than I was. "Who was that calling so early?" he groaned.

I went on into the kitchen to make coffee. "Mrs. Edwards," I told him. "Peters' baby-sitter. She's looking for him."

"He didn't come home?"

"No."

"Stayed out all night? That doesn't sound like him."

"That's what I told her."

When I went back into the living room, Ames was sitting on the side of the bed with the blanket wrapped around his shoulders, holding his head with both hands. I tossed him the aspirin bottle.

"Hung over?" I asked.

"A little," he admitted. He opened the bottle, shook out a couple of white pills, and popped them into his mouth. "What do you think happened?"

I shrugged. "Got lucky," I said. "He's probably screwing his brains out and is too busy to call Mrs. Edwards and ask for permission."

Ames chuckled at that. "I didn't know Ron had a girlfriend," he said.

"I wouldn't call her a girlfriend exactly. It's someone he just met this week. A teacher."

"What'd he do, start hanging out in singles' bars?"

"When would he have time for singles' bars? He met her at work."

"Really?"

"Where else? You don't find single women hanging out at Brownie meetings or in the grocery store."

"I heard otherwise," Ames commented. "Someone told me the best place for meeting singles is in the deli sections of supermarkets."

"I wouldn't know. I haven't tried it. Do you want coffee or not?"

"Please," Ames said.

Despite what I had told Mrs. Edwards, I didn't try calling anybody. Ames and I each drank a cup of coffee. I expected the phone to ring any minute. I figured Peters had ended up spending the night with Andi Wynn and had planned to sneak back into the house early before anyone woke up. He had probably reckoned without the Saturday morning cartoons, however, which start the minute "The Star-Spangled Banner" ends. Even kids who have to be dragged out of bed by the heels during the week manage to rise and shine in time for their Saturday morning favorites.

Two cups of coffee later I dialed Ron Peters' number again. Maxine Edwards answered. "Oh, it's you," she said, sounding disappointed when she recognized my voice. In the background, I heard a whining child.

"No, Heather, it's not your daddy," Mrs. Edwards scolded. "Now go away and let me talk to Detective Beaumont."

At that Heather pitched such a fit that eventually Mrs. Edwards gave in and put the girl on the line.

"Unca Beau," Heather said in her breathless, toothless six-year-old lisp. "Do you know where my daddy is?"

"No, Heather, I don't. But I can probably find him. Have you eaten breakfast?"

"Not yet."

"Well, you go eat. I'll make some phone calls."

"Do you think he's okay?"

"Of course he's okay. You just go eat your breakfast and do what Mrs. Edwards tells you, all right?"

"All right," she agreed reluctantly. It was clear Maxine Edwards had her hands full.

"Put Mrs. Edwards back on the phone," I ordered. In a moment the baby-sitter's voice came on the line. "I still haven't found out anything," I told her. "But I'll let you know as soon as I do."

When I hung up, I dialed the department. The motor pool told me Peters had turned his vehicle back in at nine the previous evening. That didn't help much.

I headed for the shower. "What are you going to do?" Ames asked me on my way past.

"Go and see if his car is still in the parking garage down on James."

"Wait for me. I'll go along."

It turned out the Datsun was there. It sat, waiting patiently, in a tiny parking place up on the second floor of the parking garage. So much for that. Wherever Peters was, he wasn't driving his own car.

I walked back down the ramp of the garage to where Ames waited in the Porsche.

"It's here," I told him.

"What does that mean?"

"I don't know."

"What are you going to do now?"

"Check in with the department and see if he stopped by his desk when he dropped off the car."

He hadn't. Or, if he had, he had left nothing showing on his desk that gave me a clue about his next destination. I paused long enough to try checking with a couple of night-shift detectives to see if they had seen Peters.

To begin with, you don't call guys who work night shift at ten o'clock in the morning unless you have a pretty damn good reason. I got my butt reamed out good by the first two detectives who told me in no uncertain terms that they hadn't seen anything and wouldn't tell me if they had and why the hell was I calling them at this ungodly hour of the morning.

The third one, a black guy named Andy Taylor, is one of the most easygoing people I've ever met. Nothing rattles him, not even being awakened out of a sound sleep.

"Ron Peters?" he asked once he was really awake. "Sure, I saw him last night. He came in around nine, maybe a little later."

"Was he alone?" I asked.

Andy laughed. "Are you kiddin'? He most certainly was not."

"He wasn't?"

"Hell no. Had some little ol' gal in tow. Looked like the two of them were havin' a great time."

"Auburn hair? Short?" I asked.

"You got it."

"And did Peters say if they were going anywhere in particular?"

Again Andy laughed. "He didn't say, but I

sort of figured it out, if you know what I mean."

"Yes," I said. "I guess I do."

"How come you're checkin' on him, Beau? You afraid he's gettin' some and you're not?"

"Up yours, Taylor," I said, then hung up.

While I was using the phone at Peters' desk, Ames had been sitting at mine, listening with some interest to my side of the conversation. "So where's our little lost sheep?" he asked when I put the phone down.

"Being led around by his balls," I replied.

"Is that what you're going to tell Maxine Edwards?" I looked at Ames. He was grinning like a Cheshire cat.

"No, God damn it. That's not what I'm going to tell Mrs. Edwards."

"What then?"

"That he's working and he'll call as soon as he can."

I did just that, punching Peters' telephone number into the receiver like I was killing bugs. Mrs. Edwards answered after only one ring. She must have been sitting on top of the phone. "Hello."

"Hi, Mrs. Edwards. Beau here. I haven't located Peters yet, but I understand he's working. He'll call home as soon as he can."

"And I should just stay here with the kids?"

"Why not take them to a movie. It'll get their minds off their father."

"That's a good idea. Maybe I'll do just that."

As I stood up to leave, Ames handed me a yellow message sheet that he had plucked off my desk. "Did you see this?" he asked.

The message was from Don Yamamoto in the crime lab, asking me to call. I did. Naturally, on Saturday morning, Don himself wasn't in. The State Patrol answered and tried to give me the runaround. When I insisted, they agreed to have Don Yamamoto call me back.

"It's about the flour container," he said when we finally made the connection.

"What about it?"

"We got a good set of prints off Ridley's belt and also off the inside of the flour container. We're sending them to D.C. to see if we can get any kind of match."

"Great," I told him. "That's good news."

When I hung up the phone the second time, I told Ames what the crime lab had said as we marched out of the office.

Despite the good news from Yamamoto, I was still mad enough to chew nails. It was one thing if Peters wanted to get his rocks off with someone he had just met. I didn't have any quarrel with that. Peters' sex life was none of my concern, one way or the other. What burned me was that he had been so irresponsible about it. If not irresponsible, then certainly inconsiderate. Mrs. Edwards was upset.

His kids were upset. So was I for that matter.

The least he could have done was call home, give some lame excuse or another, and *then* go screw his brains out. That way I wouldn't have been dragged out of a sound sleep and neither would Andy Taylor.

"So where are we going," Ames asked me once he caught up with me on the street. "Back to your place?"

"Not on your life. I'm not going to spend all day sitting there fielding phone calls for some wandering Romeo. And I'm not going to try calling his girlfriend's house, either."

"Why not?" Ames asked.

"Because I don't feel like it. Want to go whack a few golf balls around a golf course?"

Ames stopped in his tracks. "You really are pissed, aren't you? I've never once heard you threaten to play golf before."

"Nobody said anything about playing golf," I muttered. "I want to hit something. Hitting golf balls happens to be socially acceptable."

"As opposed to hitting someone over the head?" Ames asked. "Ron Peters in particular?"

"That's right."

"Golf it is," said Ames. "Lead the way."

C H A P T E R
24

The Foster Golf Course in Tukwila was the only place a couple of rank amateurs could get a toehold and a tee time on a sunny Saturday afternoon in March. We chased balls for eighteen holes' worth and were more than happy to call it quits. Ames wanted a hamburger. Just to be mean, I dragged him to what used to be Harry and Honey's Dinky Diner, until Honey ran Harry off and removed his name from the establishment. We had cheap hamburgers before returning to my apartment late in the afternoon.

On the kitchen counter, the little red light on my new answering machine was blinking cheerfully, announcing a message. Grudgingly, I punched the play button and waited to see what would happen. The machine blinked again, then burped, whirred, and beeped.

"Beau, I just . . ." a voice began, followed by the dial tone and then an operator's voice announcing, "If you wish to place a call, please hang up and dial again. If you need help, hang up and dial your operator."

Ames came out of the bathroom and wandered into the kitchen just as I punched the play button again. "Who was it?" he asked.

"I don't know. I think it's Peters," I told him. "He sounded funny, though. Hang on a minute. I'm playing it again."

When I heard the message the second time, I was sure the caller was Peters, but once more he was cut off, practically in mid-word.

"That's all?" Ames asked. "Are there any other messages?"

"No, just this one."

I picked up the phone and dialed Peters' number in Kirkland. Tracie, Peters' older daughter, answered the phone instantly. Disappointment was evident in her voice when she realized I wasn't her father.

"Oh, hi, Uncle Beau. Is my daddy with you?" she asked.

"No, he's not."

"When will he be home?"

"I don't have any idea, sweetie. Let me talk to Mrs. Edwards."

"She's taking a nap. I'm taking care of

Heather for her. Should I wake her up?"

"No, never mind. She's probably tired. I'll call back later." I hung up.

"He's still not there?" Ames asked.

"No, and that message on the machine has me worried."

Ames nodded. "Me, too. Mind playing it again?"

I did. It proved to be no different from the first two times we had heard it. The message simply ended in mid-sentence with no reason given.

"You're right. It sounds strange," Ames commented after the message had finished playing. "He seemed upset."

"That's what I thought, too. I've got a bad feeling about all this."

"Why not try the department once more," Ames suggested. "Maybe he showed up there while we were out playing golf."

I tried, but no such luck. No one had heard from him. For a long time I stood with the phone in my hand, my dialing finger poised above the numbers, wondering what I should do. There was a big part of me that wanted to go on living in a fool's paradise, believing that everything was hunky-dory, that Peters was just getting his rocks off with Andi Wynn and didn't care if the sun rose or set. But there was another part of me, the partner part of me, that said something was wrong. Dead wrong.

I finally dialed Sergeant Watkins at home. Watty has been around Homicide two years longer than I have. He's virtually unflappable. "What's up, Beau?" he asked when he knew who was on the phone.

As briefly as possible I summarized what I knew, that Peters had stayed out all night, that he had been fine when he dropped off the departmental vehicle at nine, that he had been seen on the fifth floor in the company of a young woman, and that he had left an abortive message on my answering machine at home.

"So what are you proposing?" Watty asked when I finished my recitation.

"File a missing persons report for starters," I said.

"Missing persons or sour grapes?" he asked.

"Watty, I'm serious about this. It's not like him to go off and not bother to call home."

"Now look here, Beau. Let's don't hit panic buttons. You know as well as I do how long it's been since Peters' wife took off. And you know, too, that he's had his hands full with those two kids of his. In other words, he hasn't been getting any. Give the guy a break."

"But Watty . . ."

"But Watty nothing. We don't accept missing persons reports for at least twenty-four hours. You told me yourself that Andy Taylor saw him at nine o'clock last night. Nine o'clock is still a good five hours away. If you go ahead and file a report, he'll probably show up and be pissed as hell that you're advertising his love life all over the department."

"But . . ." I tried again.

"No, and that's final."

Watty hung up and so did I.

"I take it he didn't think much of the idea," Ames observed mildly.

"Right."

I paced over to the window and stared down at the street below. It was Saturday and the area of the city around my building was like a deserted village. No cars moved on the street. No pedestrians wandered the sidewalks. Only a live bum kept company with the bronze one in the tiny park at the base of what I call the Darth Vader Building at Fourth and Lenora.

"So what are you going to do?" Ames asked. "Are we just going to sit around here and do nothing?"

"No, we're not," I replied. "I'm going to go to Candace Wynn's place, pry that worthless bastard out of the sack, and knock some sense into him. After that, I'll hold a gun to his head and make him call his kids."

Ames nodded. "Sounds reasonable to me," he said.

"Are you coming along, or not?" I asked.

Ames shook his head. "I think you'd better

take me over to Kirkland and drop me off at Peters' house. You've got a bad feeling about it, and so do I. Somebody should be there with his kids, just in case."

One look at Ames' set expression told me his mind was made up. I shoved the paper with Andi Wynn's address into my pocket. "Good thinking," I agreed. "Let's get going." After I jotted down Candace Wynn's address from the file, Ames and I took off.

I didn't let any grass grow under my steel-belted radials as we raced across the Evergreen Point Bridge toward Kirkland. For a change there was hardly any traffic. The needle on the Porsche's speedometer hovered around seventy-five most of the way there. I screeched off the Seventieth Street exit on 405 and slid to a stop in front of Peters' modest suburban rambler.

I glanced at Ames. His ashen color told me we had made the trip in record time.

Heather and Tracie were out in the front yard tossing a frisbee back and forth. They dashed over to the car, pleased to see me and thrilled to see Ames. Ralph was the person who had bailed them out of their mother's religious commune in Broken Springs, Oregon. He is also one of the world's softest touches as far as little girls are concerned. They look on him as one step under Santa Claus and several cuts above the Tooth Fairy.

The two of them smothered him with hugs and kisses while he scrambled out of the Porsche.

"Call as soon as you can," he said, leaning back inside the car to speak to me. "I'll hold the fort here."

As I turned the car around in the driveway, he was walking up the sidewalk into the house with a brown-haired child dangling from each arm. Ames is my attorney, but he's also one hell of a good friend. He somehow manages to be in the right place at the right time, just when I need the help. No matter what was going on with Peters, Heather and Tracie couldn't have been in better hands.

Relieved, I flew back across the bridge. My mind was going a mile a minute, rehearsing my speech, the scathing words which would tell Detective Ron Peters in no uncertain terms that I thought he was an unmitigated asshole. In my mind's ear, I made a tub-thumping oration, covering the territory with pointed comments about rutting season and bitches in heat. In my practice run, Andi Wynn didn't get off scot-free, either. Not by a long shot!

The area west of the Fremont Bridge and north of the Ship Canal is a part of Seattle that hasn't quite come to grips with what it wants to be when it grows up. There's a dog food factory, a dry cleaning equipment repair shop, and a brand-new movie studio soundstage.

Added into the mix are Mom-and-Pop businesses and residential units in various stages
of flux, from outright decay to unpretentious
upscale.

Andi Wynn's address was actually on an
alley between Leary and North Thirty-fifth, a
few blocks north of the dog food factory. The
fishy stench in the air told me what they were
using for base material in the dog food that
particular day.

I remembered Andi had told us that she
lived in the watchman's quarters of an old
building. The place turned out to be an old,
ramshackle two-story job with a shiny metal
exterior stairway and handrail leading up to a
door on the second floor. An oil slick near the
bottom of the stairs testified as to where Andi
Wynn usually parked her pickup truck. Right
then, though, the Chevy Luv was nowhere in
sight.

I parked the Porsche in the pickup's parking
place and bounded up the stairs. Halfway to
the top, I tripped over my own feet and had
to grab hold of the handrail to keep from fall-
ing. I caught my balance, barely. When I let go
of the rail, my hand came away sticky.

The paint on the handrail wasn't wet, but it
was fresh enough to be really tacky. The palm
of my hand had silver paint stuck all over it.

"Shit!" I muttered, looking around for
somewhere besides my clothes or the wall to

wipe the mess off my hand. I turned and went back down the stairs. Partway down the alley, an open trash can sat with its cover missing. Whoever had painted the rail had used that particular can to dispose of painting debris, from old rags to newspapers. I grabbed one of the rags, mudded off my hand, and started back up the stairs.

Pausing where I had tripped, I examined the damage I'd done to the fresh paint. There, clearly visible beneath the fresh silver paint, was a scar. A deep blue scar.

I'm not sure how long I stood there like a dummy, gazing at the smudge in the paint. My eyes recorded the information accurately enough, but my mind refused to grasp what it meant.

Blue paint. What was it about blue paint?

When it finally hit me, it almost took my breath away. Flakes of paint, blue metal paint, had been found in Darwin Ridley's hair! And around the top end of the noose that had killed him.

"Jesus H. Christ!" I dashed on up the stairs and pounded on the door. "Police," I shouted. "Open up!"

There was no answer. I'd be damned if I was going to ass around looking for some judge to sign a search warrant, or call for a backup, either.

The first time I hit the door with my foot, it

shuddered but didn't give way. The second time, the lock shattered under my shoe. With my drawn .38 in hand, I charged into the tiny apartment.

Nobody was home.

J. P. Beaumont rides to the rescue, and nobody's there. It's the story of my life.

Cautiously, and without holstering my .38, I gave the place a thorough once-over. By the time I finished, I was beginning to worry about kicking down the door.

As nearly as I could tell, nothing seemed amiss in the apartment. There was no sign of any struggle. It looked like the bed had been slept in on both sides. I found nothing to indicate a hurried leave-taking. The closet was still full of clothes, and the dresser drawers contained neat stacks of female underwear.

Finally, I put my gun away, picked up the phone, and dialed Sergeant Watkins. At home. I figured I was going to get my ass chewed, and I wanted to get it over with as soon as possible.

Watty was particularly out of sorts when he came on the phone. It sounded like he was out of breath. I had a pretty fair idea what Saturday evening activity my phone call might have interrupted.

"I just broke into Candace Wynn's apartment," I told him without preamble. "Nobody's here."

"You what?" he demanded.

"You heard me. I broke into her apartment, hoping to find Peters. They're not here. Now I need some help."

"You're damn right about that! You need more than help. You need to have your goddamned head examined! You ever hear of a fucking search warrant? You ever hear of probable cause?"

"Watty, listen to me. That's what I'm trying to tell you. I've found something important. Remember the blue paint on the rope that killed Ridley and the chips of paint they found in his hair? I think I've found where it came from. I want a crime scene investigator from the crime lab over here on the double."

"Over where?" he asked. "To a place you've broken into without so much as a by-your-leave, to say nothing of a search warrant?"

"Did you hear what I said?"

"I heard you all right. Now you hear me. No way is someone coming over there until you have an airtight search warrant properly filled out, signed, sealed, and delivered. Understand?"

"But Watty," I objected. "It's Saturday night. Where am I going to find a judge at this hour?"

"That's your problem, buster. And you make damn sure it's a superior court judge's signature that's on that piece of paper. I don't want someone throwing it back in our faces later because it's just some lowbrow district court judge. You got that?"

"I don't want to leave here, though," I protested lamely. "What if they come back while I'm gone and find the door broken?"

"You pays your money, and you takes your choice," Watty told me. "You get your ass out of there and don't go back until you have that warrant in your hot little hand."

Watty was adamant. There was no talking him out of it. "All right, all right. I'll go get your fucking search warrant. But we're wasting time."

"You'll be wasting even more time if somebody files a breaking-and-entering or illegal-search complaint against you. Now, give me the address. I'll get somebody over there to watch it until you get back."

Grudgingly, I drove back down to the Public Safety Building, parked in a twenty-four-hour loading zone, and went upstairs to type out the proper form. When I finished typing, I grabbed the list of judges' home phone numbers and started letting my fingers do the walking. I didn't know it, but I was in for a marathon.

Fifteen no answers and three answering machines later, I finally spoke to a human being, a judge's wife, not a judge. She sounded more than a little dingy. According to her, all the judges she knew, including her husband, were in Olympia for a retirement banquet for one of the state supreme court justices. She would have been there herself, she assured me, but she was just getting over the shingles.

The lady must have been pretty lonely. She was so happy to have someone to talk to that she could have kept me on the phone for hours, giving me a detailed, blow-by-blow description of all her symptoms, but I was in a hurry. I cut her off in mid-diagnosis. "Where in Olympia?" I asked.

"I beg your pardon?"

"The banquet," I said, pulling her back on track. "Where is it?"

"Oh, at the Tyee," she answered. "At least I think that's what the invitation said. Since I wasn't going, I didn't pay that close attention."

I thanked her and hung up. Olympia is sixty miles or so south of Seattle.

Fortunately, the Porsche was still there when I went back outside. It hadn't been towed. It didn't even have a ticket plastered to its windshield. The parking enforcement officers must have been taking a coffee break. So was the State Patrol on I-5. I had clear sailing, and I drove like an absolute maniac—forty minutes flat from the time I left the Public Safety Building until I pulled into the parking lot at the Tyee.

I had driven the last twenty miles with my bladder about to burst, so my first priority was to find a restroom and take a leak. A dapper little guy in a suit and tie was having a hell of a time aiming. He was a little worse for wear, but I thought I recognized him.

"You wouldn't happen to be a judge from Seattle, would you?"

He grinned fuzzily. "That's right. Do I know you?"

He didn't then, but by the time he finished signing the search warrant, we were old pals. I grabbed the paper out of his hand and beat it back toward the car. I was back on the Fremont Bridge thirty-eight minutes later.

Happily, Sergeant Watkins hadn't been sitting around playing with himself in my absence. He had alerted the crime scene team and had worked out a treaty with King County for them to bring their laser printfinder along to the apartment. The King County Police crime scene van was parked in Candace Wynn's parking place.

Watty must have pulled out all the stops to conjure up that kind of interdepartmental cooperation on such short notice on a Saturday evening.

There was quite a crowd gathering between the alley and Leary Way. In the process of rounding up everybody we needed, Watty had inadvertently summoned the fourth estate. I found an unwelcome welcoming committee of reporters waiting for me behind the police barricade.

I parked the Porsche and started to make my way through the crowd. Somebody stopped me. "What's happening, Detective Beaumont?" a reporter asked, shoving a microphone in my face. "What's going on in there?"

Someone else recognized me. "Hey, Detective Beaumont, this another homicide? How many does that make this week? You guys going for some kind of record?"

Ignoring the cameras, I pushed on, wondering if there wasn't some other kind of work I could do that wouldn't put me in daily contact with the press.

When I finally reached the bottom of the stairway, I stopped to examine the motley crew Watty had assembled—two latent-evidence examiners from the crime lab, a beefy sheriff's department deputy packing what looked to be a large suitcase, a King County ID person, two night-shift homicide detectives from the department, and a uniformed S.P.D.

officer. Each of them nodded to me in turn, but no one said anything.

Sergeant Watkins himself was waiting at the top of the stairs. He stood blocking the doorway, glaring down at me, arms crossed truculently across his chest. He looked like what he wanted was a good fight. "Give it to me," he demanded when I came up the stairs.

"Give you what?" I asked.

"The warrant, for chrissakes!" He held out his hand. I removed the warrant from my inside jacket pocket and slapped it into the palm of his hand. Holding it up to the dim glow of a street lamp half a block away, he studied it for a long time.

"All right," he said finally. "Break the door down."

For the first time, I looked at the door. Sure enough, while I had been driving up and down the freeway to and from Olympia, someone had jerry-rigged the door back together.

"How'd it get fixed?" I asked. "Did she come back home?"

"I fixed it, you asshole," Watty whispered through clenched teeth. "Now break this motherfucker down, and make it look good. I want a picture of this on every goddamned television station in town."

I understood then why Sergeant Watkins was at the top of the steps and everyone else was waiting down below. Watty's nobody's fool. He was looking out for my ass, and his, too. It was all I could do to keep from laughing out loud as I kicked Candace Wynn's door in one more time. Once more with feeling. Take it from the top. J. P. Beaumont does "Miami Vice."

The only problem was, I kicked the door like it was really locked, like it hadn't been wrecked only hours before. I almost broke my neck when it caved in under my foot.

Once inside, Watty motioned the rest of the troops to join us. It turned out the suitcase contained King County's laser printfinder. The deputy, huffing, lugged the case up the stairs and put it down in the middle of Candace Wynn's living room.

The printfinder weighs around eighty pounds or so, and it works off a regular 110 volt plug-in. He fired it up, plugging it into an outlet right there in the room. The crime scene investigators dusted the various surfaces in the room with a fluorescent powder. Then, one of them donned a pair of goggles.

"Okay, you guys," the other said. "Here go the lights."

With that, he turned out all the lights in the room. We were plunged into darkness. The only illumination was the finger of light from the printfinder as it played over the glowing powder and the periodic flashes from a 35-mm camera as the other investigator snapped pictures.

I felt like a kid who had stumbled into a midnight session with a Ouija board. There was nothing to do but stand there with my hands in my pockets and wait as the investigator ran the lens in the end of a length of fiber optic cable over everything that wasn't readily movable and bagged up everything that was.

He picked up prints from everywhere—the table, the refrigerator, the bathroom counter and mirror, the couch and chair in the living room, all the while recording the prints on film for later examination. Not only did the laser pick up prints, it also located other bits of trace evidence—hairs and fiber fragments that would have been tough to find with the naked eye.

Finally, tired of doing nothing, the rest of the team went outside. The other homicide detectives gathered a series of paint scraping samples from the handrail on the stairs. I showed them which garbage can had held the painting debris I had discovered earlier in the evening when I had been looking for something to use to clean my hands.

Fascinated by the workings of the laser, I went back inside and followed the deputy around like a puppy. I was so intrigued with the process that I failed to notice when one of the crime lab boys came to the door and motioned Watty aside. Moments later, Watty switched on the lights.

"Hey, why'd you do that?" the laser operator griped.

"Can you take that thing outside?" Watty demanded. He looked more anxious, more upset, than I had ever seen him. His whole demeanor vibrated with unmistakable urgency.

"Now?"

Watty nodded.

"I guess we can finish up in here later," the tech grumbled. "But I'll have to get the van to fire up the generator. I thought we were going to be inside. Nobody told me we'd be working outside. I need a place to plug all this shit in."

"What's up?" I asked Watty as soon as they called the deputy back upstairs to carry the equipment down to the alley. "What did they find?"

"Come see for yourself," Watty said grimly.

I followed him outside and down the steps. The King County van had been moved farther down the alley and was parked next to the garbage can. The deputy was busy hauling out power cables to hook the laser up outside.

As we started away from them without acknowledging their presence, the members of the press put up a hell of a fuss.

"Ignore them," Watty ordered. I was only too happy to oblige.

We walked down the alley and gathered

around the garbage can like a group of male witches around a mysterious cauldron. Standing to one side, I watched as the laser operator lowered his cable into the can. The brilliant light illuminated only a tiny area at a time. Someone had removed the top layer of paint-sodden rags. I moved even closer to see what had been unearthed, what the light was focusing on.

It was a bottle, a tiny medicine bottle, the kind liquid narcotics are stored in before someone sucks them into a syringe.

I turned to Watty then. "Morphine?" I asked.

He nodded, saying nothing.

"Oh, shit!" I muttered. Sick with dread, I turned to walk away.

Just beyond the police barricade, a cameraman caught me walking back down the alley. As I passed him, I was aware of the red light from his videocam shining full on my face. It was then I realized I had never called Ames to let him know what was going on, and here I was, live, on the eleven o'clock news.

I wanted to grab the camera out of the man's hands and shove it down his throat. I didn't.

Excessive common sense is one of the few side benefits of advancing middle age.

Unfortunately, it's also a symptom of despair.

C H A P T E R
26

We went back into Candace Wynn's apartment, eventually, after the deputy had used the laser to go over everything of interest in the garbage can. By then, Watty was as serious as hell. The morphine bottle was no joke. He watched over our shoulders while the crime scene team, the other two Seattle P.D. detectives, and I scoured the place inch by inch. We found a number of useful items, including the automobile license renewal form on Andi's Chevy Luv. Watty phoned the license number in to dispatch and told them to put out an APB on Candace Wynn.

I lost all track of time. Long after one in the morning somebody thought to reach down behind the couch cushions. There, stuck in the crack between the springs and the back of the couch, we discovered a small, dark, leather wallet. I recognized it at once.

"That's Peters'," I said.

Sure enough. Inside we found both his badge and his departmental ID. I felt like somebody had kicked me in the stomach.

Right up until then, I suppose I'd kept hoping I was wrong. Hoping that, despite the mounting evidence, Peters would show up and chew my butt for pushing panic buttons when he was just out knocking off a piece of ass. Finding his badge corked it for me. Cops don't get separated from their badges without a fight. Or without a reason.

When we finally left Candace Wynn's apartment, Watty and I took our separate vehicles and drove back downtown to the Public Safety Building. I went upstairs to write my report while a team from the crime lab night shift went to work as fast as they could on comparing the prints we'd found on the things in Joanna Ridley's trunk with the prints in Candace Wynn's apartment.

With every moment vital, it was frustrating to realize that the process, which would take several hours of manual labor, could have been done in a matter of seconds with a computerized fingerprint identification unit. The last request for one had been turned down cold by the state legislature.

When I finished my report, I stamped

around the fifth floor, railing at anybody who
would listen about goddamned stupid legis-
lators who were penny-wise and pound-fool-
ish.

In the meantime, another team downstairs
had tackled the paint samples. It turns out that
paint samples take a hell of a lot less time to
compare than fingerprints. My friend, Janice
Morraine, called me at my desk about three-
thirty in the morning to let me know that the
samples taken from Candace Wynn's porch
matched those taken from Darwin Ridley's
hair as well as those from the rope found in
Joanna Ridley's trunk.

That one little chip of information told me
who. It didn't tell me why or how. And it
didn't give me a clue as to where she was right
then.

I left the office about four. I had caught my
second wind. Instead of driving home to my
apartment, I headed for Kirkland. I needed to
talk to Ames and tell him what we had found,
to say nothing of what we hadn't. I also
needed his calm assessment of the situation.

Much to my surprise, even at that late hour
the lights were blazing in Peters' living room.
I peered in the window of the door and caught
a glimpse of Ames' head peeking over the
back of a chair. His face was pointed at a
snowy, otherwise blank television screen on
the other side of the room.

A series of light taps on the window brought Ames scrambling to his feet. "Who is it?" He opened the door, then stood back, rubbing his eyes. "Oh, it's you," he mumbled. "Did you find anything?"

Ames led me into the kitchen, where we scrounged around for sandwich makings while I told him what I knew. He nodded as I talked.

"I watched the news at eleven," he commented somberly. "The reporters didn't have any idea what was going on, but I could tell it wasn't good."

"Did Heather and Tracie see it?" I asked.

He shook his head. "Mrs. Edwards finally talked them into bed about ten."

"Good."

Over a thick tuna sandwich, I finished the story, including all the minute details I could remember, from the paint samples and the morphine bottle to Peters' ID holder hidden in the couch.

Me and my big mouth.

When I ended my story, the room got quiet. It was then I heard the sound of a muted whimper coming from the other room.

Hurrying to the pocket door between the kitchen and the dining room, I slid it open. There, crouched on the floor, I discovered Tracie, her whole body shaken by partially muffled sobs.

"Tracie, what is it? What's the matter?"

I picked her up and held her against my chest. "You didn't find my daddy. You promised you would and you didn't."

I touched her brown hair, smoothing it away from her tearstained cheeks. "Shhh, sweetie," I whispered. "It's all right."

She pulled away and looked at me reproachfully. "It's not all right. He's dead," she declared. "I know he's dead."

"No, Tracie. Your daddy's not dead. He's lost, and we're going to find him. You wait and see."

"But what if he is," she insisted stubbornly. "That's what happens on TV. The bad guys and the good guys shoot each other. Usually, the bad guys die. But sometimes the good guys die, too."

Ames came over and gave Tracie's head a comforting pat. "This isn't TV, Tracie. Everything's going to be all right. You'll see."

"But what if?"

"Don't you worry. You go back to bed and let Uncle Beau and me handle it. It's late. Mrs. Edwards said you have to go to Sunday school in the morning."

"I don't want to go to Sunday school."

"Too bad." Ames reached out and took Tracie from my arms. She went without objection. He carried her out of the room and down the hall. When he returned to the kitchen, he was alone.

"Will she stay in bed?" I asked.

"We'll see," he answered.

"Goddamned television," I muttered.

Ames sat down across the kitchen table from me, a small, tight frown on his face. He rubbed his forehead wearily. "What would happen to the girls?" he asked.

"You mean if something happened to Peters?"

Ames nodded again. "Has he made any arrangements? Do you have any idea?"

I shrugged. "We've never talked about it."

"Somebody should have talked about it long before this," he said grimly. "And that somebody should have been me. It's my job."

"Come on now, Ralph. Don't blame yourself. We're all doing the best we can."

Unconvinced, Ames shook his head. "In a custody case like this, especially one where the mother is out of the country, I should have taken care of it."

I had come to Kirkland hoping Ames would make me feel better. Instead, he succeeded in doing just the reverse. The two of us sat there conferring miserably until fatigue finally caught up with us.

It was starting to get light outside when I bailed out and told him I had to get some sleep. Neither one of us went near Peters' bed.

We rummaged around in a linen closet and found blankets and pillows. Ames took the couch. Stripped down to my T-shirt and shorts, I settled down on the floor.

I must have fallen asleep the instant my head touched the pillow. I was dead to the world when thirty-five pounds of kid did a belly flop onto my chest, knocking the wind out of me.

"Unca Beau, Unca Beau," Heather lisped. "Can I use the blanket, too?"

Unable to speak, I held up the blanket. A chilly, pajama-clad kid wormed her way into my arms, snuggling contentedly against my chest.

"Is Daddy still asleep?" she asked.

"I don't know, Heather. He's not here."

She sat up and looked at me accusingly. "He isn't? You said you were going to find him."

"I'm trying, but I haven't been able to yet."

"When will you?"

"I don't know. I can't say."

She got up and stood glaring scornfully down at me, both hands on her hips. "I want him home *now*," she announced. With that, she turned, flounced down the hallway without a backward glance, marched into her bedroom, and slammed the door.

"Sounds like 'Unca Beau' is in deep shit," Ames observed dryly from the couch.

I struggled clumsily off the floor with my

bad back screaming at me. I'm too old to sleep on floors. " 'Unca Beau' is going to get the hell downtown and find out what the fuck is going on," I growled, throwing the wad of bedding onto a nearby chair.

I glanced at the couch, where Ames still lay with the blanket pulled up to his chin. "Are you coming or not?"

"Not. I'll stay here," he said. "I think it's best."

I had to agree. When I finally got moving, I discovered the hour or so of sleep had done me a world of good. I was awake and alert as I started toward the city. I drove with my mind racing off in a dozen different directions at once: Why? And how? And where? Those were the basic questions, but where was the most important.

Where could they be? With every passing hour, that question became more critical. I was convinced Peters was being held somewhere against his will. As time passed, Andi Wynn had to be getting more and more desperate. And dangerous.

Through a series of mental gymnastics I had managed to keep my mind from touching on the bottom-line question, the question I had fought to avoid all night long. But as I crossed the bridge to return to Seattle, the question asserted itself, surging full-blown to the surface: Was Detective Ron Peters still alive?

Yes, he was alive, I decided, feeling my grip tighten involuntarily on the steering wheel. He couldn't be dead. No way. Like Heather, I wanted him home and alive. Now.

Fighting for control, I took a deep breath. In the twenty-four hours since Mrs. Edwards had first called me, I had worked my way through a whole progression of feelings, from being pissed because Peters was out screwing his brains out to being worried sick that he was being held someplace with a gun to his head.

But once the idea of death caught hold of me, I couldn't shake it. It filled up the car until I could barely breathe.

The badge and ID told me Peters wasn't in control when he left Candace Wynn's apartment. The morphine bottle hinted at why. I suspected morphine had given Andi the edge both with Darwin Ridley and with Peters, providing a chemical handcuff every bit as effective as the metal variety.

And if Andi Wynn had indeed killed Darwin Ridley, then I had to believe she was capable of killing again. It was my job to find her, to stop her, before she had the chance.

Downtown Seattle was a ghost town at seven-fifteen on Sunday morning. I parked the Porsche in front of the Public Safety Building and hurried inside. There were only two people visible in the crime lab when I was led into the room. One of them was my friend, Janice

Morraine. She reached into her lab coat pocket, removed a package of cigarettes, and nodded toward the door. "Let's go outside," she said.

As soon as we were out in the elevator lobby, she lit up. "Did you find Peters?" she asked, blowing a long plume of smoke toward the ceiling.

I shook my head. "Not yet. What's the scoop on the stuff we brought in?"

She shrugged. "We've got matches every-where—the prints from Ridley's clothes, from the flour container, from the Fremont apart-ment, and from Joanna Ridley's house as well."

I felt the cold grip of fear in my gut. Looking at Janice's somber face, I could see she felt it, too.

"What does that say to you?" I asked.

"That the killer doesn't give a damn whether you catch him or not."

The knot in my gut got a little tighter, a little colder. I pushed the call button on the eleva-tor.

"That's what I was afraid you'd say, but it's a her," I added.

Janice blew another plume of smoke and ground out the remains of her barely smoked cigarette in the sand-filled ashtray in the hall. "Good luck," she said softly.

I stepped into the elevator. "Thanks," I told her. "We'll need it."

When the elevator stopped on the fifth floor, I was almost run over by two detectives who charged through the open door. One of them grabbed me by the sleeve and dragged me back inside as the door slid shut.

"Hey, wait a minute. I wanted off."

"You'd better come with us," Big Al Lindstrom ordered.

"How come? What's up?"

"Somebody just spotted that missing Chevy Luv," he answered.

"No shit? Where?"

"Parked in front of Mercer Island High School. That's where we're going."

"Who's we?" I asked.

"Baxter here and me. You, too, if you want. Mercer Island Police say they have the place pretty well sealed off, but they called us to let us know."

Big Al and Baxter got off at the garage level. I had to ride down to the lobby and charge down the street half a block to where I had parked, but once I fired up the Porsche, there was no contest. I passed Big Al and Baxter on the bridge like they were standing still.

I'm not sure if it was because the Porsche was a better car or because Peters was my partner.

Actually, it was probably a little of both.

C H A P T E R
27

We raced to the high school, only to find ourselves stuck behind a police barricade along with everybody else.

The next hour and a half was an agonizing study of affirmative action in action. From a distance, I caught a glimpse of the new Mercer Island Chief of Police—a lady wearing a gray pin-striped suit and sensible shoes with a dress-for-success polka-dot scarf knotted tightly around her neck. She had definitely taken charge of the situation.

When Marilyn Sykes, assistant police chief in Eugene, Oregon, was hired for the job on Mercer Island, there had been a good deal of grumbling in law enforcement circles. The general consensus was that, in this particular case, the best man for the job wasn't a woman. I hadn't paid a whole lot of attention to the debate since half the complainers said she was too tough and the other half claimed she was too soft. I figured the truth was probably somewhere in between.

Right then, though, watching the action from an impotent distance, my inclination was to dismiss Marilyn Sykes as a pushy broad, one who didn't have enough confidence in herself and her position to let any other cops within consulting distance, as though she was afraid our advice and suggestions might undercut her authority.

It's something I'll remember as one of the most frustrating times of my whole life. It was only an hour and a half, but it seemed much longer. I wanted to *do* something, to take some physical action, like knocking down the barricade and making an unauthorized run for the building.

Candace Wynn's pickup had been parked right in the middle of the high school lot, with no attempt to conceal it. Chief Sykes had sealed off the entire campus and was in the process of deploying her Emergency Response Team. Directing the operation from her car, she had the team secure one building at a time.

As a cop, I couldn't help but approve of her careful, deliberate planning. It was clear the safety of her team was uppermost in her mind. But I wasn't there as just a plain cop. I was there because Peters was my partner. Marilyn

Sykes' deliberateness drove me crazy. I wanted action. I wanted to get on with it.

The interminable wait was made worse by the fact that our Seattle P.D. personnel were stuck far behind the lines, rubbing shoulders with reporters and photographers, all of them angling for an angle, all of them snapping eagerly toward any snippet of information. It was clear from the questions passing back and forth between them that the names of the missing officer and the missing teacher had not yet been released. I thanked Arlo Hamilton for that. At least Peters' girls wouldn't hear it from a reporter's lips first.

As the minutes ticked by and the tension continued to build, my fuse got shorter and shorter. Finally, I turned to Big Al, who was standing beside me. His face was grim, his hands jammed deep in his jacket pockets.

"God damn it!" I complained. "Why the hell doesn't she send 'em into the gym? I'd bet money they're in the girls' locker room."

Just then someone tapped me on the shoulder. I turned around and found myself eyeball to eyeball with Chief Marilyn Sykes herself. She was a fairly tall woman in her mid-forties, with sharp, hazel eyes and a tough, overbearing way about her.

"Are you Detective Beaumont?" she demanded.

I nodded. "I am."

"As I'm sure you realize, Detective Beaumont," she continued severely, "we've got a potentially dangerous situation here. What I don't need is a Monday-morning quarterback second-guessing my decisions, is that clear?"

Chastised, I gave the only possible response I could muster: "Yes, Ma'am."

She turned on her heel. "Come with me," she ordered over her shoulder.

I looked at Big Al, whose only consolation was a sheepish shrug of his shoulders. Without a word, I followed. She led me back to where her car was parked before she stopped and waited for me. By then, we were well out of earshot of all the reporters.

"The detective who's missing, Detective Peters. He's your partner?"

"Yes."

Turning away, she reached into her car and pulled out a handheld walkie-talkie. She flicked a switch. "Come in, George. Have you cleared the way to the locker-room door yet?"

"Check," a voice crackled from the device in her hand. "Just now."

"All right. I've got someone here, Detective Beaumont from Seattle P.D., who thinks they're in that locker room. I'm sending him in with you."

I pulled my .38 from its holster and started scrambling out of her car. "Just a minute, Detective Beaumont," she snapped.

I stopped. Chief Sykes picked up a long roll

of paper from the floor of the front seat. When she spread it out on the backseat, it was a detailed architectural drawing of the high school plant. With a slender, well-manicured finger, she traced a line from where we stood to the girls' locker room.

"This is the part we've secured," she said. "Don't go any other way, understand?"

"Right," I said.

"And no heroics. You want to see your partner alive, and so do we."

Once again she reached into the front seat. This time she brought out a bulletproof vest. "Put this on," she said. "Now get going."

I shrugged my way into the flak jacket and paused for just a moment before I bailed out of the car. Marilyn Sykes met my gaze without flinching. She was tough, all right, but not in the way her detractors meant. There was a soft spot, too. Not the kind of softness that translates into weakness, but a certain empathy that told me sometime in her past she, too, had lived with a partner in jeopardy, that she knew the terrible helplessness of doing nothing.

Someday, when we had time, Chief Marilyn Sykes and Detective J. P. Beaumont would have to sit down, have a drink, and talk about it. But not now.

"Thanks," I said, then took off.

I trotted through the buildings, careful not to deviate from the path she had laid out. My footsteps echoed through the silent walkways. I'm not prone to prayer, but I found myself muttering one as I ran. "Let him be safe, God. Please let him be safe."

A uniformed Mercer Island officer motioned me into the gym. "They're waiting for you by the door to the locker room," he whispered as I passed.

Waiting they were. Three officers, all wearing bulletproof vests, crouched against the wall on either side of the door. One of them motioned for me to join him. When I was in position behind him, he raised a bullhorn to his lips.

"Come on out, Mrs. Wynn. You're surrounded. Give yourself up."

There was no answer. The blank, silent door gave no hint of what was happening on the other side. We waited one endless minute. We waited two.

"Come on out, Mrs. Wynn. Come out before we have to come in after you."

Still there was nothing. No sound. Images of bloody carnage raced through my mind. Too many years on homicide had left my imagination with too much fuel for the fire. I pictured Peters lying facedown in a pool of blood or dangling on the end of a rope with his head flopped limply to one side. In the silence I heard an imaginary hail of bullets slice into the door when we attempted to push it open.

"On the count of three, we're coming in. One . . . Two . . . Three . . ." One of the members of the team on the other side of the door reached out and tried to open it. Nothing happened. It was locked.

The leader, the man beside me, nodded to the guy on the other side. "Big Bertha it is."

The third man came forward carrying a handheld battering ram. He popped the door twice before the lock crumbled. As the door swung open, the silence was deafening.

Crouching low, weapon in hand, I followed the leader into the darkened locker room. We switched on the lights. Inside, we wormed our way around first one bank of lockers and then another. The place was empty.

Peters wasn't in the locker room, and neither was Candace Wynn. They had been there, though. At least someone had.

The locker, the one with the list in it, the Mercer Island High School cheerleader trophy list, had been smashed to pieces by someone wielding a heavy object. I could make out only one or two letters from the battered piece of metal that had once been the inscribed ceiling.

"All clear in here, Chief," the leader said into his walkie-talkie. He put the microphone into his pocket, then walked up closer to the damaged locker.

"What do you suppose went on here?" he asked.

"Beats me," I told him. Quickly, I moved away to the other side of the room, out of casual conversation range but close enough to hear him give the all-clear to Chief Sykes via his walkie-talkie. I tried my best to become invisible. Just because Chief Sykes had been kind enough to include me in the operation didn't necessarily obligate me to full disclosure. I didn't want to tell them everything I knew. That locker list might somehow still be useful.

Marilyn Sykes strode into the locker room about that time. She glanced in my direction, then walked up to join the man by the locker. "Vandalism?" I heard her ask.

The man shrugged. "I give up. It's funny, but it looks like this is the only locker that was damaged." For a moment, Chief Sykes gazed at the mangled pile of sheet metal.

"Somebody went to a hell of a lot of trouble to destroy this one," she said. Then she turned to me. "What do you think, Detective Beaumont?" she asked.

Whether or not I wanted to be, she had pulled me back into the conversation. "Do you think this has anything to do with your partner's disappearance?"

By aiming her question directly at me, Chief Marilyn Sykes created an instant moral dilemma. I owed her, goddamnit! She had let me through the barricades onto her turf, and I owed her.

"I'd have the crime lab take a look at it if I were you," I suggested. That let me off the hook without my having to give up too much.

She nodded. "All right."

Wanting to get away quick, before she could ask me anything more, I turned and walked out of the locker room. Halfway down the walkway, I ran headlong into Ned Browning rushing toward the gym. "Hello there, Ned," I said.

He stopped cold when he saw me. He was uncharacteristically agitated. "Oh, yes, Detective . . . Detective . . . I'm sorry, I don't remember your name."

"Beaumont," I supplied. "Detective Beaumont."

"You'll have to excuse me. I understand there's been some difficulty in the gym. I'd been trying to get through, but they wouldn't let me until just now. Somebody called me at home when I came back from church."

"Church," I grunted with contempt. "That figures."

Browning started forward again, but I stopped him. "I'm going to want to talk to you, too," I said. "As soon as they finish with you."

"I don't have time, Detective Beaumont. My

family is waiting for me. We're having guests."

"I don't give a shit if it's the pope himself, Ned. I want to talk to you alone. About the cheerleading squad, remember them? I'm sure you remember one or two of them fairly well."

An almost audible spark of recognition passed over his face. He paled and stepped back a pace or two. "What do you mean?"

"Don't play dumb. You know what I mean," I said menacingly. "I'll wait for you at Denny's, here on the island."

"All right," he said, crumbling. "I'll meet you as soon as I'm finished here."

You're finished, all right, pal, I thought to myself, but I didn't say it aloud. I didn't have to. And I wouldn't have to lift a finger to make it happen, either. Chief Marilyn Sykes and the Washington State Patrol's crime lab would take care of all those little details.

Meanwhile, while Ned Browning still thought there was a way he could wiggle off the hook, while he still thought there was a way to save his worthless ass and his career, I'd play him for all he was worth, see if I could wrangle any helpful information out of his scared little hide.

That's one thing I've learned over the years. If you have the slightest advantage, use it. And don't worry about it after you do.

Creeps don't have any scruples.

Cops can't afford them.

C H A P T E R
28

When I walked back to the Porsche, old man trouble himself, Maxwell Cole, stood slouching against the door on the driver's side.

"Get away, Max. You'll scratch the paint," I told him.

He didn't move. "Hey, there, J. P. How's it going?"

"Get out of the way. I don't have time to screw around with you." Bodily, I shoved him aside far enough so I could put my key in the lock.

"I'll bet it is Peters, isn't it? That's the rumor, anyway," he said, grinning slyly under his handlebar mustache. "I mean, he's not here, and you are. Same thing happened last night, over in Fremont, or so I hear."

"Will you get the fuck out of my way?"

"And what's the teacher's name? Candace Wynn, isn't that it?"

"I'm not talking. Leave me alone, Max."

"I won't leave you alone. I want to know what's going on. Why won't they release any names? All Arlo Hamilton does is read prepared speeches that have nothing to do with what's going on. I want the scoop, J. P., the real scoop."

"You won't get it from me, asshole. Besides, it sounds to me like Hamilton is giving you guys just what you deserve."

"What do you mean?"

"What Arlo tells you is bullshit. What you write is bullshit. Sounds like an even trade to me."

Max took an angry step toward me, but thought better of it and stayed out of reach. He glared at me for a long moment before dropping his gaze, his eyes watery and pale behind the thick lenses of his glasses. "You're not going to tell me about Peters, then?"

"You're damn right."

I flung the Porsche's door open, bouncing it off Cole's ample hip for good measure. Just to make the point. He finally moved aside.

The problem with Max is that I'm so used to avoiding him that in the crush of worrying about Peters I had forgotten I needed to talk to him. Instead of starting the car, I got back out. Max moved away from me.

"You leave me alone, J. P."

"Where'd you get the picture, Max?"

"The picture? What picture?"

"The one you wrote about but didn't print. The one of Darwin Ridley and the cheerleader."

He smirked then. "You scratch my back, I'll scratch yours."

I didn't have time to mess around with him. I turned on my heel and got back in the car.

"All I want to know is if it's Peters or not."

"Fuck you, Max."

He looked offended. "I have other ways of confirming this, you know," he whined.

"So use 'em," I told him. "Be my guest, but you'd damn well better keep your facts straight, because I'll cram 'em down your throat if you don't!"

With that, I started the engine and laid down a layer of rubber squealing out of the parking lot.

I took a meandering route to the Mercer Island Denny's through the maze of interminable road construction that has screwed up traffic there for years. Surprisingly, lots of other people had evidently done the same thing.

The restaurant was busy, jammed with the after-church/Sunday-brunch crowd. I waited almost fifteen minutes before they finally cleared out the line and showed me to a table, a short-legged two-person booth in the center of the room.

During the few minutes I was there alone, I couldn't help reflecting. The last time I had been in the room I was with Peters and Andi Wynn together, that afternoon when we finished questioning the students. That time seemed years ago, not days. Since then, my life had been run through a Waring blender. Fatigue and worry weighed me down, threatening to suck me under and drown me.

Then Ned Browning entered. He rushed through the door and stopped abruptly by the cash register to look for me. Now, starting forward again, he slowed his pace, walking deliberately and with some outward show of dignity, but nothing masked the agitation that remained clearly visible on his face.

My transformation was instantaneous. Adrenaline surged through my system, pulling me out of my stupor, putting every nerve in my body on full alert. By the time he reached the booth, my mind was honed sharp. I was ready for him.

He held out his hand in greeting, but I ignored the empty gesture. Instead, I motioned for him to sit down opposite me. If he thought I had invited him over for a nice social chat, he was wrong. The sooner Ned Browning understood that, the better.

He paused and looked down at his hand,

first comprehending and then assessing the message behind my refusal to shake hands. Maybe he had convinced himself that he had mistaken the meaning in what I had said about the cheerleaders.

My insult wasn't lost on him. Ned Browning was caught, and he knew it. Flushing violently to the roots of his receding hairline, he sat down.

"What do you want?" he asked in a hoarse, subdued whisper.

It was time for poker. Time to play bluff, raise, and draw. I happened to have a pretty good hand. "What did you use?" I asked obliquely for openers.

"I beg your pardon?" He frowned. He may have been as genuinely puzzled as he looked, or he may have been playing the game.

"What did you use to smash the locker, Ned? A sledgehammer? A brick? A rock?"

He drew back in his chair as though I'd slapped him squarely across the face. His unhealthy flush was replaced by an equally unhealthy pallor. "I don't know what you're talking about!"

"Yes, you do. You know very well."

He stood up. "I've got guests waiting at home. I didn't come here to play games."

I caught the sleeve of his jacket and compelled him back into the booth. "Fuck your guests," I snarled. "Believe me, this is no game."

His eyes darted warily around the room, checking to see who was within earshot, to see if there was anyone nearby who might know him or who had overheard my rude remark.

He made an attempt to retrieve his old stuffiness. "I don't think it's necessary to use that kind of language, Mr. Beaumont."

Once upon a time I had been briefly impressed by his outward show of high-toned values. That was no longer true. His high-toned values were a sham.

"Don't pull that bullshit on me. I'm not one of your students, Ned," I reminded him. "I'll talk to you any damn way I please."

His hands dropped to his lap, but not before I caught sight of a nervous tremor. An involuntary tic touched the muscle of his left jaw. A rush of gleeful satisfaction passed through me. I was definitely making progress. Visible progress.

Just then, our waitress appeared. "Can I get you something?" she asked.

"No, nothing for me," Browning murmured shakily.

"Toast," I said. "Whole wheat. And two eggs over easy." I nodded as the waitress offered and poured coffee. Browning refused that as well. When the waitress left, I picked up my spoon and began stirring my coffee with slow deliberation. Ned Browning was already nervous. Any delaying tactic, anything that would make him sit on his powder keg a little longer, would work in my favor.

Carefully, I put down the spoon, took a long sip of coffee, then leaned forward, thrusting my face toward his, invading the body space, the distance, he had created around himself.

"Let's get down to brass tacks, Ned. When did you find out about the list?"

"What list?" He was determined to play dumb. I was in no mood to tolerate it.

"The one with you on it, Ned. The pep squad scorecard. As I recall, your name is on it more than once."

In the previous few minutes, a little color had returned to his face. Now it drained away again, leaving him a pasty gray. That took the fun out of it for me, calling a halt to the game. I prefer someone who offers a little more of a challenge, a worthy adversary who fields the questions and makes me work for my answers. Ned Browning caved in so easily, I almost laughed out loud.

"You know about that?"

"Lots of people know about it. More than you'd expect. They also have a pretty good idea what it took to get on it."

"But . . ."

"When did you find out about it?" I insisted. "And how?"

"But she said . . ."

"Who said?"

"Candace. Mrs. Wynn."

"What did she say?"

"That if I destroyed the locker, no one would ever know."

"Right. And why do you suppose she told you that?"

"I don't have any idea."

"When did she tell you?"

"Saturday morning. She called me at home."

"What time?"

"It must have been around ten. I was out working in the yard when she called and asked me to meet her at school."

"And you did?"

"She said it was urgent, something I needed to know."

"Where did you meet? In the locker room?"

"No. In my office."

"All right, so after you met, what happened then?"

"She told me about the list. Said she'd just found out about it the night before, at Darwin Ridley's memorial service."

The little orange warning light in the back of my head started flashing. I had a vivid memory of Candace Wynn looking at the list in the locker after Peters and I found it. She had known about it for sure since then, and maybe even before that. Why had she lied to Browning about when she found out, and what had made it so urgent?

"So what happened?" I urged impatiently. "Go on."

"She said if anyone else found out about it, it would be awful for everyone. She thought the best idea would be to get rid of it, both for the girls' sakes and for the men as well."

"My, my, a concern for public relations. A little late for that, wouldn't you say?"

He frowned and said nothing. The waitress brought my food and set it in front of me. Browning stared miserably at my plate as though the very idea of food sickened him.

"So you got rid of it," I commented after the waitress walked away. "Pounded the locker to pieces. Right then or later?"

"Right then. She said she had a sledgehammer in the back of her pickup. I used that."

"You used it. She didn't? Did she go with you?"

"No. She waited in my office while I got the hammer from the truck and did it."

"Where was it?"

"The hammer? I just told you, in the back of her truck."

"Not the hammer. Where was the truck?"

"Parked in front of the school. Right where it is now."

"She hasn't moved it since then?"

"I can't tell for sure, but I don't think so. It looks to me like it's in the same place."

"Who left first and when?"

"I did. About eleven-thirty or so. She said she needed to pick up something from her office. She was still at the school when I drove away."

"And there was no one with her?"

"I didn't see anybody. There wasn't anyone in the truck when I got the hammer out or when I took it back, either. I didn't see anyone else on the grounds the whole time we were there."

"Any other cars parked in the area?"

"No, just her pickup and my Olds."

"How did she leave there, then?"

Browning shrugged. "I don't know."

I stirred my coffee again, trying to make sense of what he had told me. It didn't work. Finally, I said, "Candace Wynn worked for you for several years. Did you know anything about her personal life?"

Again he shrugged. "Nothing much. She was divorced. Her father died a year or so back. Her mother's been sick for several years."

"I remember seeing a bumper sticker on her truck. Something about sailing. Do you know anything about that?"

"She's supposed to be part owner of a boat over on Shilshole. I don't know the name of it or the names of any of the co-owners."

"And her mother's sick."

"She has cancer."

"I already knew that. Do you know where she is?"

"A hospital somewhere around here. A cancer unit, I believe."

"What's her mother's name? Any idea?"

"No."

I paused for a moment, wondering if there was any easier way to track down Candace Wynn's maiden name. "Is there a blank on the school district's employment form that calls for a maiden name?"

Browning shook his head. "No."

"What about the group insurance form? If she wasn't married and didn't have any children, she might have listed her mother as beneficiary."

"That's possible, but all that information is confidential. It's in the district office."

"Can you get it for me or not?"

"Not on a weekend. I could probably get it tomorrow morning. Why do you need it?"

"Because I've got to find Candace Wynn before she kills someone else," I said.

I pushed my plate aside, picked up the bill, and stood up. Ned Browning sat motionless, shocked by my words. He stared up at me. "Kills?" he repeated.

Obviously, none of the Mercer Island Police

Force had chosen to clue him in on what was happening.

"And because tomorrow may be too late," I added.

I left him sitting there in Denny's, a man frozen in stunned silence. His past had just caught up with him, and his guests waiting at home were long forgotten.

As I started the car, I didn't feel sorry for Ned Browning. Whatever disgrace was coming to him wasn't undeserved. After all, he had been on the list twice, not once. Once was once, but twice was twice.

I did feel sorry for Mrs. Browning, however. She was probably a nice enough lady, one I would never meet even though I was changing her life forever. Whoever she was, wherever she was, her world, like Joanna Ridley's, was about to fly apart. She didn't have the foggiest idea it was coming, but J. P. Beaumont was sending trouble her way.

It was just as well we would never meet.

CHAPTER
29

The only thing to do was to find Candace Wynn's mother. Somehow.

I was sitting in my car with the engine running when I realized I was going off half-cocked. I waited until Ned Browning came out of the restaurant. Expecting me to be long gone, he turned like he'd been shot when I hailed him from the Porsche. He approached the car cautiously. "What now?" he asked.

"Do you have a picture of Candace Wynn?"

"No."

"Maybe not a separate picture, but wouldn't she be in a yearbook? Do you have any?"

He nodded. "I do have one of those, at school, in my office."

"Good. Let's go get it."

He started to object but thought better of it. He led the way back to the school, where a tow truck was just hooking on to Candace Wynn's Chevy. Avoiding the crowd in the parking lot, he took me into his office and handed me a copy of the current yearbook. Mrs. Wynn's picture was there, alongside her angelic crew of cheerleaders. There was another picture as well, a more formal one, in the faculty section of the book.

"Thanks," I said. "I'll bring it back."

"Don't bother," Ned Browning told me.

If I had been in his shoes, I wouldn't have wanted to keep a copy of that particular yearbook, either.

When I left him, he was standing in the middle of his office, looking at it the way someone looks when they're getting ready to pack up and move on. Ned Browning was a man who had worn out his welcome.

The next three hours were hard on me. They shouldn't have been, I suppose. After all, I'm a homicide detective. We're supposed to be tough, right?

But tracking through those hospitals, trying to locate Candace Wynn's mother, carried me back some twenty-odd years, back to my youth and to my own mother's final illness.

Maybe part of it is that you never get over your mother's death, no matter how long you live. Being in those polished corridors with their antiseptic odors and their stainless steel trays made it seem like yesterday, not half a lifetime ago.

Pain was all around. The patients had help for theirs, however fleeting the hazy comfort of drugs might be, but my heart went out to the empty-eyed visitors I found walking the halls, lingering in the rooms. There was no prescribed medication available to lessen their hurt.

I remembered only too well when I had stumbled blindly among them, holding tightly, stubbornly, to each grim crumb of hope. And then, eventually, the day had come when all hope was gone. I had resigned myself to my mother's loss, knowing the how. That was inevitable. But for three long years I had spent every resource at my disposal, delaying as long as possible the unpredictable when.

Walking the hospital halls that bright spring afternoon, knowing the difference between the budding promise outside and the burgeoning grief inside, I could relate to Candace Wynn just a little bit. Maybe, after fighting a losing war for far too long a time, she had cracked under the strain.

I started with the obvious, the Fred Hutchison Cancer Research Center on First Hill. A lady at the front desk cheerily told me they had a master list of all the cancer patients in Seattle, but without a name, she couldn't help me. She did, however, point me in the direc-

tion of the hospitals with known cancer units—
Swedish, Providence, Cabrini, and Virginia
Mason on Pill Hill—and later, University Hos-
pital, Overlake, and Northgate.

I drove like a maniac from place to place,
speeding on the way, leaving the Porsche in
patient-loading zones with the hazard lights
flashing when I went inside.

And all the while I was driving, I kept coming back to the same question: Why had Candace lied about the locker? Why had she
pretended to have heard about it only the
night before, and why had she encouraged
Ned Browning to destroy it? She knew we
knew about it. The list wasn't something that
could simply be swept under the rug and forgotten. There was some reason for her telling
Browning on that particular day in that particular place. I drove and wished I had the answer.

At each hospital, it wasn't a matter of waltz-
ing up to the head nurse, showing her Candace Wynn's picture, and getting a straight
answer.

Straight answers aren't to be had from either
doctors or head nurses. They're usually too
close to God to talk to mere mortals. I went
looking for orderlies, for hospital volunteers,
for candy stripers—little people who might
feel some sense of importance in being asked
to help.

And help me they did. They were happy to look at the picture of Candace Wynn, and over and over they shook their heads. No, they were sure no one like that had visited any of the patients who were in that hospital right then.

And with each shake of the head, with each negative answer, the icy knot in my gut got bigger. I wasn't getting any closer. A terrible clock was ticking in my head, telling me that time was running out. I tried to tell myself it was just from being in hospitals, from seeing so many people who were sick or dying or both. But that didn't help me shake it.

The lady at Fred Hutchison had given me a list of board-approved cancer units. I visited them one by one and came up empty-handed each time. By the time I reached the last one, I was pretty discouraged.

Instead of leaving the lights flashing, I searched around and found a real parking place in the lot outside Northgate General Hospital. I ignored the noisy horde of teeny-boppers on their way to the latest teenybopper movie. They were having a great time, laughing and joking and shoving one another around. I wanted to tell them to shut up and pay attention, that there was a real world out there waiting for them.

Back in my car with yet another failure, I sat for a moment, resting my head on the steering wheel. I had struck out. Tired beyond bearing, I was determined to go on, if I could just figure out where I ought to go.

I tried to collect my thoughts. It was like corralling a herd of frightened, milling sheep. I kept after it, though, and gradually, as I sat there, order returned.

Going over every conversation with Candace Wynn, playing back each one in my mind, I picked out only those things she had told me about her mother. I remembered her saying she had visited her mother in the hospital during the third quarter of the game. That had to have been fairly late in the evening. After eight o'clock. Dave Rimbaugh had told us that much. To get to a hospital from Seattle Center before visiting hours ended, it must have been one fairly close at hand.

I got out of the car and walked back through the movie-going kids and into the waiting room at Northgate General Hospital. I walked up to the main desk.

"What's the closest hospital to Seattle Center?" I asked the young black receptionist. She turned to a much older lady sitting next to her.

"What do you think, Irene?"

Irene shrugged. "Group Health up at the end of Denny, or maybe Ballard Community."

I felt a faint surge of hope. Ballard Community wasn't that far from Seattle Center, and it wasn't that far from Fremont, where

Candace Wynn lived, either. I charged out the door and back through the parking lot. When I started the Porsche and peeled out of the place, I left a few young high school bucks staring after me in openmouthed envy.

Parking on N.W. Fifty-third, I dashed into the hospital and was directed to their medical/surgical floor, 5-E. There, I tackled a lady in a bright pink jacket pushing a cart full of paperback books and newspapers down the hall. Her name tag said Mrs. Rasmussen—a good, old-fashioned Scandinavian name.

"Excuse me," I said. "I'm with Seattle P.D. I'm trying to locate a patient."

She pointed down the hall. "If you'll just go down to the nurses' station, they have a list of all the patients there."

"No, you don't understand. I don't know the patient's name." I had conducted the same conversation over and over the whole afternoon. I opened the yearbook to where a piece of paper marked Candace Wynn's smiling picture. "This is her daughter."

Mrs. Rasmussen fumbled in the pocket of her pink jacket and brought out a pair of gold-framed glasses. She perched them on her nose and peered down at the picture. "Oh, her!" she said. The disgust in her voice was unmistakable.

"Her? You mean you recognize her?"

"You say you're from the police? Well, it's

about time, that's all I have to say."

"What do you mean? What are you talking about?"

"I was telling Betty just the other day that somebody should see to it that girl goes to jail."

"But why?" I was sure that if I ever got Mrs. Rasmussen on track, she was going to tell me everything I needed to know and then some.

"You know, some of the patients complain about their kids, that they do stuff behind their backs, give away their things, move into their houses whether they want them there or not. But I was there the day she made her mother agree to sell the house. It was awful. It made me sick. Mrs. Scarborough cried and cried about it afterward."

"That's her name? Mrs. Scarborough?"

"Yes. Elaine Scarborough. Second room on the left. The bed by the window." Mrs. Rasmussen took off her glasses and patted them back into her pocket. "That's not all, either."

"It isn't?"

"She kept saying that at home her daughter sometimes wouldn't let her have her pain medication."

"Did anyone do anything about it?"

"The doctor said he was sure the visiting nurses made certain that kind of thing didn't happen. But you should have seen how happy she was to be in a hospital so she could get medication when she needed it. She was in such pain! What kind of a monster would do a thing like that? I just can't understand it!"

Mrs. Rasmussen stood there glaring at me with one hand on her hip as though she expected me to come up with an instant explanation. What kind of monster indeed! There's no understanding that kind of human aberration.

A hefty nurse came rustling officiously down the hall. Mrs. Rasmussen beat a hasty retreat into the nearest doorway, saying a cheerful "Good afternoon" to whomever was inside.

Uncertainly, I paused in the hallway for a moment too long. The nurse, observing my indecisiveness, stopped beside me. "May I help you?"

"Yes. I wanted to see Mrs. Scarborough."

"Are you a family member?" the nurse inquired.

"No. Not really." I stopped short of pulling out my badge and identifying myself. It didn't make any difference.

"I'm sorry. Mrs. Scarborough is gravely ill. Her doctors have limited visitors to family members only, and even those are allowed to stay for just a few minutes at a time."

"But it's important . . ."

The nurse took my arm and guided me firmly back toward the elevator. "There is

nothing more important than our patients'
well-being," she said stiffly. "If the information you have for her is so important, then it
would be best if you would contact one of the
family members to deliver a message."

"Could you give me the names on the ap-
proved list?"

The nurse looked at me disapprovingly and
shook her head. "Now if we really were a
friend of the family, we'd know those names,
wouldn't we."

Yes, we certainly would.

The elevator door opened, and I got on. The
nurse made sure of it. I was surprised she
didn't ride all the way down to the lobby and
see me out onto the street. I would have made
more of an issue out of it, but I figured having
the family name was enough.

I made one stop before I left the building, at
the pay phone in the lobby. A frayed Seattle
phone book lay on the shelf under the phone.
Unfortunately, there were six Scarboroughs
listed. None of them said Elaine.

Rummaging through my pockets, I dredged
out a collection of quarters. I dialed the first
three numbers and asked for Elaine, only to be
told no one by that name lived there. On the
fourth call, Candace Wynn herself answered
the phone. I recognized her voice.

"Hello?"

"Wrong number," I mumbled, disguising

my voice as best I could. I hung up the phone, made a note of the address, and raced toward the hospital exit door, almost smashing into the glass when the electric door in the lobby didn't open quite fast enough to let me through.

Hospital doors aren't generally timed for people moving on foot at a dead run.

C H A P T E R
30

It took exactly thirteen minutes to drive from Ballard Community Hospital to Thirtieth Avenue South and South Graham. Nobody stopped me for speeding. That's always the way. Where are all the traffic cops when you need one?

Had one pulled me over, I would have sent word to the department for help. As it was, I decided to go to the Scarborough house first, try to get some idea of the lay of the land, and then call the department for a backup.

Driving east after crossing Beacon Avenue, I spotted a small Mom-and-Pop grocery store with a pay phone hanging beside the ice machine outside. I figured I'd come back there to use the phone as soon as I knew what was coming down.

As plans go, it wasn't bad. Things just didn't work out that way.

At Graham and Thirtieth South, a towering electrical transmission line dissects Beacon Hill and cuts a huge green north and south swath through the city. The Scarborough address in the phone book was 6511 Thirtieth Avenue South.

The seriousness of my miscalculation became apparent the moment I saw the house. North of Graham, Thirtieth was a regular street with houses on one side facing the wide clearing under the power lines. On the south side, though, the 6500 block dead-ended in front of the only house on the block, 6511—the Scarborough house.

So much for sneaking around. So much for subtlety. Guard red Porsches are pretty goddamned hard to camouflage on dead-end streets when there's only one house on the block and the rest is nothing but wide-open spaces.

Instead of turning right onto Thirtieth, I hung a left and drove north, ditching the Porsche three houses north of Graham behind a vagrant pickup truck sitting on jacks. I figured I had a better chance of getting close to the house unobserved if I moved on foot rather than in the car. All I needed to do was get close enough to have some idea of what was going on.

There wasn't much cover, even for someone on foot. The Beacon Hill transmission line was built in the twenties and thirties to bring power from the Skagit Valley power plants into the city. The right-of-way was purchased from farmers along the route. Later, the city grew up around the power line.

Directly under and for twenty-five or thirty yards on either side of the long line of metal towers, emerald green grass sprang to life. It looked as though the power line had driven every other living thing but the grass out of its path.

Here and there, looking down the line, a few houses remained, almost on the right-of-way itself. These were mostly remnants of the original farmhouses, most of them still occupied and still in good repair.

The Scarborough house was one of those, a sleepy-looking relic from another era with a steeply pitched gray roof and a graceful white porch that stretched across the entire front of the house. Two matching bay windows, opening onto the porch, were carefully curtained so no one could see inside. To the right of the walkway leading up to the house stood a "For Sale" sign with a "Sold" sticker stuck across it.

I returned to Graham. Attempting to look casual, I sauntered east, hoping for a wider view of the house as it dropped behind me. A short distance up the street was a bus stop. I stopped under the sign and turned to look behind me.

I was far enough away that, for the first time, I could see the south side of the house. Parked next to it, almost totally concealed from the street, was the corner of a school bus. A van actually. A yellow team van.

As I stood watching, the front door swung open. Candace Wynn stepped outside, carrying a suitcase in either hand. With brisk, purposeful steps, she moved to the bus, opened a side door, and placed the suitcases inside.

Watching her, I had moved unconsciously into the middle of the street, drawn like a metal chip toward a powerful magnet. Too late I realized she was moving toward the door on the driver's side of the van. She vaulted into the driver's seat and slammed the door behind her. I heard the engine start and saw the backup lights come on.

Suddenly, behind me, squealing brakes and a blaring horn brought me to my senses as a car skidded to a stop a few feet from me. I scrambled out of the way only to dash into the path of another car. Blind to everything but the moving bus. I charged toward it.

It was only when the bus backed out and swung around to turn toward the street that I saw Candace Wynn wasn't alone in the vehicle. Peters sat slumped on the rider's side, his head slack and drooping against the window.

"Stop! Police!" I shouted, drawing my .38 from its shoulder holster. I saw Candace glance across Peters in my direction. Our eyes met briefly across the narrowing distance in a flash of recognition. She saw me, heard me, recognized me, but she didn't stop. She didn't even pause. Instead, the van leaped forward like a startled rabbit as she hit the accelerator. I saw, rather than heard, the side of Peters' head smack against the window.

What's the matter with him, I wondered. Is he asleep? Why doesn't he do something? "Peters!" I shouted, but there was no response.

I ran straight down Graham toward Thirtieth, hoping to intercept the van where the two streets met. As I charged forward, Candace must have read my mind. As she approached the intersection, she gave the steering wheel a sharp turn to the left. The van shuddered and arched off the rutted roadway, tottering clumsily onto the grass.

Good, I thought. She's losing it. But she didn't. Somehow she regained control. The van pulled onto Graham, skidding and sliding, a good ten feet in front of me. She gunned the motor and headed west. I put on one final burst of speed, but it was too little too late.

The Porsche, three houses up the street behind me, was too far away to be of any use. There was only one chance.

The drawn .38 was in my hand. I was tempted to use it. God was I tempted. But just then, just as I was ready to squeeze the trigger, another car met the van on the street. It was a station wagon loaded with people, two women with a bunch of kids.

I couldn't risk it, not even for Peters. I couldn't risk hitting a tire and sending the van spinning out of control to crash into innocent bystanders.

A second car stopped behind me with a screech of brakes. Horns blared. One driver rolled down his window. "What the hell's going on here?"

I rammed the .38 back into its holster and turned to race toward the Porsche in the same motion only to stumble over a little black kid on a tiny bicycle who had pedaled, unnoticed, up behind me.

"Hey, man, you a cop?" he demanded.

I sidestepped him without knocking him down and ran up the street with the kid trailing behind. When I reached the Porsche, I struggled to unlock the door, unable to fit the key in the lock.

"Hey, man," the kid repeated. "I axed if you was a cop. How come you don't answer me?"

Finally, the key slipped home. I glanced at the kid as I flung the door open. He wasn't more than five or six years old.

"Yes, I am," I answered. I fumbled in my

pocket, located a loose business card with my name on it, and tossed it to him. Deftly, he plucked it out of the air.

"Do you know how to dial 9—1—1?" I asked.

He nodded, his black eyes huge and serious. "Sure."

"Call them," I ordered. "Tell them there's trouble. Serious trouble. I need help. My name's on that card."

The Porsche's engine roared to life. I wheeled the car around and drove into the confusion of cars still stopped to sort out the excitement. As I swung onto Graham, the boy was hightailing it up the street on his bicycle, pumping furiously.

I'd have given anything for flashing lights about then, or for a siren that would have forced people out of my way. As it was, I had to make do with the horn, laying into it at every intersection, raging up behind people and sweeping them off the road in front of me.

As I fishtailed around a stopped car at the Beacon Avenue intersection, I caught sight of the lumbering van. It was far too unwieldy for the sports car rally speed and terrain. Half a mile ahead, it skidded into the wrong lane, around a sharp curve. I don't know how she did it, but Candace Wynn dragged it back onto the road. She could drive like hell, damn her.

As she disappeared behind the hill, I

slammed the gas pedal to the floorboard and the Porsche shot forward. I was gaining on her. No way the van would be a match for my Porsche. No way.

I raced down Graham, swooping around the curve, over the top of the hill, and down the other side, with its second sharp curve. The traffic light at the bottom of the hill turned red as I approached. Despite my frenzied honking, cars on Swift Avenue moved sedately into the intersection.

One disinterested driver glanced in my direction as I tried to wave him out of my way. Another, a semidriver, flipped me a bird. I finally moved into the intersection all right, but only when my light turned green.

While I was stopped, I had looked up and down Swift, searching for her, but I saw no sign of the van. There was only one other direction she could go at that intersection, only one other choice—onto the freeway, heading north.

I shot across Swift and sliced down the on ramp. Far ahead, a glimpse of yellow school van disappeared around yet another curve, swerving frantically in and out of the otherwise leisurely flow of homeward-bound Sunday afternoon traffic.

I dodged from one lane to another. Where the hell was she going? Why did she have Peters in the car with her? My heart thumped in my throat as we came up the straightaway by the Rainier Brewery. I was closing on her fast, looking for ways I could cut her off, force her to the side of the road.

Just north of the brewery, I was right behind her, honking and motioning for her to pull over. Suddenly, without warning, she veered sharply to the right. With a crash of crumbling metal, the van smashed through the temporary guardrail on a closed exit ramp and bounced crazily over a railroad tie barrier.

I skidded to the shoulder. I couldn't follow her in the Porsche. It never would have cleared the railroad tie. Throwing myself out of the car, I tumbled over the shattered remains of the guardrail and raced up the ramp on foot.

Nobody clocked me, but I was moving, running like my life depended on it, wrestling the .38 out of its holster as I went. I knew how that exit ended. In a cliff. A sheer drop from thirty feet in the air over Airport Way.

I topped the rise. She must have thought the exit was one of the almost completed ones that would have swung her back onto Beacon Hill. At the last moment, she tried to stop. I saw the flash of brake lights, but it was too late. She was going too fast.

The van skidded crazily and then rammed into the two Jersey barriers, movable concrete barricades, at the end of the ramp.

I stopped in my tracks and watched in horror. For the smallest fraction of a second, I thought the barrier would hold. It didn't. The two pieces split apart like a breaking dam and fell away. Carried forward by momentum, the van nosed up for a split second, then disappeared from view.

An eternity passed before I heard the shattering crash as it hit the ground below. Riveted to the ground, frozen by disbelief, I heard a keening horn, the chilling sound of someone impaled on a steering wheel.

Sickened and desperate, I turned and ran back the way I had come. Within seconds, the wailing horn was joined by the faint sounds of approaching sirens. I recognized them at once. Medic One. The sirens did more than just clear traffic out of the way. They said help was coming. They said there was a chance.

"Hurry," I prayed under my breath. "Please hurry."

As I reached the Porsche, I saw two squad cars speeding south on the freeway, blue lights flashing. The boy on the bicycle had made the call. They were coming to help me.

Nice going, guys!

C H A P T E R
31

It took three illegal turns to get off the freeway and reach the area on Airport Way where the van had fallen to earth. By the time I got there, someone had mercifully silenced the horn.

Naturally, a crowd had gathered, the usual bloodthirsty common citizens who don't get enough blood and gore on television, who have to come glimpse whatever grisly sight may be available, to see who's dead and who's dying. Revolted, I pushed my way through them. An uncommonly fat woman in a bloodied flowered muumuu with a plastic orchid lei around her neck sat weeping on a curb. I bent over her, checking to make sure she was all right.

"Look at my car," she sobbed. "That thing fell out of the sky right on me. My poor car! I could have been killed. If someone had been in the backseat . . ."

I looked where she pointed. A few feet from the van sat the pretty much intact front end of an old Cadillac Seville. The rear end of the car, from the backseat on, had been smashed flat. All that remained behind the front door was a totally unrecognizable pile of rubble.

A few feet away lay the battered van, surrounded by hunks of shattered concrete. The van's engine had been shoved back to the second seat. It lay on its side like a stricken horse with a troop of medics and firemen scurrying around it.

My knees went weak. I felt sick to my stomach. The sweet stench of cooking grain from the brewery mixed with the odor of leaking gasoline and the metallic smell of blood. The concoction filled my nostrils, accelerating my heartbeat, triggering my gag reflex.

I attempted to stand up, hoping to get away from the smell and to escape the lady in the flowered dress, but she grabbed onto my arms, pulling herself up along with me. Once we were both upright, she clung to me desperately, repeating the same words over and over, as if repetition would make sense of the incomprehensible.

"It just fell out of the air. Can you imagine? It landed right on top of me."

Prying her fingers loose one by one, I broke

away from her. "You stay here," I told her. "I'll send someone to check on you." I walked toward the wreck. A uniformed officer recognized me and waved me past a police barricade.

Just then a second Medic One unit arrived at the scene. A pair of medics hurried to the woman's side. I turned my full attention on the van.

Paramedics, inside and outside the vehicle, struggled to position their equipment, trying to reach the injured occupants of the van. I knew from experience that their job would be to stabilize the patients before any attempt was made to remove them from the vehicle, place them in ambulances, and transport them to hospitals.

Standing a little to one side, I waited. I didn't want to be part of the official entourage. I didn't want to ask or answer any questions. I was there as a person, a friend, not as a detective. The less anyone was aware of my presence, the better.

Dimly, I observed the gathering of reporters who showed up and demanded to know what was going on. Who was in the van? What school was it from? How had it happened? Were there any children involved?

Not directly, I thought. Only Heather and Tracie, whose father lay trapped in that twisted mass of metal. I thought of them then for the first time, of two girls waiting at home for me to bring them word of their father.

A paramedic crawled out of the vehicle and walked toward the lieutenant who was directing the rescue effort. In answer to the captain's question, the paramedic shook his head.

Dreading to hear the words and yet unable to stay away, I moved close enough to overhear what they were saying despite the roar of nearby fire truck engines.

"She's gone," the paramedic said. "What about the guy?"

"Lost a lot of blood," the lieutenant answered. "I don't know if we'll get him out in time or not."

I dropped back out of earshot, trying to make myself small and inconspicuous. I didn't want to hear more. The paramedic's words had confirmed my own worst fears. They didn't think Peters would make it.

I didn't, either.

I retreated to the curb and sat down a few feet away from where the woman in the flowered dress was being treated for cuts and bruises. I closed my eyes and buried my face in my hands. I kept telling myself that Seattle's Medic One was the best in the country, that if anyone could save Peters' life, they could. My feeble reassurances fell flat.

Peters was still trapped. How could they

save his life if they couldn't even get him out of the van?

I forced myself to sit there. While the paramedics worked furiously to save Peters' life, they didn't need someone like me looking over their shoulders, getting in the way, and screwing up the works.

Detectives are ill-suited to doing nothing. It goes against their training and mind-set. Sitting there, staying out of the way, took tremendous effort, a conscious, separate act of will for every moment of inactivity. Watching the paramedics and the firemen on and in the van was like watching an anthill. Everyone seemed to be doing some mysterious specialized task without any observable direction or plan.

Then, suddenly, the anthill of activity changed. There was a new urgency as firemen moved forward, bringing with them the heavy metal shears they call the jaws of life. Without a wasted motion, they attacked the side of the van. Within minutes, they had cut a hole a yard wide in the heap of scrap metal. Leaning into the hole, they began to ease something out through it. They worked it out gradually, with maddening slowness, but also with incredible care.

Peters lay on a narrow wooden backboard with a cervical collar stabilizing his head and neck. Blood oozed from his legs, arms, and face. Carefully, they placed him on a waiting stretcher and wrapped his legs in what looked like a pressurized space suit, then carried him ever so gently toward a waiting medic unit. A trail of IVs dragged along behind them.

I was grateful to see that. The IVs meant Peters was still alive, at least right then.

As the medic unit moved away, its siren beginning a long rising wail, I was surprised to discover that darkness had fallen without my noticing. Floodlights had been brought in to light the scene so the paramedics and firemen could see to work. It was dark and cold and spitting rain. I had been so totally focused on the van that I had seen and felt none of it.

Chilled to the bone, I straightened my stiffened legs and walked to where the paramedics were busy reassembling and packing up their equipment. I buttonholed one I had seen crawl out of the van just before they brought Peters out.

"Is he going to make it?" I demanded.

"Who are you?" the paramedic returned without answering my question. "Do you know him?"

I nodded. "He's my partner."

"Do you know anything about his medical background? Allergies? Blood type?"

"No."

"We couldn't locate any identification.

What's his name so I can call it ahead to Harborview."

"Peters," I said quietly. "Detective Ron Peters, Seattle P.D."

Just then a uniformed officer caught sight of me. "Beaumont! There you are. We were responding to your distress call when this happened. We heard you were here, but we couldn't find you."

I didn't tell him that I had been hiding out, that I hadn't wanted to be found. I shook my head. The paramedic I had been talking to moved toward me with an air of concern. I must have looked like hell.

"Are you all right?" he asked.

"I'm okay," I muttered.

A uniformed female patrol officer with an accident report form in her hand stepped forward and addressed the paramedics in general. "You found no ID of any kind? Any idea how the accident happened?"

"Nope." The paramedic pointed toward me. "He says the guy is a detective with Seattle P.D."

She turned to me, looking for verification. Sudden anger overwhelmed me, anger at myself mostly, but I focused it on her. She was handy. She was there.

"It wasn't an accident, stupid. Call Homicide. Get 'em down here right away."

I turned on my heel and stalked away. She followed, trotting to keep up.

"Who are you?" she demanded.

"I'm Detective Beaumont, Homicide, and that's Ron Peters, my partner, in that medic unit."

"You know that for sure?"

"Yes, I know it for sure! Now call Homicide like I told you."

"If you know something about this, I've got to talk to you," she snapped back.

She was right and I was wrong, but I kept walking. "They're taking him to the trauma unit at Harborview. If you need to talk to me, that's where I'll be."

My Porsche was parked at a crazy angle half on and half off the sidewalk. The flashers were still flashing. The woman followed me to the car and persisted in asking questions until I slammed the door in her face and drove off.

When I reached Harborview, Peters' empty medic unit sat under the emergency awning with its doors still open and its red lights flashing. The hospital's glass doors slid silently open and the two paramedics wheeled their stretcher back outside.

"Is he going to be all right?" I asked as they came past me.

"Who?" the one asked. "The guy we just brought in?"

"Yeah," I replied gruffly. "Him."

"Talk to the doctor. We're not allowed to answer any questions."

Talking to the doctor turned out to be far easier said than done. I waited for what seemed like hours. I didn't want to call Kirkland and talk to Ames until I had some idea of what to tell him, until I had some idea of what we were up against.

Word traveled through the law enforcement community on an invisible grapevine. The room gradually filled with people, cops keeping the vigil over one of their own. Captain Powell and Sergeant Watkins were two of the first to arrive. Shaking his head, the captain took hold of the top of my arm and gripped it tightly. He said nothing aloud. I felt the same way.

Margie, our clerk, came in a few minutes later, along with several other detectives from the fifth floor. It wasn't long before the officer from the scene showed up, still packing her blank report. Watty sent her away. I think we all figured there'd be plenty of time for filling out forms later.

At last a doctor emerged through swinging doors beside the nurses' station. A nurse directed him to me. He beckoned for me to follow him. I did. So did Watty and Captain Powell. He took us down a polished hallway to a tiny room. A conference room. A bad news room.

The doctor motioned us into chairs. "I understand Detective Peters is your partner?" the doctor said, turning to me.

I nodded.

"What about his family?"

"A couple of kids."

"How old?"

"Six and seven."

"No wife?"

"No." I took a deep breath. "Should someone go get the kids? Bring them to the hospital?"

The doctor shook his head. "No. He's in surgery now. It'll be several hours. If he makes it through that . . ." His voice trailed off.

"Look, doc. How bad is it?"

He looked me straight in the eye. "Bad," he said quietly. "His neck's broken. He has lost a tremendous amount of blood."

His words zinged around in my head like wildly ricocheting bullets. "But will he make it?" I demanded.

The doctor shrugged. "Maybe," he said. The doctor spoke quietly, but his words washed over me with the crushing roar of breaking surf.

Stunned, I rose from the chair. I couldn't breathe. I scrambled away from the doctor, from the brutal hopelessness of that maybe. I battled blindly for a way to escape that tiny, oppressive room before its walls caved in on me.

Powell caught me by the arm before I reached the door. "Beau, where are you going?"

"To Kirkland. To talk to his kids."

"I can send somebody else," Powell told me. "You don't have to do it."

"This is unfortunate," the doctor said. "Perhaps it would be better if someone else . . ."

I turned on him savagely. "Unfortunate?" I bellowed. "You call this unfortunate!"

Powell gripped my arm more tightly. "Hold it, Beau. Take it easy."

I glared at the doctor. "I'm going to Kirkland," I growled stiffly through clenched jaws. "Don't try to stop me."

I shook off Powell's restraining hand and strode from the room. They let me go.

When I pushed open the swinging door at the end of the hall, the waiting room was more jammed than it had been before. I recognized faces, but I spoke to no one. The room grew still when I appeared. Silently, the crowd stepped aside, opening a pathway to the outside door.

On the outskirts of the crowd, just inside the sliding glass door, I saw Maxwell Cole. He stepped in front of me as I tried to walk past.

"I just heard, J. P. Is Peters gonna be all right?" he asked.

I didn't answer. Couldn't have if I had tried.

Max gave me a clap on the shoulder as I went by him. "Too bad," I heard him mutter.

He made no attempt to follow me as I got into the car to drive away.

Maybe Maxwell Cole was growing up.

Maybe I was, too.

CHAPTER
32

I started the engine in the Porsche. Instantly, a mantle of terrible weariness fell over me. It was as though all my strength had been sapped away, all the stamina had drained out of me and into the machine. Gripping the wheel, I felt my hands tremble. I was chilled, cold from the inside out.

It was well after ten. I understood why I had hit a wall of fatigue. The days preceding it, to say nothing of that day itself, had taken their toll.

Common sense ruled out hurrying to Peters' house to tell his girls. It was long past their bedtime. They were no doubt already in bed and fast asleep. Let them sleep. The bad news could wait.

I decided to go home, shower, and change clothes before driving to Kirkland. Mentally and physically, I needed it. Besides, a detour to my apartment gave me a little longer to consider what I'd say, what I'd tell Heather and Tracie when I woke them.

When I got to the Royal Crest, it was all I could do to stay awake and upright in the elevator. I staggered down the hallway, opened the door to my apartment, and almost fell over what I found there. My newly recovered recliner had been returned and placed just inside the door. How Browder had gotten it done that fast I couldn't imagine. But he had.

Unable to walk through the vestibule, I turned into the kitchen. There on the counter sat my new answering machine with its message light blinking furiously.

I counted the blinks, ten of them in all. Ames had told me that each blink indicated a separate message. I pressed rewind and play.

The first two were hang-ups.

The third was a voice I recognized as that of Michael Browder, my interior designer, telling me he was on his way to downtown Seattle. He was bringing the chair in hopes of dropping it off on his way.

The fourth call was Browder again, calling from the security phone downstairs this time, asking to be let into the building.

The fifth call was from the building manager, explaining that he was letting someone deliver a chair and that he hoped it was all right with me.

The sixth was someone calling to see if I was interested in carpet cleaning.

The seventh was from Ned Browning. He didn't say what day or time he was calling. He said he had just discovered that the keys to the Mercer Island team van were missing from his desk. Checking in the district garage, he had discovered that the van was gone as well. He had reported it missing, but did I think it possible that Candace Wynn had taken the keys from his desk while he was down in the locker room?

I stopped the answering machine and re-played Browning's message. Possible? It was more than possible. You could count on it. So that was why she had insisted on meeting Browning at school, why she had pretended to have just learned about the names in the locker the night before. She had lured Browning there so she could get the keys and steal the van.

But why? That still didn't give me the whole answer. Parts of it, yes, but not the whole story. Maybe she had known we were getting close and had wanted to use another vehicle in case we were already looking for her truck. But why a school van? Surely she must have known that by Monday at the latest someone would have noticed and reported it missing.

Unless, by then, she no longer cared whether she got caught. I remembered the fearless, single-minded way she had crashed through the barriers onto the exit ramp. Maybe she had reached a point where being caught was no longer the issue. Now, with Candace Wynn dead, hope faded that I would ever learn the answers to those questions.

I turned back to my answering machine to play the next message. The eighth one was from Joanna Ridley, asking me to call her as soon as I could. She left her number.

The ninth and tenth messages were both from Ames, looking for me, wondering what was going on, and had I learned anything.

The machine clicked off. I dialed Joanna's number, but there was no answer. I poured myself a tumbler full of MacNaughton's and dialed Peters' number in Kirkland. Ames answered on the second ring.

"It's Beau," I said.

"It's about time. Did you find him?"

"Yes."

"It sounds bad. Is it?"

"He's in the hospital, Ralph. The doctors don't know whether or not he'll make it..."

"And...?" Ames prompted.

"Even if he does, he may be paralyzed. His neck's broken."

There was a stricken silence on the other end of the line.

"Are the girls in bed?" I asked eventually.

"Mrs. Edwards put them down a little while ago. I told them we'd wake them up if we heard any news."

"Don't get them up yet. Wait until I get there," I said. "I'm at home now. I need to shower. I'll come prepared to spend the night."

"Good," Ames said. "That sounds like a plan."

"I'll be there in about an hour," I told him. "Captain Powell was to give the hospital that number in case they need to reach us. Is there anything you need over there?" I asked as an afterthought.

"As a matter of fact, bring along some MacNaughton's."

"In addition to what's in my glass?"

"Bring me some that hasn't been used," he replied.

The shower helped some. At least it gave me enough energy to gather up a shaving kit and some clean clothes. I drove to Kirkland in the teeth of the roaring gale. Waves from Lake Washington lashed onto the bridge and across my windshield, mixing with sheets of rain and making it almost impossible to see the road ahead of me.

The storm's fury matched my own. J. P. Beaumont was in the process of beating himself up and doing one hell of a good job. What if I had called for help before I ever left Ballard? Was it possible that a patrol car could have reached the Scarborough house in time to keep Candace Wynn from getting away, from making it to the freeway? What could I have done differently so Peters' life wouldn't be hanging in the balance?

In the end, I couldn't ditch the singular conclusion that it was my fault. All my fault.

Ames met me at the door. He looked almost as worn and haggard as I felt. "Tell me," he commanded, taking the bottle of Mac-Naughton's from my hand and leading me into the kitchen.

Ames poured, and I talked. Off and on I tried Joanna Ridley's number, but there was still no answer. Between calls, I told Ames every detail of what had happened that day, down to the doctor's last words as I left the hospital. When I finished, Ames ran his hands through his hair, shaking his head.

"God what a mess! What are we going to do?"

"About what?"

"The kids."

"What do you mean? What'll happen to them?" I asked.

"That depends," Ames said quietly. "If Peters lives long enough to make his wishes known, he might have some say in it. Otherwise, with their mother out of the country, the state may very well step into the picture and decide what's best."

"You mean hand the girls over to Child Protective Services or to a foster home?"

"Precisely."

"Shit!" I had seen the grim results of some foster home arrangements. They weren't very pretty.

"Has Peters ever mentioned any plan to you? A relative of some kind. Grandparents maybe? An aunt?"

"No. Never."

Ames poured us both another drink. He looked at me appraisingly when he handed it to me. "What about you, Beau?"

"Me?" I echoed. I was thunderstruck.

"Yes, you. God knows you've got plenty of money. You could afford to take them on without any hardship."

"'You're serious, aren't you!"

"Dead serious. We've got to have some kind of reasonable plan to offer Peters at the first available moment, before the state drops down on him and grabs Heather and Tracie away. And we've got to have something to tell the girls in the morning."

"But, Ames, I'm not married."

"Neither is Peters, remember? But you've raised kids before, two of them. And from what I've seen of them, you did a pretty commendable job of it. You could do it again."

"I've just bought a place downtown," I protested. "No grass. No yard. No swings."

"Children have grown up in cities for as long as there have been cities. Besides, if they don't like it, you can move somewhere else."

Ames was talking about my taking on Peters' kids with the kind of casual aplomb that comes from never having raised kids of his own. People talk that way about kids and puppies, about how cute they are and how little trouble, only when they've never pulled a six-year-old's baby tooth or housebroken an eight-week-old golden retriever.

Ames spoke with the full knowledge and benefit of never having been in the trenches. His naiveté was almost laughable, but he's one hell of a poker player. He had an unbeatable wild card—my sense of responsibility for what had happened. And the son of a bitch wasn't above using it.

"So what do we do?" I asked. He read my question correctly as total capitulation.

"I'll draw up a temporary custody agreement," he replied. "As soon as Peters is lucid enough for us to talk to him about it, we'll get it signed and notarized."

"Signed?" I asked.

"Witnessed," he corrected.

"And what if that's not possible? What if he never is lucid enough to agree to it?"

"We use the same agreement. It just costs

more money to put it in force, that's all," Ames replied grimly.

I knew from experience that Ralph Ames had the moxie to grease the wheels of bureaucracy when the occasion required it.

It was one-thirty in the morning when we finally called it quits. The decision had long since been made to wait until morning to tell the girls. There was no sense in waking them up to tell them in the middle of the night.

For a long time after Ames went to bed, I lay awake on the floor mulling our conversation. Ames was right, of course. I was the only acceptable choice for taking care of Heather and Tracie. I had the most to offer. And the most to gain.

It was probably just a sign of fatigue, but by five-thirty, when I finally fell asleep, it was beginning to seem like a perfectly reasonable idea.

Heather bounded into my room an hour later. "Unca Beau," she squealed, climbing gleefully on top of me. "Did you find him? Did you?"

It was a rude awakening. Tracie, more reticent than her younger sister, hung back by the door. I motioned to her. With a kind of delicate dignity, she sat down beside me.

I swallowed hard before I answered Heather's question. "Yes, I did," I said slowly.

"Well, where is he, then? Why isn't he in

his bed?" Heather's six-year-old inquisitiveness sought answers for only the most obvious questions.

"He's in the hospital, girls."

Tracie swung around and looked up at me. "He's hurt?"

"I'm afraid so."

"Will he die?"

"I don't know. Neither do the doctors."

"I don't want him to die," Heather wailed. "He can't. I won't let him."

Tracie continued to look up at me, her eyes wide and unblinking. "What will happen to us?" she asked.

Bless Ames for asking the question first, for coming up with a plan. "We talked about that last night," I assured them. "If your father approves, maybe you can stay with me for a while. Downtown."

"But you're moving."

"To a bigger place. There'd be more room."

My heart went out to Tracie. She was very young to be so old, to carry so much responsibility for what was happening around her.

Heather's sudden outburst quieted as suddenly as it had come. "Would we ride in a elevator?"

"Every day."

I reached over and tousled Tracie's long brown hair. "We'll take care of things, Tracie.

Ames and Mrs. Edwards and I will do the worrying. You don't have to."

Tears welled in her big brown eyes. She turned around and launched herself at my neck, clinging to me like a burr.

I'm glad she didn't look up at me right then. I was busy wiping my own eyes.

CHAPTER
33

Ames had talked to Mrs. Edwards while I
was telling Heather and Tracie. By the time we
came out to the kitchen, the housekeeper, red-
eyed but under control, was busy making
breakfast. She dished out huge bowls of oatmeal. "You've got to eat and keep up your
strength so your daddy won't have to worry
about you," she said. Then she went over to
the sink and ran water to cover her sniffles.

None of us ate the oatmeal.

I was pushing my chair back from the table
when the phone rang. It was Margie, Peters'
and my clerk from the department. She
sounded pretty ragged, too.

"Sorry to bother you, Beau, but there's a
message here I thought you should know
about. It's been here since last night. From
Harborview."

"From Harborview! Why didn't they call me here?" I demanded. "Powell was supposed to tell them."

"I don't know what happened, but here's the number."

I took it down and dialed it as soon as I heard the dial tone.

"Emergency," a woman answered.

"My name is Beaumont. I had a message to call this number."

"One moment. Here it is. You're to call 545-1616."

My frustration level was rising. I dialed the next number. "Maternity," someone said.

"Maternity? Why am I calling Maternity?"

"I wouldn't know, sir. This is the maternity wing at University Hospital. Is someone in your family expecting a baby?"

"No, I can't imagine . . ."

"What is your name, sir? I may have a message here for you."

"Beaumont. J. P. Beaumont."

"That's right. Here it is. Hold on. It's early, but I can connect you."

Ames, who had heard the entire conversation, looked at me questioningly. I shrugged my shoulders. Why the hell would Maternity at University Hospital have a message for me?

"Hello." At first I didn't recognize the voice.

"This is J. P. Beaumont. I had a message to call."

"Oh, Beau. Thank you for calling."

"Joanna?"

". . . tried to get hold of you yesterday, but then my water broke, and they took me to the hospital."

I was so relieved it wasn't bad news about Peters that it was all I could do to make sense of what she was saying.

"You had the baby, then? What is it? A boy or a girl?"

She didn't answer. "I've got to talk to you. Right away. Can you come down here?"

"To University Hospital? Sure, I guess so." I held the phone away from my mouth and spoke to Ames. "She wants to see me."

"Go ahead. Mrs. Edwards and I will hold down the fort."

I drove to Harborview first. I went directly to the intensive-care-unit waiting room. Big Al Lindstrom, one of the night-shift homicide detectives, was sitting upright on a couch, his massive arms folded across his chest, apparently sound asleep. His eyes opened, though, as soon as I stepped into the room.

"Hi, there, Beau. Me and Manny are spelling one another. We'll be here all day."

I was glad to see him. "Any word?"

"It's touch and go. He's still heavily sedated. Understand you're looking after his kids." I nodded. "You handle that end of it. We'll take care of this."

"Thanks, Al." I didn't say anything more. I couldn't.

Leaving Harborview, I drove north to University Hospital. Joanna Ridley was in a private room at the end of the maternity wing. Her door stood partially open. I knocked on it softly.

"Come in."

I entered the room. Joanna was not in her bed. Wearing a white, gauzelike nightgown, she sat in a chair near the window, gazing across a still green, stormy Lake Washington.

"Hello, Joanna," I said quietly.

She didn't look up. "I read about your partner in the paper," she said. "Is he going to be all right?"

"His neck's broken," I told her. "If he lives, he'll probably be paralyzed."

"I'm sorry," Joanna murmured. She looked up at me. "I met her, you know. She had the nerve to stand right there and invite me to Darwin's memorial service." Her eyes filled with tears. "I'm glad she's dead," she added.

I stood there awkwardly, not knowing quite what to say. "Why did you want to see me?"

She pointed toward the closet. "There's a box over there, in my suitcase. Would you bring it here?"

The box was a shoe box, a red Nike basketball shoe box, size thirteen. I handed the box to her and she motioned for me to sit on the bed. She remained in the chair.

For a time after I handed it to her, she sat looking down at the box in her lap, her hands resting on the cover. When she finally raised her face to look at me, she met my gaze without wavering.

"I never knew it was the same woman," she said softly.

"Who was the same woman? I don't understand."

"Candace Wynn and Andi Scarborough. Darwin never wanted me near school. I thought that was just his way. It was one of those little peculiarities. I never questioned it. I never knew it was because of her."

"Joanna, I still don't understand."

"Darwin and Andi Scarborough went together in high school. Actually, they were in grade school when it started, back in those days when blacks and whites didn't mix at all, not socially. Their mothers broke it up, both of them. Darwin wrangled a scholarship to UCLA, a basketball scholarship. That's where I met him."

Slowly, the light began to dawn. "Darwin and Candace Wynn were childhood sweethearts?"

Joanna nodded. "I knew about her, at least I knew about a white girl named Andi Scarborough. His mother told me about her when

Darwin and I were just going together. But I never knew her married name was Wynn. And I never knew she worked with him at school."

The lights came on. I began to fill in some of the blanks. "So they met years later and reestablished their relationship."

Joanna patted the box in her lap. "He kept her letters, locked in his desk at school. I found them yesterday when I started to sort through the big box the principal sent home."

"I'm sorry," I said.

She drew her chin up and squared her shoulders. "Don't be," she answered. "I'm glad I found them and read them. It makes it easier to go on. I didn't lose anything. It never existed."

A nurse poked her head in the door. She saw me sitting on the edge of the bed and frowned in disapproval. "You'll have to leave now. We're bringing the babies to nurse."

I started to my feet. Joanna caught my hand. "Don't go," she said.

The nurse glared at me. "Are you the baby's father? Fathers can stay."

"He's a father," Joanna said evasively. "I want him to stay."

The nurse clicked her tongue and shook her head, but eventually she gave in, led Joanna back to bed, helped her get ready for the baby, and then brought a tiny bundle into the room.

I sat self-consciously on the chair by the window, unsure what to do or say.

I couldn't help remembering those first few tentative times when Karen had nursed Scott when neither of them had known what they were doing. That wasn't the case here.

When I glanced up at Joanna, she was leaning back against the bed looking down contentedly at the bundle nestled in her arms. "I've decided to name him Peter," she told me.

Without her having to explain, I knew why and was touched. It was a nice gesture toward Peters, one I hoped he'd appreciate someday.

"It's a good name," I said.

It was quiet in the room after that. The only sounds came from the lustily sucking infant. This part of parenthood made sense to me. It seemed straightforward and uncomplicated. Joanna Ridley made it look deceptively easy.

But still there was an undercurrent beneath her placid, motherly surface. I sensed there was more to the story, more she hadn't told me. I didn't know if now was a good time to ask her about it. Fools rush in where angels fear to tread.

"What was in the letters?" My question broke the long silence between us.

Joanna answered my question with one of her own. "Do you remember when Detective Peters asked me if Darwin had a separate checking account or credit cards?"

I nodded. "You told us no."

"I was wrong. There was a lot I didn't know, including an account at the credit union, a joint account with her, with Candace Wynn. I never saw the money. It was deducted from his paycheck before it ever came home, and he had all the statements sent to him at school. Between them they must have had quite a sum of money. Part of it came from Darwin, and part came from her. According to the letters, she had been systematically gutting her parents' estate for years. They used the money to buy a boat."

"A boat?"

"A sailboat. It was supposedly a partnership made up of several people. In actual fact, there were only two partners, Candace and Darwin. They planned to run away together until I found out something was going on. Then, even after she knew I was expecting a baby, she still kept talking about it in her letters, that eventually it would be just the two of them together."

Joanna paused and took a deep breath before she continued. "From the letters, it sounded like she understood about me, about the baby, but when she found out about the cheerleader, that Bambi whatever-her-name-was, she snapped."

The quote came unbidden to my mind. I repeated it aloud. " 'Hell hath no fury like a woman scorned.' Isn't that what they say?"

Joanna didn't answer me. I watched as she took the baby from one breast, held the child, patted his back until he burped, then gently moved him to the other breast. Once more I was struck by her beauty, by the sudden contrasts of black and white, skin and gown, sheet and blanket, mother and child. Sitting there in a splash of morning sunlight, Joanna Ridley was the epitome of every Madonna I had ever seen.

Beautiful and serene, yet she, too, had been scorned, betrayed. Where was her anger, her fury?

"What about you, Joanna?"

She looked up at me and gave me a wry grin. "I wasn't scorned, honey," she drawled with a thick, southern accent I had never heard her use before. "I was suckered. There's a big difference."

───◆───

C H A P T E R
34
Epilogue

The next few weeks were a blur. I camped out in Kirkland with the kids and Mrs. Edwards until school got out.

I took a leave of absence so I could look after the kids and run back and forth to the hospital. The girls kept wanting to go see their dad, but he was far too sick for visitors. Peters' health remained precarious, and the doctors told us it would be months before he was entirely out of the woods.

Before Ames returned to Phoenix, we spent hours trying to second-guess what the long-term implications were, but other than sorting out the custody arrangement, we decided to hide and watch and not make any other plans until we had some clear direction from the doctors. Mostly, they weren't very informative, but they did hint that the fact that Peters had been unconscious at the time of the wreck was probably the only thing that kept him from being killed. The doctors vacillated between saying he'd never be able to live on his own again and voicing cautious hope that he might recover.

There were occasional times when Peters was fairly lucid. During one of those periods, I asked him if he remembered anything about his time with Candace Wynn. He said no. The doctors tell me that it's not unusual for a person who has suffered a traumatic injury to totally forget the events surrounding the injury.

Considering what I discovered, his amnesia was probably a good thing. Joanna let me read Candace Wynn's letters. In the last one, one written the Thursday before Darwin Ridley died, she raged about Bambi Barker. She had somehow gotten hold of Molly Blackburn's negative. Alternately threatening Darwin and pleading with him to run away with her, she ended the letter with the impassioned statement that if she couldn't have him, nobody would.

She must have gone over the edge then. From what the homicide detectives were able to piece together, she somehow convinced Darwin Ridley to come home with her, slipped him some of her mother's morphine, put a noose around his neck, and pushed him off the second-floor landing over her truck. All she had to do then was cut him down, hose him off, cover him up, and haul him away. The crime lab found bits of trace evidence in the truck that indicated she had used it to transport Ridley back to the dumpster where he was found. No one ever figured out for sure why she went to the trouble of stripping him, unless she used his clothes in a futile attempt to frame Joanna.

Eventually, Maxwell Cole came forward with the envelope and his copy of the Ridley/Bambi photo. The typeface on his envelope matched that on Joanna Ridley's envelope. It was also the same typeface on Candace Wynn's love letters to Darwin Ridley. The remains of the typewriter were found crushed in the wreckage of the van, along with a suitcase of small bills and Molly Blackburn's missing negatives. Peters' .38 was there, too.

Candace must have sent the pictures to the Barkers, Joanna, and the press, just as she had planted the evidence in Joanna Ridley's trunk in hopes of throwing us off the track.

She and Peters hit it off like a couple of starstruck kids. Maybe she was on the rebound. Maybe she liked playing with fire. Somehow, while he was at her apartment, Peters must have discovered something that alerted him, something that told him Candace was behind Ridley's death. Since she went to the trouble of painting the rail, he may have discovered the chafed place on the upright where the noose was tied off.

Whatever it was, when she overheard him trying to call me, she stopped him. That explained the cryptic message on my machine.

Ned Browning resigned on the first of April under a cloud of Chief Marilyn Sykes' making. His case won't come up for several months, but when it does, I doubt he'll be involved in the educational system anymore.

As for me, I'm beginning to get used to being a parent again. According to Ames, who just called from Phoenix, it's just like riding a bike. Once you learn how, you never forget.

He could be right about that.